The
EARL
of
Arundel

The EARL of Arundel

ANGELA JOHNSON

SWEETWATER
BOOKS

AN IMPRINT OF CEDAR FORT, INC.
SPRINGVILLE, UTAH

ISBN 13: 978-1-4621-3781-7

Published by Sweetwater Books, an imprint of Cedar Fort, Inc.
2373 W. 700 S., Springville, UT, 84663
Distributed by Cedar Fort, Inc., www.cedarfort.com

Library of Congress Control Number: 2020937911

Cover design by Shawnda T. Craig
Cover design © 2020 Cedar Fort, Inc.

Printed in the United States of America

10 9 8 7 6 5 4 3 2 1

Printed on acid-free paper

For Athenia, Sjayna, Braden,
Bridger, Brooklyn, Jaxtin,
Joslynn, Journey, and June

May you all find ways to
make your dreams a reality.

One

PHILLIP SAT AT THE PIANOFORTE, fingers moving across the ivory keys with a smoothness that came from years of practice and enjoyment. The instrument represented much to him; his father had presented him with it when he was fifteen years old as an *apology*. This piano sat in a private library, which was also a gift. Over the years his father, the Duke of Ashby, had presented him with books, rare finds of poetry, short stories, and his favorite, Shakespeare, all of which came as an *apology*.

The song he played was his composition that he had written for his mother. The melody reminded him of the caring way she raised him. As he played, he allowed the music to fill his mind and body. He realized he was rushing through the piece, so he slowed the tempo and moved with each note. He turned when a knock sounded on the door.

"Come in," he called as he played. His mother entered, followed by Ashby, and smiled in appreciation, recognizing the tune. Phillip stopped playing to give attention to his father. His parents were accompanied by Lady Olivia Harrison and her parents, the Duke and Duchess of Norland.

"Phillip." Ashby stood in the middle of the group. He was a tall, intimidating, and stiff man. "You are acquainted with Lady Olivia?"

"Yes, Father." The Duke of Ashby and the Duke of Norland had been friends and enemies since their days at Oxford. Each year, Norland and his family visited Wentworth Hall for the summer months.

1

Phillip and his identical twin brother, Edward, had spent more time in the outdoors on horses and childly pursuits than with Olivia, but he had seen her every summer since he was four years old.

Ashby cleared his voice with a nervousness, which was rare. "Norland and I have an announcement to make." He shuffled his feet as he spoke. It was by far the oddest behavior his father had ever exhibited. Ashby's posture wasn't as stiff as normal. With the way he was standing, Phillip was able to meet his eyes without having to look up. Although they both had blue eyes, Ashby's were usually clouded with anger and intrigue. "Norland and I have agreed to a marriage between Arundel and Olivia."

Phillip didn't care for titles. To men like his father and Norland, titles meant everything. A man without a title was as good as a servant to both dukes. As the oldest son, he would inherit the title of Duke upon his father's death. It was rare for his father to refer to him as anything other than Arundel.

Phillip's heart sank. He didn't want an arranged marriage.

"The marriage will take place four weeks from today," Norland stated. "The banns will be read in both our parish and the parish here at Wentworth Hall."

Clearing his throat to get back into the conversation, Ashby took Phillip's hand and placed it in Olivia's. "You should spend time together over the next four weeks. I believe it is better to know a little about each other before the wedding night."

Speechless, Phillip watched as his parents and her parents left the room. Phillip turned to make certain the door to the library was open due to propriety. He let go of Olivia's hand and tried to think of something to say so he didn't sound ignorant or foolish. Before he could gather his thoughts, she dipped her head, curtsied, and left the room.

He waited until he could no longer hear her in the hallway before he exited the library. He walked to his father's den and found his parents conversing in low tones.

"May I speak with you?" he asked, after a soft knock on the door.

His father gave him a frustrated glare but allowed him to enter. Shutting the door so the conversation would not be overheard,

Phillip gathered his thoughts to find the best possible way to approach the subject.

"Father, I realize I have not taken the last few London seasons seriously in regards to finding a wife. I am but twenty-three years old, and I hoped to wait at least another two years before getting serious about marriage."

"This has nothing to do with the fruitless London seasons," Ashby said, sitting behind his desk.

Phillip noticed the similarities and differences between himself and his father. They both had blue eyes and were tall, but the similarities stopped there. His father's face was commonly marked with a scowl, which he claimed came from the stress of his position in society. His father also had dark brown hair, where Phillip's was a dirty blond. Phillip preferred to smile and dream about the future. His father lived day by day.

"Mother, can you not help me with this?" Phillip turned pleading eyes toward her.

"Your father is responsible for the engagement. I don't have a say in it." She looked down at her hands, and he could see the remorse in her face.

"We realize this has been a shock for you and Olivia. We will allow four weeks for you both to come to terms with the engagement," his father continued.

"Four weeks is not enough time to know the woman I am supposed to spend the rest of my life with. I prefer to be in charge of my life."

His father stood and walked around the desk. This time he stood to his full height. There was no reservation in his posture. Phillip looked up into his father's eyes, making an effort to match the angry stare. He walked so close to where Phillip stood, Phillip was forced to take a small step backward for comfort. "You should be out there getting to know your bride. And don't think about breaking the engagement. If it is to be broken, she will have to be the one to do it."

"Why?" It seemed like an idiotic question to ask. If he broke the engagement it would ruin Olivia's reputation. But the tone his father used made him think the statement was more of a threat to him than a desire to preserve Olivia.

Ashby stood looking at him as though he were trying to decide if he should answer the question. After a short internal deliberation, he spoke. "Norland and I have a small bet between old friends. It isn't anything for you to concern yourself over."

"You've gambled my life away?" Incredulous over his father's lack of care for him, he paced the room, trying to find something to say to stop the madness. His father had never taken Phillip's feelings into consideration, and this engagement was a prime example. "You and Norland created an engagement for what purpose?"

"If Lady Olivia pulls out of the engagement, I get Norland's lands, money, and titles."

"And if I end the engagement?"

"You won't be the one to end it, Arundel. The only way out for you is through death."

Speechless, he stared at his father's angry red face. He had to find a way out of the engagement, but it needed to be beneficial for both his father and Norland. Instead of begging to end the contract, he decided to ask for more time. "Please, Father. I beg of you, at least give us a year."

"Four weeks, Arundel."

"Father—"

He could tell when he had pushed his father too far, but his senses must have been off due to the shocking news of the betrothal. Focused on his father's eyes, in an effort to match him look for look, he didn't see his father's hand come up until it was too late to move out of the way.

Ashby hit him on the side of his face. The sting of the blow hurt, but he wasn't going to let a visible expression of the pain show for Ashby's enjoyment. In a raised voice, his father continued. "Do I need to speak louder for you to understand the situation?" He hit Phillip again in the same spot.

There has to be a red outline of a hand on my face now, he thought as he glared into his father's uncaring eyes.

"Are you finished arguing?"

Phillip moved backward and nodded in understanding. He left the room, rubbing the side of his face and hoping the sting of the rebuke would dissipate. In an effort to gather his thoughts, he walked out to the stables. The goal was to saddle his horse, Bassanio, and head out for a ride. *I'll marry the chit*, he thought, hearing the bitterness.

His brother Edward sat waiting for him. Rushing over, Edward asked, "What is going on? Father and Norland spent half the morning in the den."

"I'm expected to marry Lady Olivia in four weeks," he said, shrugging as though he didn't care.

"They expect you to marry in four weeks?" Edward asked, surprise written on his face.

"Yes."

Laughing at the absurdity, Edward asked, "What do you plan to do?"

"I suppose I will have to get to know my *bride*, as Father now refers to her." He emphasized the word "bride" and heard the angry tone in his voice. He wouldn't be able to hide his distaste for the situation.

Pointing to the stable yard where two horses stood saddled and ready, Edward said, "I already saddled horses. Do you mind if I join you?"

"You're welcome to ride with me, as long as you don't talk about this engagement," Phillip said, walking ahead of his twin brother to mount Bassanio.

The first Sunday as the banns were read, Phillip looked into Olivia's brown eyes to assess her reaction. He thought he saw defiance and wondered if she would dare object when the vicar asked if there was a just cause known for the marriage not to proceed. But she stayed silent and the meeting continued forward.

"Lady Olivia?" he asked, running to catch up with her as they left the services.

"Yes?" she asked, her posture and voice showing annoyance at his presence.

"Will you walk back to Wentworth Hall with me?" He extended his arm as a gentleman offering to a lady.

"I suppose," she said, "if I must." The latter part of her statement was under her breath, and he wondered if he heard correctly.

Deciding to ignore her rudeness, he walked in companionable silence with her. The weight on his arm was uncomfortable—not because it was heavy, as she was a dainty woman, but it was more the tension in her body language and the stiffness of her posture. She never once laid her arm on his. Instead she held it in a stiff hover.

He looked up to the trees and thought about pointing to the birds and asking her if she enjoyed nature. But when he said the words in his mind, he decided it was a terrible way to start a conversation. Instead he found a topic he enjoyed.

"Have you read any good books lately?"

"Why did you want to walk with me?" she asked, pulling away from him.

At least she is speaking to me, even if she hasn't any manners. But her rudeness caught him off guard, and he stared at her for a moment while he processed a response.

"I think we should at least be cordial if we are going to be married," he finally said.

"We aren't going to marry."

Her abrupt words continued to surprise him. He had always seen her as a quiet and dignified woman. He realized he had never known her, and he did not like her.

"I am trying to make the best of this situation, and I would prefer to know you before we are wed. We are stuck in this engagement, so we should try to get along."

"I don't want to get to know you, *my lord*." She uttered his title with so much contempt he had to wonder why she had such a dislike for him. She turned and walked away. He didn't realize the speed a dainty woman could walk when angry. Her blonde hair danced as she ran to get away from him.

"Have I done something to make you not want to know me?" he called after her and increased his speed to catch up.

She turned and almost ran into him. "I would prefer to find a match without help. I don't need my parents to *sell* me to someone I don't want."

"I understand," he said, trying to make peace with her. "As you are aware, I have also been blindsided by this engagement, and I don't have a choice."

She stared at him as though she wanted nothing more than to hit him. The situation was not his fault. It was their fathers who had caused this issue.

"Then why are you going along with it? Can you not convince your father of the imprudent match we would make?"

"Have you spoken to your father?" he asked, throwing her challenge back to her. He had gone to his parents, and Ashby had left a bruise on Phillip's upper cheek in response. He was not going to argue with the duke again.

"Yes. He won't relent."

"Neither will mine."

Phillip had spent more than enough time over the last week thinking about a marriage to a woman he didn't love. It wasn't the perfect situation, but then the upper class rarely made decisions of marriage based on love. He came to realize that even if he had found a woman of his choosing during the London seasons, it would've had to be a woman in his same social class with connections.

"My mother told me marriage does not have to be love," she said as she continued to glare in his direction.

"As have my parents informed me," he responded, turning his head to look away from her.

She looked as though she wanted to confide in him. He waited for her to begin speaking but realized if they were going to make it back in time for the garden party his parents were hosting, they would have to start walking. He held his arm out to her again and pointed toward Wentworth Hall.

As they walked, again in a deafening silence, he wondered why she was so adamant against the marriage. He was not happy with the situation, but he'd consigned himself to his fate.

"Is there someone else?" he asked, and then wanted to take the question back as she glared at him and pulled her arm away. She again increased her speed.

Emboldened now he had put the question out in the open, he also increased his speed and tried to goad her into answering. "Am

I correct? You have another man you are hoping to marry and this ruins your plans?" He couldn't stop the smile from crossing his face as he said the words, realizing he'd figured out her indifference.

She turned to him and pushed him away. Then, without any warning, she stomped on his foot and kicked him in the shins. She ran toward Wentworth Hall while he hopped on one foot, trying to ease the pain before putting pressure on it again.

He entered the house, to find his brothers, Edward and Charles, laughing and his sisters holding hands over their faces to hide their amusement.

"You're getting along rather well," Edward chimed.

"Amusing," Phillip said, glaring as he passed by them. He'd give up the position as heir to get out of the engagement.

He continued into the hall and heard Olivia complaining to her parents regarding his manners and inappropriate questions. He raised his eyebrows as he passed by. Ashby gave him a questioning look, but he shrugged and continued up to his bedchamber to change before the guests arrived.

Phillip pulled the bell cord to summon Edward's valet, as his was out of town. While Phillip waited, he brooded over the engagement contract. He didn't want to be the heir and wanted to make the choice when it came to marriage.

"My lord?" Thomas asked as he came in the room.

Phillip turned in surprise as his own valet entered. "I didn't realize you were back. When did you arrive?"

Thomas crossed the room and pulled two options of jackets from the wardrobe. "I arrived an hour ago, my lord."

"How is your mother?" Phillip didn't realize Thomas would return so soon, as his mother was ill. Thomas had left the previous week to visit and care for her.

"She passed away, my lord."

Phillip looked at him in surprise. "Why didn't you tell me she was so ill? Why aren't you in full mourning? Thomas, you should take more time to mourn. Edward's valet can help me."

"No, my lord. I would prefer my mother's passing be kept silent."

"If you change your mind, you have my permission to take leave. I'm sorry for your loss." Confused, he allowed Thomas to continue to help him. He didn't understand the desire to keep the death silent.

"Thank you, my lord. I wouldn't want to cause distress to you and your family. My mother wouldn't be happy to know I told you. Please forget about it." Thomas was stiff and distant in his attention to Phillip. "Which jacket would you like to wear to the party?"

"The brown. I think I will escape early and go for a ride."

"Where do you plan to ride, my lord?"

"The meadow. Do you think the pockets are big enough to pack a book?" Phillip loved reading in the meadow. The stream and the spring budding trees made reading Shakespeare's sonnets come to life.

"I can put a book in your saddlebags."

"I don't know what I did without you, Thomas. I'm happy to have you back." Phillip walked to his side table and grabbed the sonnets. He handed the book to Thomas and rushed from the room. The sooner he arrived at the party, the sooner he could escape.

The garden party turned out to be a boring affair. A group of women gossiping was not an ideal way to spend the day. He watched as Edward made rounds of the room. The women were talkative, and he could tell they knew how to stroke his brother's ego. Edward had always been the favorite among the *ton*.

Phillip's wit was more literary than Edward's, who was just a plain flirt when he had a group of women around him. Charles, their younger brother, was more like Edward when it came to women. He danced and chatted with them during the London seasons, and there were more than a few broken hearts when the Watson boys left town each year without making a match.

Phillip sat next to Olivia for a great deal of the party and was attentive to her as his mother asked him to be. He offered to get her punch multiple times and her wrap when a light spring breeze went through the patio and caused her to shiver. He played the role of adoring fiancé, while she played the role of an indifferent and angry forced bride. She made certain to inform anyone who would listen she was not happy with the arrangement, and how she was forced into the match.

Olivia gained the sympathies of the young women around her. She also gained the sympathies of some of the young men, as she was a beautiful young lady. Phillip thought to himself, *If they knew her temper and ornery ways, they would not be so quick to sympathize with her as they should with me.* He was going to be stuck with her indifference for the rest of his life.

Giving up on the party, as he decided he'd spent more than enough time socializing, he left to go out to the stables.

"You're escaping?" Lord Folly asked from a perch on the fence.

"Is there a reason I should stay? You've found solace out of the chattering of the party."

"I only just escaped," Folly said with a smirk. "If I'd stayed another minute, I might have fallen prey to a few débutantes looking for a younger son."

The idea was amusing. He'd known Folly since Oxford, and he knew Folly had his fair share of beautiful women seeking after him during the season.

"Why the escape?" Folly asked again with a more direct look.

"I need some time to think. There's a wonderful meadow waiting for me. I plan to spend my afternoon reading instead of listening to the chatter of women." He didn't mind sharing his destination with Folly.

"Arundel," Folly said as he jumped off the fence. He looked as though he'd burst if he didn't speak. Phillip could see a visible tension in his posture. "I need to speak with you about Lady Olivia." Phillip watched as Folly gathered his thoughts. Folly made agitated movements, ran a hand through his hair, and balanced between both feet. He finally gained the courage to speak. "I am in love with Olivia. We planned to marry this year."

"Are you in earnest?" Phillip asked the first question that popped into his mind. Without allowing Folly to respond, he added, "Does Norland know about this?"

"Yes. I asked permission and I was turned away."

"Why did Norland refuse you?"

"I am not heir to my father's title. I am the younger son. Also . . ." Folly hesitated and looked around as though he didn't want to be overheard. "My father is bankrupt. Norland doesn't feel it would be a good connection."

"*Bankrupt?*" Folly's father in a compromised financial situation surprised him. There hadn't been any gossip or whispers among the *ton*. In an effort to hide his surprise, Phillip nodded in understanding. "I would release Olivia from the engagement if my father would let me."

"This agreement they have, what is it?" Folly asked in frustration.

"I don't know the details." Giving the information to Folly would be a betrayal of his father. He also feared the information would spread through society faster than a woman's ruined reputation, if whispered to the wrong person. He didn't like telling a falsehood, but it was the best way to sidestep the question.

Folly's face fell. He said in dismay, "I know you haven't made a match, but I am in love with Olivia. Please, what can I do to make this engagement go away?"

"My father has made it clear; the only way I can get out of it is through my death."

Folly's eyes fell to the ground. "There isn't another way?"

"Olivia would have to break it."

"Norland won't allow her to."

Phillip nodded. "There isn't a simple way out of the arrangement. Olivia and I will marry in a month's time. Instead of fighting it, we will consign ourselves to the fate we've been dealt. And you should find a bride with a substantial dowry." He hated himself for speaking the words as they escaped his mouth. It was almost as if he said it more for his own benefit than Folly's. The statement caused an uncomfortable silence to blanket the conversation. "I believe my horse is saddled and waiting for me." Without another word, Phillip walked away.

Before he mounted his horse, he turned and watched as Folly went back to the party. He looked defeated. Angry with himself, Phillip rode off into the countryside with the goal to return once the party was over.

He led Bassanio to a large shade tree and dismounted to give the horse a rest. The tree sat along a shallow stream, so he tied the horse to a branch with enough tether to drink. As he relaxed, he pondered again over the mess Ashby had caused for him. Anger flared in him, which went back to resignation due to his father's response when he asked for the engagement to end. *One consolation to marriage is Ashby will no longer expect me to spend my days at Wentworth Hall.* Escaping his father's clutches for a large part of the year would be a relief.

He stood and picked a rock off the ground and looked at the stream. The rock had a smooth side to it, perfect for skipping across the water. He was able to forget the annoyance of the entire engagement for a short time as he focused on finding stones. After he grew bored of skipping rocks, he again sat with his back against the tree trunk and read the sonnets. Phillip looked up from Sonnet 13 to think about the words when a slight movement to the right caught his eye.

He looked over to see who it was, but upon first glance there was no one around. Standing to make certain he didn't miss the person he thought he had seen, he looked toward the trees to the right but again couldn't see anyone.

Uneasiness caused him to go over to the horse and give up his solitude for the day. "Bassanio, we should go back to the house." As he said the words, a gunshot sounded through the spring air. Phillip ducked behind the tree and waited until his heart no longer pounded to mount and ride away.

It could be a hunter, he rationalized. *I overreacted,* he told himself as he rushed to mount and ride back to Wentworth Hall. He had gone a short distance through the meadow when he knew he heard another horse behind him.

"Is someone there?" he called out as he brought Bassanio to a stop. Although he was still in the open meadow, the rider hid among the trees. One of the reasons he loved the meadow was due to the private enclosure the beech trees afforded the area. He now cursed the exposed feeling he had and the way the forest around him offered concealment to the other rider. The other person must not have expected him to stop, because he could hear the other horse. Again, there was no answer.

It is a hunter, he repeated to himself. Deciding to investigate, Phillip turned Bassanio toward the right. He would find this person. The forest alight with crunching leaves and tree branches caused chills to run up and down his spine. The nervousness must have translated to the horse, because Bassanio missed a step and startled.

"Hey boy," Phillip said as he leaned forward to pat Bassanio's neck. "I don't think there is anyone out there," he said as a way to calm his horse and himself. "We should go home." Imagination shrouded rational thought, and it wasn't a pleasant experience.

Frightened, he turned Bassanio back toward Wentworth Hall and put him into a canter so he could get out of the woods with speed. Again, he could see from the corner of his right eye a man on a horse as he kept pace with Phillip. His temper flared. In anger, he turned and decided to cut the man off, but the man anticipated the move and also turned.

It was a quick glance, but Phillip noticed Bassanio was the superior horse. He couldn't go fast in the woods without hurting the horse. Phillip shook his head in annoyance. The other horse looked familiar, but he was too far away to be sure. Whoever was out in the woods with him didn't want to be engaged. As another gunshot sounded through the late afternoon sky, Phillip decided he'd had enough. He pointed Bassanio back toward Wentworth Hall as the bullet grazed his right arm. Pain shot through his arm. He passed the reins to the left hand and glanced down to see the damage. For the small bit of blood on his jacket, he was in a severe amount of pain. As he rode a short distance further, Bassanio suddenly shook his head and neighed. The horse stopped and refused to move. Phillip tried to get the horse to go forward by squeezing his legs against the horse's body, but he continued to stay still.

Dismounting, he walked around, checking to see if there was a rock or a thistle stuck in Bassanio's hooves. As he came back to the front of the horse, he rubbed the horses' face. "What's wrong?" he asked. "We have to get home."

The horse continued to shake his head and whinnied in a way Phillip had never heard from Bassanio. "Let's get home, boy," he said, patting the horse again on his neck. He walked for a short time and allowed the horse to get used to moving forward again before mounting.

It took some coaxing, but as soon as they were moving, the tension in his body calmed. He'd not realized the lateness of the hour until he noticed the sun was setting. He was nearing the edge of the woods when he saw the rider again, this time on his left. He had an internal struggle. He wanted to go after the person, but he also knew he should go home and get help. This person had shot at him twice. His arm was injured, and he wasn't a match for the gun since he didn't have one.

In an unwise, split-second decision, he decided to veer off to the left and go after his shadow. *I'm an idiot*, he said as he raced after the other rider, who sped up to stay out of Phillip's view. Phillip was gaining on him when Bassanio again reacted in a strange way. The horse increased speed and moved off to the right. Although he'd traveled through these woods since he was a boy, he was lost. It could have been fear impeding his mind and sense of direction as he hadn't lost enough blood to be confused.

"Whoa," he said to the horse, trying to get him to slow down, but the horse again increased in speed running without direction. Phillip pulled the reins back as he called out again, "Whoa, Bassanio." But again, the horse didn't listen. He heard the other horse on his left and turned in time to see the barrel of a gun right before a shot rang through the woods.

"Yah!" Phillip kicked the horse in his sides to make him go faster. He realized he was lucky the horse had not stopped when he had wanted him to; otherwise he would have been a still target for the other rider.

Phillip pushed the horse faster, knowing the rider who shot at him was still behind him. Although he was riding a Darley Arabian, each horse had a limit and he'd not yet found the limit for Bassanio. He had a terrible feeling he was about to find out how far and long this horse could run without a break.

The sun was nearly down when the horse slowed beneath him. He was going to be stuck out in the dark. And if he kept running Bassanio the way he was, he was going to injure him. He needed to get out of the woods and find a safe place to lay low and figure out who would try to kill him. As he thought about the horse being tired, Phillip realized he was also losing stamina. He blinked and shook his head, trying to keep his eyes open. He didn't know how long he'd been riding, but exhaustion plagued his mind and body.

Bassanio continued to slow when Phillip heard another gunshot. This time the shooter was successful. The bullet pierced his right shoulder. Pain raced through his body, and he let go of the reins. He squeezed his legs in an effort to stay mounted, but the latest wound made him weak and he fell.

Phillip woke. He was lying on the ground, with a tree root stabbing him in the back. He registered pain throughout his body. Ready to give into the pain and sleep, he heard a tree branch snap and leaves crunch under footsteps. Although the night sky lacked a moon, Phillip knew the assailant was nearby and would find him at any moment. The anxiety of this thought made him want to crawl away. He had to find a way to escape this person.

Phillip pulled himself forward with his left arm. He let out an involuntary gasp of pain and then a cry as his right arm scraped against the ground. He couldn't be sure, but he thought at least one leg was broken from the fall. Crawling proved to be a painful challenge.

Before he could get far, the assailant found him. Phillip looked up to see who it was but was unable to focus his eyes. Without care for the bullet wound, the assailant took both of his arms and dragged him down the hill. Phillip didn't know if he cried out, because rational thought left him. His mind went blank from the pain of the right arm being pulled over his head.

Going in and out of consciousness, Phillip registered rocks and debris scraping against his body. *When is this going to end?* Phillip howled in his mind. He couldn't form words, as the pain was too intense. A small amount of relief went through him as his body fell into the water. He floated; the cold water caused a shock to his system and he again fell unconscious. The last thought to go through his mind was, *I'm going to die.*

Two

THE WEATHER IN NORTHERN ENGLAND was cold and a bit breezy. Miss Emma Parker loved taking advantage of the cool air during the end of spring and opening days of summer. She sat in the parlor by an open window with her mother, two brothers, and sister. Their father was expected to arrive at some point in the evening. He had business in Lincolnshire and had been gone for a fortnight. She enjoyed sitting in a seat near the window so she could look out at the trees and flowers surrounding Springhill Abby. She sat entertaining herself with a book of Shakespeare's sonnets.

Not for the first time, Emma read Sonnet 116 and wondered what Shakespeare must have been thinking when he wrote the beautiful lines of love. As a young lady of eighteen, she had attended her first season in London the previous year. Her parents hoped her older sister would marry before Emma entered society, but after Anne's third season she was still unmarried.

Due to her inexperience with love, Emma often imagined finding her future husband. The daydream included him walking toward her across a ballroom and asking her father if he could be introduced. The gentleman would then tell Emma he had dreamed of her his entire life, and it would be love at first sight.

Her mother, father, and brothers would think she was silly if she told them her dream. But Anne listened and for a while told Emma to keep dreaming of her handsome gentleman, for Anne had not found many gentlemen in London. The previous season Anne had a near engagement to Mr. Christian Bennett, but before an offer of marriage arrived, Mr. Bennett left London and didn't return for the rest of the season. Anne returned to Springhill Abby with a broken heart and changed her advice to her sister. She told Emma to forget about love and the dream of romance. She advised Emma to find a match to give her a comfortable life and hope for happiness in marriage. If happiness didn't come from the gentleman, then hope would come in the form of children.

Distracted from her thoughts, she watched as her father's carriage approached. It was going much faster than normal.

"Father is here," she called out as she closed her book.

"I was beginning to worry," her mother said, looking up from her stitching.

"I think something is amiss," she said, her voice trailing off as she stood from her seat.

"What do you mean?" Henry asked, walking over to look out the window.

Emma watched as her father lifted a man from the carriage. She found herself running along with her brother out of the parlor and into the entryway, where her father was giving orders and servants were rushing to do as he said. Her eyes rested on the man they carried. He was wet and covered in blood and mud. Compassion filled her when she saw blood dripping on the floor as they carried him past her.

"Put him in the green room," her mother called, stepping in to take charge of the situation. "Henry, send for Doctor Price."

Emma followed her parents to the green room and watched as they laid the man on the bed. She wanted to help but wasn't certain how.

"Emma, get blankets," her father yelled.

"Anne, bring warm water and towels. Now!" their mother yelled as she continued to remove his clothing.

Emma ran down the hall and grabbed blankets out of a linen closet. She'd never seen anyone this badly injured. She turned to run back to the room and bumped into Meg, the maid in charge of building fires in the grates. Meg carried an arm full of wood, which spilled out of her hands as they collided.

"I'm sorry, miss. I didn't see you," Meg cried out, bending to gather the wood.

"It is my fault, Meg. Please let me help you."

"Emma, where are the blankets?" her mother called out.

"Please, miss, I will gather the wood. Take the blankets," Meg whispered while scrambling to gather the fallen items.

Emma nodded her understanding and continued down the hall to the green room. "I have the—" her words cut off as she saw the man's unclothed legs. She blushed and walked into the room.

"Leave the bed clothes and go out of the room," her mother said, pointing to the end of the bed.

Meg scurried into the room, arms burdened with wood. She dropped the wood as she saw the man's legs. Emma ran over and helped her. She moved the wood over to the fireplace and helped stack it when she heard the man moan.

"Is he awake?" Emma asked, jumping up from the floor. She wanted to help but knew she should leave as her mother had asked.

"Go out, Emma. We need to clean him," her father said, pulling the blankets down.

As she walked out of the room, Anne hurried in with a bucket of hot water and towels. Their housekeeper, Mrs. Lampton, rushed into the room with her.

"Anne, go with Emma back to the parlor," their mother said. "When the doctor arrives, have Henry escort him in."

"I don't know if he will live. A lot depends on the internal injuries." The doctor put his tools in a bag. "I will send a nurse to care for him. She should be here by morning."

"How long before we will know if his injuries are fatal?" her father asked.

"The nurse will watch his breathing. If he starts to cough blood, or if his lungs fill with fluid, he won't survive. We also need to watch the bullet wound for further bleeding."

Emma pulled the chair from the side desk and set it next to the bed. She sat down to look at the man. His face and head were covered in bandages, along with his legs and arms. There wasn't an uninjured part of his body. "I will stay with him until the nurse arrives." Perhaps it was the romantic within her, but she wanted to give this man some kind of comfort.

"Anne, you will stay in here with your sister," their father said, refusing argument from either of his daughters.

Emma walked to the drawing room and grabbed the book of Shakespearean sonnets she had been reading and her sketchpad and pencil. She wanted to read out loud but also wanted to let the man sleep. She decided to spend time on the landscape in her sketchbook.

Imagining the seaside as she had seen it during a trip to Liverpool with her father, she attempted to finish the drawing from memory. As she drew one of the ships, she looked over to see Anne was sleeping in the plush brown chair near the window. She went back to drawing and again looked up after a moment to look at the injured man. She wondered what color his eyes were. Blue would look dashing with his hair. She'd always loved men with blue eyes.

He could be described in one word: handsome. His blond hair had streaks of light brown. She could see from the streaks the sun had begun to bleach his hair. He had a scar near his left eye, untouched by the damage done to his body. The silent sleeping face showed a vulnerability rarely seen in men. She was used to her brothers and father showing constant strength, and she had a feeling this man would be the same when awake. But as he slept, she imagined he had a very tender side.

The romantic within her hoped he loved Shakespeare, her favorite writer. She imagined reading to him and looked back at the book of sonnets she had brought with her. Again, she looked over at her sister to see she was asleep.

In a split-second decision, she decided to draw the man in front of her. She had never tried her hand at portraits, but she found herself inspired to draw this man in his current circumstances: injured, vulnerable, and handsome.

Three

EDWARD STOOD IN THE PARLOR with his family, waiting to go into dinner. Phillip had not yet arrived, and everyone was waiting for him. It wouldn't be an inconvenience if it was just their family, but they had a house full of people due to the upcoming wedding. He looked over at his parents, who were conversing with their guests and wondered what punishment his father would deal out when Phillip arrived.

The butler, Mr. Hodgens, entered the room and walked over to the duke. The room erupted into questioning whispers when Ashby announced, "We will go into dinner now."

Edward took Charlotte's arm and escorted her into the dining hall. The only vacant seat at the table belonged to Phillip, and it was next to Lady Olivia. He saw a smile cross Olivia's face as the footman helped her into her chair and she viewed the vacant spot. *Well, at least someone is happy he isn't here,* he thought as he watched her happiness increase with each round of the meal arriving and Phillip's chair remaining empty.

The party didn't break up until three o'clock in the morning, and Phillip had still not arrived. Edward checked his brother's room, library, and their father's den. He walked out to the stables as the party ended and noticed Bassanio standing in the yard, saddled and roaming.

Edward walked forward and took hold of the reins. He pulled Bassanio to the fence and tied him off. Using the lamp, he walked around the horse and experienced a jolt of surprise when his hand ran across a sticky wetness. He brought his fingers up to the lamp. Before he could process the word *blood*, Edward set off for the house.

"Father," Edward said as he rushed into the parlor. "I'm going to search for Phillip."

"Not tonight. If he isn't back by morning, we can start a search."

Edward held his fingers up. "Bassanio is in the yard. He's covered in blood."

The room erupted for the second time as his father started calling out orders. Although everyone was exhausted from the long day, horses were saddled and the men split into search groups. Edward rode out with his father and Charles.

They checked the meadow near the stream where Phillip spent the majority of his time relaxing. When they did not find him, they rode around the meadow, searching under each tree. Frustration loomed as they rode the property and found zero evidence of his brother.

As the sun rose, they rode back to the house to see if anyone had better luck. Edward was ill as he heard the reports coming in. No one had found him.

His mother had the serving staff provide breakfast to the men before they set out again. Edward was exhausted but nearly lost his temper when he saw Olivia flirting with Lord Folly.

"She doesn't look worried about Phillip's disappearance," Edward growled as he glared at Olivia.

"She made it clear during the garden party she wants nothing to do with this marriage," Marianne said as she stifled a yawn. "She told more than one of our guests Phillip can't find a wife during the London season and so our father negotiated to trap her in a marriage with him."

Edward raised his eyebrows and with a disbelieving chuckle responded, "The Earl of Arundel can't find a wife? And these women believed her?"

"I don't think they believed her," Charlotte said as she put a calming hand on Edward's shoulder. "We all know Phillip does not have a hard time finding women to flirt with, even if he does not have your humor."

"We have to have a way for people to tell us apart if they don't see the scar by his eye," he said by way of explanation.

Their father approached and put his hand on Edward's shoulder. "Constable Adams is organizing a search party in the yard."

"I'm going out again." Edward wouldn't stay behind.

"Your Grace," Constable Adams called out, walking through

the stable, "I've given the leaders of each group a map of the area and an assignment of where to search. If any of them find the earl or any sign of him, they will shoot a flare in the air."

"Thank you, Adams. Arundel disappeared yesterday morning," his father said as he took the reins of his horse, ready to leave again.

"Within the next few hours it will be full daylight and it will warm up. The night temperatures dropped low, so time is crucial. He's injured and will need a physician." Constable Adams finished by taking his horse by the bit.

By supper, the room was eerily silent with Phillip's continued absence. Edward sat looking at the food on his plate. He couldn't bring himself to eat when his brother was injured and lost. Many scenarios ran through his mind. Had he been abducted? Was he dead? Did he fall from his horse?

"Edward," Duchess Ashby said in a whisper, "if you're going out again you will need your strength."

He nodded and took a bite of a roll. He knew his mother was correct, and he didn't want to be left behind if he didn't have enough strength. As he was cutting the beef on the plate, Hunter, the stable hand, came running into the dining room.

"Your Grace," he called out. Then as though he remembered he was entering the home of a duke, he bowed and tried to stand with some grace. "They found blood."

"Where?" Ashby asked, jumping to his feet.

Edward and Charles both flew out of their chairs, along with a few others in the room.

"Near the hill." Hunter bent over, hands on knees, taking a deep breath.

"Did you find my son?"

Hunter looked up. It was obvious he didn't want to answer the question, but he continued. "Constable Adams believes he fell down the hill. He sent men to search."

Letting Hunter's words sink in, Edward asked, "Blood?"

"Yes, my lord," Hunter whispered.

Although it was already dark, Edward and his father moved toward the stables. "Hunter, saddle my horse," Ashby called.

Four

"'SHALL I COMPARE THEE TO a summer's day? Thou art more lovely and more temperate: Rough winds do shake the darling buds of May—'" Emma looked up when she heard a moan. "Nurse Brown, he's coming around."

He blinked a few times. She could see from his expression he was in pain.

"I'm going to send for the doctor," Nurse Brown said as she placed her embroidery aside and moved toward the door.

"Please have a maid bring a bowl of broth." Emma turned back to him and noticed he fell back to sleep. She watched as his eyelids twitched. "Are you sleeping? Or are you in pain?" she asked out loud, hoping her voice would pull him into consciousness. She moved his dirty blond hair off his face and thought about how long it had grown in the weeks he had been in their home.

"He's sleeping again?" the doctor asked as he approached the bed.

Emma pulled her hand back, regretting her decision to touch his hair. "Yes, but his eyelids keep twitching as though he is trying to wake up."

The doctor moved around the bed to examine the man. She watched the man's face and wondered what he could be dreaming about when his eyes flew open.

"Doctor, he is awake again," she said as he looked at the gunshot wound in the shoulder.

The man opened his mouth to speak but let out a moan instead.

"Welcome to Springhill Abby." Emma moved aside as her father approached. "This is my wife and daughter. My name is Lord Anthony Parker. Nurse Brown and Doctor Price are caring for you."

The doctor looked up from the shoulder after replacing the bandages. "Nurse Brown has some broth to feed you. It will help you regain strength." Turning to the others in the room he said, "Let's go out and give him some time. Waking up in an unknown place can cause unneeded stress, and right now we don't want him stressed."

Emma watched as the nurse gave him half-spoons of broth. A great deal of it ran down the side along his neck, as if he were a small child learning to eat.

Emma left the room as he fell back into unconsciousness. She wanted to hear the doctor's diagnosis.

"He is healing. Keep him in bed and try to get food into him whenever possible."

Emma read the words, "Let me not to the marriage of true minds admit—"

"Do you always read Shakespeare's Sonnets, or do you branch out to his other works?" the man asked, cutting her off in the middle of the reading. His voice cracked from non-use and dryness.

She startled a little at his question. "I do enjoy his other works as well." She smiled and said conspiratorially, "Nurse Brown was certain you were a mute."

He smiled at her jest. "Talking is painful."

"I can see the pain in your eyes," Emma said. She cringed as she heard the words. *I am transparent! But he does have startling blue eyes.* To cover her embarrassment she said, "My name is Miss Emma Parker."

"Thank you for reading to me, Miss Parker." He closed his eyes and took a raspy breath. "How long have I been here?"

The question caught her off guard. She expected him to tell her his name. She brushed over the lack of propriety and answered, "You have been here a fortnight." Gathering her courage she asked, "Can you tell me your name?"

He paused and she wondered if he was in too much pain to answer any more questions. "I don't remember my name."

She tried to hide her surprise but didn't do well. She stammered, "I will send to the kitchen to get you something to eat, and then I will send for Doctor Price." She looked to the side of the room and motioned to Nurse Brown.

"He doesn't remember his name."

"I heard. Have your father send for Doctor Price."

Emma stood by the window, watching for the doctor. She tried to imagine what it would be like to wake up in a strange home and not know her name. She thought about the beautiful blue eyes of the stranger in the green room and tried to imagine his name. They could make something up for him.

Doctor Price checked his pulse, listened to his chest for fluids in the lungs, and examined the injuries.

"Do you have any memory of arriving here?" Price asked.

The man looked around the room before answering, "No." She could've imagined it, but he looked nervous and a bit frightened.

"Do you have any memories we can use to find your family?"

"I keep thinking of the name Bassanio," he said with a hopeful tone of recognition.

"He is a character from Shakespeare's *Merchant of Venice*." Emma spoke up from her place by the door. She could tell he was educated due to his use of language and his knowledge of Shakespeare. *His knowledge of Shakespeare!* she repeated to herself. She didn't know anything about him, yet she feared she would lose her heart to him simply because he knew Shakespeare.

The doctor smiled. "Looks like you were able to hear Miss Emma during your hours of sleep."

"What happened to me?"

"You were found in the river caught in some debris. It looked as though it stopped you from going further down the river. As for your injuries, you are fortunate Lord Anthony was delayed on his journey home. Otherwise it would have been morning before you were found."

"I am in your debt, my lord."

"There is no need to thank me. We are happy to have you healing," her father responded. "Doctor Price sent out inquiries to see if a missing person has been reported matching your description. We hope it won't be long before we find your family."

Emma watched as her mother moved forward and pulled the covers up to his chin. "Until we find your family, take care to keep warm, and let us know if you need anything. We don't want you catching a cold on top of the injuries you've already sustained. Nurse Brown will continue to keep you comfortable."

"What are my injuries?"

"Your right leg is fractured in two different areas, but don't worry; you'll have full use of the leg. I've set the bone and with the lack of movement over the last fortnight, it has started healing. You had a gunshot wound in your shoulder, but it is mending. The contusions on your face and body have all but healed, and the bruising has gone down as I expected. You are on your way to a full recovery." He patted the man's good shoulder before continuing, "Of course the addition of amnesia is a setback. But a minor one. It was caused by the injuries to your head, or the shock of cold water could have done it. But it should be temporary. In time you'll regain your memories."

"How long do you think it will take for my memory to return?"

"I cannot put a time frame on this particular injury. Fractures and contusions heal over a few weeks, but the mind is a different type of medicine. I believe to increase the chances of your memory returning, it will be necessary for us to find your family. You need to be surrounded by familiar people and places."

"I don't even know what town I am in."

"You are in Stafford," the doctor stated as he gathered his instruments.

Emma left the room to get some air. She walked out to the garden and thought about the nameless man. She was going to have to come up with a name for him.

Five

"Have you had any memories come back?" Emma asked as she pushed him through the garden in a wheelchair.

He was allowed to leave his room in a wheelchair and for short visits to the garden.

"I keep seeing a face," he said.

"Is it a woman's face or a man's face?" she asked, feeling as though she was transparent.

"A woman's face," he said in response.

"Do you think it could be your mother? Or a sister?" She was making a complete fool of herself prying into his memories.

"I'm not certain."

She wanted to scream; every answer he gave was short and to the point. He didn't elaborate on anything, and he gave very little information.

"Do you have any feelings when you see her face?"

"Somewhat," he responded.

She continued to push him through the garden, hoping he would say more, but he remained silent. She decided to push him over to a bench where she could sit and enjoy the air as well.

Emma was surprised when he asked, "Will you tell me about your family?"

She considered the information to share with him for a moment and started, "My father is the youngest son of a duke. This is the home he inherited. His brother inherited everything else."

"It is a beautiful home," he said. "Which of your brothers will inherit?"

"Henry is the oldest."

"He looks too young to be the oldest."

"He is twenty-four years old. Are you saying Anne looks old?" she asked, raising her eyebrows with a large smile to show she was teasing him.

"I would never suggest a woman looks old," he responded with mock abhorrence.

"I think this is the first smile I've seen on your face since you've been here," she said. A strange sensation came over her as she bent toward him. She wondered what it would be like to have him touch her face or hold her hand.

"I haven't had much to smile over. Or perhaps it is all of the contusions healing on my face. If I smile too much, they could reopen."

Pulling herself out of her thoughts, she giggled a little. "I've never heard such a ridiculous excuse."

"Tell me more about your family."

"Richard and I are the youngest. Richard wants to go into the clergy. He is twenty. Anne is twenty-two. Last year we thought Anne would be married by the end of the season. Mr. Bennett spent a lot of time with her throughout the season. We were all surprised when he left London and broke Anne's heart."

"Mr. Bennett? I think I might know him."

Emma perked up and turned toward her friend. "You think you know him?"

"The name sounds familiar."

"Perhaps he will know you. My family plans on going to London for the season. If you remain with us, you will also go."

"I have a few months to start walking again; perhaps I will be able to dance by the time the season starts," he joked.

Silence followed their conversation as Emma tried to find another conversation starter. She noticed he was rubbing the sides of his head with his eyes closed.

"Are you ill?" she asked, reaching toward him.

"A headache is all. I am certain it will go away soon," he said as he continued to rub the sides of his head.

"Would you like to go back inside?"

He looked up at her and gave a sad smile. "I think it would be best. Perhaps it is the sunlight causing the pain."

She pushed him back into the house and waited as Nurse Brown helped him into his bed. The pain in his head seemed to increase from the time he was in the garden to getting him back to his room. The nurse sent her to get a servant and hot water and asked her to give him time to sleep.

Emma was not allowed into the sick room without Nurse Brown now that their houseguest was healing. Doctor Price arrived to assess the headache, so Emma decided to take some time to herself. She gathered her notebook and pencil and walked out to the orchard. She found a soft spot under a tree and looked through the drawings she had already finished. She had drawn the man in their house numerous times as he slept. Now she wanted to draw him with his face healed. She started drawing from memory as she spent so much time in his presence.

"May I join you?"

Emma looked up to see Anne walking toward her. "Yes, you may."

"Does he have any memories back yet?" she asked as she sat.

"He said he continues to see a woman's face. I thought I would die of curiosity when he would not answer my question about how he feels when he sees this woman. Do you think he could have an intended?"

She saw the knowing smile on Anne's face. "What if the woman is his wife?"

"Never say so!" Emma said while cringing.

"I worry you are allowing your romantic sensibilities to run away from you."

Emma blushed. "I know. I can't help myself."

She saw Anne's eyes focus on her pad of paper and regretted not trying to hide it when they were talking. "What have you been drawing?" she asked as she reached forward and grabbed it.

"Landscapes; they aren't very interesting," she said, trying to take the book back from her sister.

The book opened and one of the drawings of their houseguest fell out. "Oh, Emma." The pity in Anne's eyes was evident.

Emma looked down at her hands and admitted, "I'm very fond of him."

"I feared you were." She examined all of the portraits in the notebook, thumbing through each page and shaking her head. "These are very good drawings."

"A nice way to look on the bright side of the mess I'm in." She wiped the tears away as they formed.

They sat in silence as Anne continued to look through the drawings. Emma rested her head on her sister's shoulder.

Anne rubbed Emma's back. "How long have you been drawing him?"

"Since the night he arrived." She closed her eyes so she wouldn't see her sister's response. "Am I a lost cause?" she asked as her sister finished thumbing through the sketches.

"You are hopeless," Anne said with a laugh, "but we need to go inside. Mother sent me here to find you. Father and Henry are due from London."

They walked arm in arm back to the house. Emma continued to wipe the tears away, hoping her insensible romantic heart would stop hurting before they reached the house. "Has the doctor relieved his headache?"

"When I left they were administering laudanum. He should be sleeping."

Six

THE DAYS AND WEEKS BLENDED together as Edward and his family waited for information regarding Phillip. He'd been missing for two weeks. The house party ended much sooner than it was supposed to due to the disappearance. Edward continued to hold out hope of Phillip being found, as did his entire family. His moods went from worried, to anger, to fear, and finally to grief. His heart was breaking, as a part of it was missing. He and Phillip had only ever been separated for short periods of times in the past, but they always knew where the other one was.

Lord Folly admitted to seeing Phillip ride out the morning of the party. He was the last one to see Phillip alive. The thought of his brother's death caused Edward to feel like he might lose his mind. Thomas admitted to putting a book in Phillip's saddlebags. The book of Shakespeare's sonnets was found in perfect condition.

Constable Adams asked the duke and duchess for an audience with Edward. Edward paced back and forth through the parlor, wishing the conversation was over. He had a feeling he knew what the conversation was going to be. The heir to the dukedom had disappeared. They were searching for reasons anyone would want to kill him.

"Your Grace," Mr. Hodgens said as he walked into the parlor, "Constable Adams is here to see Master Edward."

"Thank you, Hodgens," his father said, standing from his place on the couch. "Please show him in."

Edward looked to his parents. Charles, Charlotte, and Marianne were all in the parlor with them. Each one expressed their desire to stay during the meeting. He wondered if the constable would allow them to stay for support. Now the constable had arrived, and Edward wished he was back to pacing and waiting.

"Constable Adams," Hodgens announced.

The man walked into the room and bowed to Ashby, Duchess Margaret, and the girls. He then turned and said, "Lord Edward, I would like to speak with you in private."

"Anything you have to say to Edward will be said in front of the rest of us," Ashby said. He spoke in a commanding voice, letting the constable know there was no need to argue.

Adams nodded his head and moved further into the room. Edward pointed toward the chair his father vacated and sat with the constable.

"Lord Edward," Constable Adams said as he pulled his notebook and pencil out of his pocket, "where were you the day Lord Arundel disappeared?"

Edward was ready for the question. "I was at the garden party."

"Which was held where?" Adams asked.

"It was held here at Wentworth Hall," Edward said in response.

"Tell me," Constable Adams continued, "can anyone verify you were at the garden party?"

"I can," Charles stated, cutting into the conversation.

"I can also," Marianne and Charlotte both said at the same time.

Constable Adams turned to look at the them. "You can verify he was at the party the entire time? There was not a single moment he was out of your sight?"

Charles chose to speak. "Certainly he was out of our sight as we were speaking with guests throughout the day. But he was here."

Constable Adams wrote on his notepad. He sat back in his chair for a moment, contemplating, and then turned to ask Edward, "When did you notice Lord Arundel was no longer at the party?"

Edward shook his head in frustration. "I don't remember when I realized he was gone."

"Why would he leave?" Constable Adams asked Edward immediately after receiving the last answer.

"He was unhappy about the engagement. He didn't want to marry Lady Olivia," Edward supplied. He looked at his father, who was facing the mantel of the fireplace.

"Where did you disappear to during the party?" Adams asked, again not giving any time between questions.

Edward stopped speaking, as he didn't expect the question. He thought his assignation with Lady Caroline had gone unnoticed.

"I have a witness who will testify you left the party after Lord Arundel. Where did you go?"

Unsure how much he should say, Edward remained silent. He looked to his parents to see the disbelief in their expressions but still said nothing. If he divulged his whereabouts, it would bring more questions, and Caroline wouldn't appreciate his loose tongue.

Adams looked up from his notepad. "Answer my question."

"What were you told about my brief outing?"

"My witness saw you leaving the party."

"So, you have no evidence of foul play, but you come here to accuse me and make my family believe I had part in my brother's disappearance?"

Adams didn't respond. Instead he fired off another question. "Did you follow Arundel into the woods and kill him?"

"Certainly not!" Edward said, anger rising in his voice.

"Why did you follow him into the woods?"

"I didn't follow him."

"Where did you go?"

"You may continue to ask, and I will continue to ignore your question. I have no intention of divulging my secrets."

"Edward," his father said in anger, "answer the constable so he can move forward in this investigation."

"I cannot, Father." Edward refused to cower. He'd always found favor with the duke and didn't have any fear of ignoring an order.

He watched as Ashby ran a hand through his hair while he considered what to say. "Adams, Edward did not injure Arundel. I can attest to his innocence."

"You believe this, yet you have no indication of where Lord Edward went during the hour he was away from the party?"

"Yes, I trust my son."

Turning to Edward, Constable Adams continued, "You are now the heir to the dukedom. Do you see how suspicious it looks? There is an hour of missing time where no one can vouch for your presence."

Edward stood, feeling anger build. It was rare for him to lose his temper, but Constable Adams had crossed a line. "I don't want to be the heir. If Phillip is gone from this world, which I don't believe he is, I will be more than happy to give the inheritance to Charles."

"Edward!" Ashby yelled. This was the first time Edward could ever remember hearing his father's voice raised toward him. Phillip always received the rebuke and punishment, because his father held him accountable for far too much. It wasn't fair to Phillip, but it was the way of their father.

"Yes?" Edward asked with defiance.

"Tell Adams where you went during the party."

"No, I cannot."

Edward wasn't expecting the impact. Just as Ashby had never yelled at him, he had never hit Edward. He should have recognized the symptoms of abuse, as he'd seen Ashby hit Phillip for as long as his memory went back, but it was a surprise to him to be hit. Edward stepped backward and stared in disbelief.

"Tell the constable where you went. *Now.*"

Edward stood tall, as Phillip had always done during the beatings. If he now was the heir, this was the future he had ahead of him. He would have to get used to the abuse. "No, I cannot divulge the information because it not only affects me but another as well. I will not ruin her reputation."

He'd said too much. His father's eyes went wide, as did his mother's. He didn't say anything more. Edward didn't mind a small flirtation with a woman. Nor did he mind meeting up for a tête-à-tête, but he wouldn't do anything to destroy a woman's reputation.

"Who is the woman?" Adams asked. It was obvious he didn't believe Edward in the slightest.

"Stop circling around the questions you want to ask," Edward said, angry with the constable and his father.

"Did you kill your brother?"

"No, I didn't."

"Did you take a gun and shoot your brother?"

"No," Edward said, anger rising in his voice, "I didn't."

"If I were to search your room, would I find evidence of your day in the woods?"

"I didn't spend the day in the woods," Edward responded. He knew the constable was trying to catch him in a lie, but there wasn't anything to hide.

"I found a ring by the river," Constable Adams said, opening a handkerchief to show the finding. "Do you recognize this?"

Edward walked forward and took the ring from the constable. Blood drain from his face. "Yes, I recognize it."

"Who does it belong to?" he asked even though the smug look on his face told Edward he already knew.

"It's mine," Edward continued. "I haven't worn it for over a year, though."

"Convenient."

"This ring has been sitting in my room. I do not know how it ended up by the river."

"You will be in my custody until further notice," Constable Adams said. He stood and took the ring back, motioning for Edward to join him.

His father walked forward and stopped Constable Adams from progressing. "You won't take Edward into custody."

"Your Grace," Adams said, defending his decision, "your heir has gone missing. The one person with motive at this time is your son next in line for the inheritance. His ring was found near a pool of blood at the river, and he disappeared for at least an hour and refuses to give evidence to save himself. Unless you have another person to suggest, I will have to take him into custody."

"Edward was the first person to suggest going out to search for his brother. Why would he make the suggestion if he was the one to kill him?" Ashby responded, trying to persuade Adams to look elsewhere for the culprit.

Constable Adams looked at Ashby. "Don't make this harder than it already is, Your Grace. I have known both Phillip and Edward since they were young boys. I have caught them in their pranks, and I have seen them grow into respectable men. This doesn't make me happy. And the loss of Phillip is not only a tragedy for your family but for the entire community."

"Do you think I don't feel the loss of my twin brother?" Edward asked, cutting into the conversation. "He is my brother. He is my double. He is my other half. I feel his loss much more than this community. But I don't believe he is dead." He finished, feeling defeated and tired.

Constable Adams looked at Edward for a few minutes before responding, "We've finished a five-mile search down the hill and the surrounding area. As you know, we were able to track his horse from an area by the stream. The route he took was erratic and didn't make much sense. Can you tell me why he would take such a strange route?"

"I can only imagine the situation for this course of action," Edward responded.

"Our tracker found Lord Arundel's riding jacket, hat, one boot . . ." The constable hesitated before finishing. "A great deal of blood."

Edward put his head in his hands. Phillip was alive; he had to be. Being a twin, Edward convinced himself he should know if his brother were gone from the world.

"So, you found blood," Edward said in frustration as he ran a hand through his hair. "Blood does not mean he is dead."

"Lord Edward," the constable said impatiently, "your brother is dead. No one could live after losing the amount we found while stuck out in the cold night air. He was shot. We found three bullets lodged in trees. One of them had blood on it."

Edward closed his eyes and took a deep breath, trying to decide on a response.

"I have no doubt after he fell off the horse he didn't live much longer. We are searching the river for a body." Constable Adams stood. "When we find his body, I will prove you did this. Now, you can either come willingly, or I will arrest you."

"This is not the answer!" Ashby yelled at the constable, punching the wall. "Edward would never kill Arundel. Never!"

Edward wanted to be thankful for his father, but he was still in shock over being hit. It happened so fast; he hadn't expected it.

His mother took hold of his arm and spoke to Constable Adams. "If you take Edward into custody, you will need to arrest me as well. I will not have my son sitting in a jail cell when he has not done anything to deserve it. He is already struggling with the loss. I will not have you add this to his stress."

In another attempt to have the constable search for Phillip, Ashby asked, "Have you checked at local farms? Or what about doing a search of local villages? Have you sent his description out?"

"Your Grace," Constable Adams said again in an effort to help the family understand they were holding out false hope. "We are searching to recover a body. We don't expect to find him living. And no, I will not send a description out. His body is at the bottom of the river."

Edward bent low over his legs, head in his lap. He couldn't handle listening to the constable announce his brother's death and accuse him of the murder. He blocked everything else out of his mind as the constable finished his statement. "It would be a miracle if Lord Arundel survived. Again, we are looking to retrieve a body."

The constable put a hand on Edward's shoulder. Edward stood without a word to anyone in his family and allowed the constable to lead him out to the wagon. Constable Adams tied his hands to the railing on the wagon seat. Edward looked back at his family as the constable drove him toward the town jail. He didn't know how long it would take for Ashby to get him released, but he knew his father wouldn't make him sit in jail for long, if only to keep society from gossiping.

He was put in a cell by himself. Edward didn't speak to the constable; he didn't eat the food brought to him for the afternoon meal or evening meal. Edward tried to sleep but couldn't get his mind to stop racing. If Phillip were dead, Edward knew his brother's spirit would be sitting with him, lending him support and comfort in the cell. He didn't realize he fell asleep until the keys to the cell hit against the bars.

"Wake up, Lord Edward," Constable Adams said, walking into the cell with a tray of food. "It's morning. You must be hungry."

Edward groggily looked up at him. "I'm not hungry. You may take the plate away."

"If you desire me to do so, I will," he said, picking up the tray. "Once you tell me where you put your brother's body, we can discuss your future."

Edward glared at the constable. "I didn't attack my brother. You are accusing the wrong man."

"Lord Arundel," Constable Adams said.

Edward looked out the cell in confusion. When he saw they were still alone he asked, "Why are you calling me by my brother's name?"

"It's now your title. Your brother is dead, which makes you the Earl of Arundel."

"My brother is still alive. He is the earl. I am not. Nor will I ever be." Edward lay back down on the cot and turned his back toward Constable Adams.

"If you say so," Adams responded.

Edward heard him leave the cell and lock it again. He didn't turn to see if Adams left the area. He stayed facing the wall and eventually fell asleep again. As the morning turned into night, Edward continued to hope his father would get him released from the cell. He heard Ashby arguing with Adams at one point during the day but wasn't allowed to see him.

Edward refused to eat throughout his entire time in the cell. On the fourth morning, he was released. His father's solicitor walked into the jail and handed over paperwork. Within an hour Edward was sitting in a carriage going home to Wentworth Hall.

Seven

HEADACHES WERE A COMMON OCCURRENCE for Phillip as his body continued to heal. Each time he was administered laudanum, he slept for long periods of time. Sometimes days would pass before the headache would dissolve.

He tried to pull out of a drug-induced sleep when his mind turned to a dream. While riding a horse, he watched from a distance as two girls ran through an apple orchard. The older girl had golden hair, and the younger had auburn. Both were dressed in frocks, indicating they were enjoying free time from daily studies with a governess. The governess followed with a scowl at a much slower pace, as she was not as young and quick as she needed to be for small children.

"Marianne. Charlotte. Don't climb the tree," the governess called out to the girls as she tried to catch up to them.

"Marianne," the older called out to her sister, "you cannot catch me."

They both ran crisscrossing through the trees farther away from the governess. It wasn't long before they were out of the governess's sight and climbing trees.

"I can climb higher than you," Marianne called over to her sister.

"You cannot reach the top like me," Charlotte challenged back.

"I can see Phillip and Edward," Marianne yelled over as she continued to climb. "I am climbing higher than you."

It was true. Marianne was climbing to the top of the tree where the branches were not as thick as they were below. The branches broke as she continued to climb. She was frightened. She cried and Charlotte called for Phillip to help.

The boys who looked like doubles were suddenly next to the tree, one climbing to the top to help his little sister down. The only difference between them was the slight difference in the color of their hair. Streaks of brown filtered through the hair of the one who stayed below the tree. The other had spent too much time in the sun, and the streaks in his hair had been bleached to be more blond than brown.

"Phillip, hurry!" Charlotte called out from the bottom of the tree. "She's going to fall."

It was true. The branches were breaking at the top of the tree. The governess found the children and was yelling at the two on the ground for allowing their sister to climb the apple tree. When the boy named Phillip reached his sister, he began talking her down the tree and guiding her as she slowly made her way to the bottom. When she was almost at the bottom, the governess grabbed her leg, thinking it would be easier to pull her down instead of waiting for her to finish the descent. As Marianne fell the rest of the way out of the tree, the governess missed catching her and she hit the ground. She burst into tears from her injury.

The dream shifted as the children were now all standing in front of a man. Although a towering man, he held his crying child in his arms and comforted her. The governess told the story from her perspective. She blamed the twin boys for encouraging their sister to climb the tree, even though neither had done so. The dream shifted as Phillip was slapped across the face. His father's ring turned, so the family crest was on the inside of his hand when he slapped the boy, causing blood to form near his left eye.

Phillip woke with a start. He pulled himself up and tried to get out of the bed. He was confused by his surroundings as he was coming out of a drugged-induced sleep, but the dream he'd just woken from had been far too real to be his imagination.

"Calm down," he heard a woman say. He turned to see Lady Amelia sitting next to him. She gently pushed him back onto the bed and pulled the covers back up. A wet cloth was placed against his forehead. The calming effect this had on him helped his heart rate return to normal, and he was able to go back into another dream-filled sleep.

When he was able to pull out of the haze caused by the laudanum, he remembered every detail of the dream, except the names of the children. He realized it was the early hours of morning, and the vigil the Parkers kept at his bed was vacant. Pulling himself to the end of the bed across from the only mirror in the room, he moved his finger over the scar next to his left eye.

The children in the dream were his siblings. He was certain of the relationship with them. The man who hit him was his father; again, there was no question in his mind to the identity of the man. The most frustrating part of waking up from a dream where a memory had come back was the lack of remembering names. The only name he did remember was Miss Hazel, the governess. Remembering her name wasn't much use to him in his situation, but it was a start.

He was able to venture out to the garden for a short walk as his headache subsided. He was still a tad murky from the laudanum, but as Nurse Brown left his room to rest, he dressed and made his escape from the confining room. He loved the sunlight and missed being in nature when he was shut in his room.

As he hobbled through the garden on crutches, he anticipated seeing Emma each time he rounded a corner or bend in the walkway, but she was absent. He wandered out to the stable yard, hoping to find her. But she was not to be found.

He didn't know why her absence bothered him. He was surprised when he woke the few times during this last headache to find she wasn't sitting near him reading. She had made a concerted effort to bring him joy by reading something from Shakespeare to him each time he had been ill. But this time she stayed away. An emptiness entered his heart without her.

"Do you know where I can find Miss Emma?" he asked when he saw one of the servants. He didn't know the man's name.

"I believe she is collecting strawberries in the field with Miss Parker, Master Henry, and Master Richard." The young man pointed toward the south end of the property.

He debated with himself on the wisdom of following them out to the strawberry patch for only a short minute. He loved strawberries. The cook at Springhill Abby made the best strawberry preserves he had ever tasted, which, as he thought about it, didn't mean much, since he couldn't remember if he had ever eaten strawberries before.

He decided to venture out to help with the collection. He found he was winded after a short time, due to having to use crutches on the dirt, grass, and weeds covering the small hill he had to climb to get to the group. He could see Emma and her siblings off in the distance and attempted to increase his speed so he could help collect and sneak a taste of the strawberries. He admired her dark brown hair, almond-shaped green eyes, and slender figure.

"What are you doing out here?" Henry asked, handing his crutches to Richard and helping him down to the ground.

"I wanted to help collect strawberries," he said, hoping Emma would come closer to him. Again, he marveled at the desire he had to be near her.

Richard grabbed a bucket and passed it to him. "You can fill this, but stay down so you don't injure yourself."

"Not a problem," he said with a laugh. "I have to admit I couldn't go much further. I'm a bit tired from the hike."

As he collected the strawberries around him, he thought again about the dream he had the previous night. He didn't mention the dream to anyone, because he didn't know how to reconcile the feelings he had toward his father and he didn't want to discuss them. His dream had been vivid, almost as if he could feel the slap across his face and the skin ripping from beside his eye.

"What are you doing out here?" Emma asked as she sat next to him. Her eyes sparkled as the sun hit them.

"I decided fresh strawberries are better than preserves," he said, popping a small strawberry in his mouth.

"How many of those strawberries have you eaten?"

He looked at his bucket; it had about two layers in it—nowhere near the amount she had in hers. He reached over and picked a few out of her bucket and bit into each one, in turn throwing the leaves and stem to the side. "I've eaten far too many of my own. I hardly have any in my bucket for the kitchen staff," he said with a mischievous smile.

She grabbed her bucket as he reached for more strawberries, trying to keep them safe from him. "You act as though you've never eaten a strawberry in your life," she chided.

"I don't remember ever eating strawberries," he responded with a smile.

She laughed out loud, which drew the attention of her brothers. He picked another strawberry out of the ground and put it in his mouth.

"What are you laughing about?" Richard asked as all of her siblings approached.

Anne sat next to Phillip, and he reached over to take a few of her strawberries from her bucket.

Pointing to Phillip, Emma said, "He can't remember if he has ever eaten a strawberry before coming here. And so he is eating as many as he can."

Henry looked over at him. "Well, at least we know you will eat strawberries. Mother has been trying to figure out what to give you to make you gain some weight."

"Give me anything with strawberries, and I will eat it," he said, stealing a few more from Anne's bucket.

Richard pulled him off the ground, and Henry handed him his crutches. He wobbled a little, feeling as though he'd stood up too quickly. He was thankful no one noticed the sway. He watched as Emma grabbed his bucket, and they slowly made their way back to Springhill Abby.

As they walked, he listened to the Parkers joking with each other and enjoying their time together as family. He hoped he and his siblings were similar to them and enjoyed each other's company.

As they neared the house, another headache pierced his head and neck. He wasn't sure how it happened, but he found himself on the ground, vomiting and shaking. All of the precious strawberries he'd picked and eaten were coming out of him through his mouth and nose.

"Get Nurse Brown," he heard Henry call out as he fell to the side.

This headache had come faster than any of the other headaches he'd experienced while at Springhill Abby. He tried to pull himself off the ground and tried to speak but could not form the words he wanted to say.

"What happened?" Lord Anthony asked as he rushed upon the scene.

His body shook from cold chills. He could feel the sweat accumulating on his head. He opened his eyes and tried to focus, but the sun was far too bright and he regretted the attempt.

"Richard, send Andy for Doctor Price," Lady Amelia said as Henry and Lord Anthony picked him up from the ground.

He knew he was mumbling. He couldn't form a coherent sentence. He wanted to ask what was happening to him. He worried the injuries to his head were so extensive he would suffer with headaches for the rest of his life. He worried he was going to be a burden on the Parkers and his family once they found him.

"What was he doing outside?" Lady Amelia asked as she pulled his one boot from his foot.

"He wanted to help pick strawberries," Emma replied. "He said he loves strawberries."

He could tell his jacket was being removed, the jacket he'd been given from Henry because his was in tatters from his accident.

"Emma, go out. You too Anne," Lady Amelia said to her daughters.

His head was ready to explode. He couldn't tell them to let him suffer without the laudanum. He hated the laudanum and knew the minute they tipped the bottle in his mouth he'd have strange dreams and groggy, muddled thoughts.

Eight

"HE NEVER SHOULD'VE BEEN OUT of this bed," Doctor Price said to the nurse in frustration.

"I apologize," Nurse Brown stammered. "I left for an hour to get rest, and when I returned he was gone."

"Doctor Price," Lady Amelia said in a calming tone, "I should have been in here so Nurse Brown could get some rest. Or I should have asked a maid to stay in here. This is as much my fault as hers."

Doctor Price changed his tune as Emma's mother took partial responsibility for the careless watch. He stammered and sputtered for a moment. "Lady Amelia, can you tell me what occurred during the dream he experienced last night?"

"Do you think it would be useful to mention the dream to him, Doctor?" her father asked.

"It could help bring back some memories. I do think we should ask him about this girl, Marianne," the doctor replied, "although I think we should have the laudanum ready in case the memory causes him stress. He is still too weak to be under a severe amount of stress. The head injuries he incurred have been far worse than I originally anticipated."

Henry interjected into the conversation, "He was joking around when he came out to the strawberry field. He was fine until we neared the house."

"I agree," Richard said, supporting his brother. "What could've caused such a vigorous headache?"

Doctor Price shook his head. "It is hard to say. I don't know what is causing the headaches."

"Could there be an internal injury we don't know about?" her father asked.

Emma closed her eyes as the doctor responded, "If there is, I can't do anything to fix the issue. He will continue to fall ill."

"Can he live like this?" her mother asked, concern etched in her face and voice.

"No, I don't believe anyone with an internal brain injury can live. He will continue to deteriorate before our eyes." Doctor Price looked back in the room as they were standing in the hall. "We need to find his family before he passes."

The thought of their guest passing away from an internal brain injury left Emma sick in her heart. She had feelings for him, and she wanted to keep him in their home forever. He was a kind and generous person. He loved to tease her, and she was fond of him. To think he was terminally ill made her want to scream.

Before the doctor left, he gave instructions to Emma's parents and Nurse Brown. Phillip was not to leave the bedchamber when he woke, and he was to eat as much as they could get down him. As Doctor Price was walking out the door he said, "It sounds as though he enjoys strawberries. Perhaps you can get your cook to put them on each plate so he will eat something."

"We will, Doctor," her mother responded.

Emma sat next to their guest, reading to him as he went in and out of the drug-induced sleep. He was incoherent for days, and this time the pain lasted longer than it should've. She held his arm as the nurse and doctor administered laudanum, because as he came out of sleep he would fight them and beg them not to give him the medication. For a week he couldn't function, and she wondered if the doctor was correct—if the injuries were inside his brain and if he would survive.

On the eighth day, Emma sat at the table, listening to her parents speaking with Doctor Price. He had come to check on the patient, and her mother had invited him to stay for dinner. As the dessert was being cleared, a maid entered the room.

"Doctor—"

Everyone turned to the maid standing in the doorway.

"He is awake. I have helped him with some porridge, although he told me he could feed himself."

"How much did he take?" Nurse Brown asked.

"He only ate a fourth of the bowl, and he drank half a glass of milk."

Everyone exchanged knowing looks. Along with the injuries that his body was attempting to heal, his appetite suffered. He ate very little, and the small amount he did eat was not enough to sustain a grown male. The doctor estimated that Phillip had lost nine kilograms since he'd arrived.

"I'm still concerned about internal injuries," the doctor said as they walked toward the green room. "It's possible a slow internal bleed could be causing the lack of appetite."

When Emma walked in the room, Phillip was sitting in a plush chair by the window with his leg propped up on an ottoman to help keep swelling down. Face pale, his blue eyes had a haunted look in them. He was rubbing the scar on the left side of his face, a scar he had before arriving at their home. She watched as the doctor sat across from him.

"Is your eye hurting?" he asked in concern.

"No," the man answered in a dreamy, far off voice.

"Lady Amelia told me about the restless dream you experienced a week ago. Does the dream have anything to do with the scar near your eye?"

He nodded his head in the affirmative.

"Did you get it when you climbed a tree?"

His head came up at the question. "Was I speaking out loud?"

"Yes. You said the name Marianne a few times," Lady Amelia said as she walked over to him. "Do you know who Marianne is?"

He smiled as he responded, "My sister. She climbed an apple tree when she was younger. She went too high, and I climbed up to help guide her down."

The doctor smiled at him and picked his hand up to check his pulse. "It's promising to have you regain a memory."

Emma wanted to cry for him when he looked over at her mother and asked, "Did I say any other names?"

Her mother shook her head. "You did call out for your father."

He looked questioningly at her mother. "I did?"

"Does this surprise you?" the doctor asked.

"I'm not certain."

Phillip turned his head and continued looking out the window. He didn't speak again as the doctor checked him.

"I believe we have given him a dose or two too much of laudanum. His mind should clear by tomorrow," the doctor said as he stood to leave.

Emma walked over to the chair the doctor vacated and picked up the book on the side table. She opened to the page he had marked as his last reading spot and read *Macbeth* to him as he continued to stare out the window.

As she read the scene where the witches predicted Macbeth would be king one day, he looked up and asked, "How do you think the story would have gone if Macbeth didn't speak to the witches?"

Emma was taken by surprise but thought it an interesting question. "I suppose he wouldn't have been power hungry wouldn't have sought the throne."

"Do you think," he asked, "Lady Macbeth would have spurred the ambition in him even without the help of the witches?"

She noticed a look of intrigue in his eyes as he spoke about the literature. The subject seemed to bring life back into him. "I believe there are some women in this world who make a living out of vexing their husbands," Emma said with a smile. "I have an uncle who would say this about his wife."

He chuckled a little before asking, "Was she a wife of his choosing? Or was it an arranged marriage?"

She was taken aback by his question. "Why do you ask?"

He shrugged. "I want to marry for love." He laughed. "I have amnesia. I have no idea if I have always wanted this or if it's new for me." He looked back out the window. "Was their marriage one of love or convenience?"

Emma smiled. "It was one of convenience. But I believe they made the match during a London season. My uncle has been known to say my aunt was looking for a husband with a title and money."

"What was he looking for when he married her?"

"I think he was looking for a wife and future heirs," she admitted. "Neither one was in it for love."

He kept his eyes on her. "Do you want a marriage of love or one of convenience?"

She knew her cheeks went red as he finished his question, but she wanted to answer him. "I want a marriage of love."

She watched as he turned his head again to look out the window. When he didn't say anything more, she picked the book back up and resumed the reading.

Nine

THE INHABITANTS OF WENTWORTH HALL were in full mourning. The family wore black as each day continued without information regarding Phillip. Edward often spent time in his brother's library, trying to feel close to him while contemplating what had happened. Why hadn't he known his brother was in trouble? As a twin, he should have known something was off. He could only attribute the lack of insight to his activities of the afternoon. Even the thought of Lady Caroline and his attentions to her made him ill. After eight weeks the constable was still unable to give the family and Ashby's solicitor conclusive information regarding the disappearance and the shooting.

The piano his brother played so well was lonely by the window. It'd been too long since Phillip sat playing songs of his composition. Edward didn't have musical abilities. Music wasn't interesting enough when they were younger, and he hadn't developed the talent. Over the years he enjoyed listening to his brother and sisters as they played, but as he sat at the piano remembering his twin, he wished he could reproduce some of the music the house had been filled with for so many years.

"Edward."

He looked over to the door as his parents entered. Lady Ashby wore a plain black dress, and Ashby had the same black band on his arm as Edward. His mother walked over, and he moved on the piano bench so she could sit next to him. Although it made him ill, every time his mother saw him she grabbed him and cried.

He and Phillip were identical, other than a scar on Phillip's face by his left eye. Before he received the scar, the only way anyone could tell them apart was by their personalities. Phillip was philosophical, musical, and a lover of classical books. Edward was a flirt, who loved to joke around and make his family laugh. Of late, he hadn't found anything to laugh about.

"Edward, your mother and I need to speak with you." Ashby sat in a plush chair close to the piano. "There isn't an easy way to say this, but our family needs to move forward."

"I don't want to move on," Edward said, holding his mother. He patted her back to comfort her.

"I understand this is difficult. But we are in the forefront of society. People watch and look to us for strength in these types of situations. If a family as strong and wealthy as ours cannot survive the loss of a child, how do we expect others with less to do so?"

"Tell people to stop looking," Edward responded. He didn't care about social expectations. If Phillip was dead, words he rarely allowed himself to think, he would need a lot more time to process the loss. "How did society respond when I was sitting in a jail cell? Was it not in the society section?"

"We don't get the luxury of spurning society. We are expected in town for Parliament. Your brother was going to start taking an active role this year." He paused as the words sunk in and the situation made itself clear. "As the spare, this responsibility now falls on your shoulders."

Edward pulled out of his mother's arms and stood, shaking his head. "No, Father. It's too early to make this decision."

"Edward, when they find your brother's body we will hold a memorial service, and we will pay our respects. But responsibility can't wait. When my father passed away, I had to take on the role of duke immediately. I didn't get the luxury of a month—"

"Father, I don't mean to be disrespectful and I understand what you are saying, but I don't believe Phillip is gone from this world. I know I would feel his loss much more than I do at present if he were . . . *gone*."

Ashby sat back against the chair, eyes closed as though he were trying to control his temper. "Edward, this is much harder on me than it is on you. I will give you another week to come to terms before I announce your move to heir and your new title."

Edward sat back down on the piano bench next to his mother and rested his head on the keys. The piano made the jumbled sound of multiple chords being hit at the same time. Phillip's title and wealth were to be given to him. *How could it be harder on him?* he thought with bitterness.

He knew a lot of people who would rejoice at the change in status from the spare to the heir, but he was not one of those men. He wanted to have his brother back much more than a title.

In an effort to forget about the change in title, Edward left the library and found his way down to the stables. He waited for the groom to saddle his horse, Winter. Winter had a coat of white with black hooves and reminded him of fresh fallen snow. Edward rode out to the hillside where they knew Phillip was last, due to the blood they had found. He navigated Winter down the hill and started to search.

Ten

PHILLIP CONTINUED TO TRY AND reconcile the dream he experienced with the feeling of anger, hurt, and fear from the memory of his father. He wanted to believe he was a strong, capable man, but the memory he experienced made him feel weak and vulnerable. The fog in his brain cleared by the following morning, but only after he experienced another dream.

The dream started with a boy sleeping under an apple tree in the same orchard he had been in before. The boy had been reading a book but decided to sleep in the warmth of the sun. He already had the scar on his face, indicating this memory took place after the previous. A younger boy snuck up on the one sleeping and took the book, then ran away.

As the book was taken, the sleeping boy woke up and chased the younger.

"Charles, what are you doing with my book?" he called out as he ran to retrieve his novel.

Charles laughed as he ran. He was taunting his older brother. It wasn't long before they came upon a river. He could tell the last days of summer were approaching and the water in the river was high and flowing faster than the last time he'd been near it. He experienced fear as he looked at the boy getting closer to the raging water.

"Charles, stay away from the water."

Without warning, while taunting Phillip by pretending to throw the book into the river, the younger boy's feet slipped, and he fell into the flowing water.

"Phillip!" Charles called as his head came above the water. "Help!" he called before his head went under again.

Phillip sprinted to the river and jumped in. As he fought to take hold of the younger boy and hold him above the water, Phillip's head went under. The thrashing of the younger boy caused the older to lose his footing. The rush of the water dragged them farther away from home and pulled them both under the water.

Relief came as Phillip grabbed hold of a tree branch and pulled himself and Charles out. His mind registered the struggle he had as he pulled both of them onto the bank of the river.

When Phillip fell on the grass, he noticed his younger brother wasn't breathing. He turned the boy on his side and started hitting him on the back, trying to release the water and causing him to choke while also coughing and releasing water from his own lungs.

"Don't die on me, Charles. Please don't die," he cried as he continued to hit his brother on the back.

Relief rushed through him as the younger boy coughed up water and let out a breath. Phillip looked up when he heard someone on his left yell. Edward and his parents were running toward him.

"Phillip, what happened? I saw you both go in the water," Edward yelled as he reached the boys. Both were still coughing to expel the excess water they had swallowed. Phillip tried to catch his breath to speak when their father and mother arrived.

"Charles. Phillip," their mother said, pulling both of them into her embrace and holding them as she cried. "I almost lost you both."

"Arundel, what happened?" his father demanded, yanking him by his arm away from his mother.

Gulping in air he replied, "Charles was running, and he fell into the river." He stopped to catch his breath before continuing. "I jumped in to pull him out. We were both pulled under and—"

His father didn't wait for the rest of the explanation before he grabbed Phillip's arm, dragged him back to the river, and forced his head into the water. His father held him down as he fought to be released. Pulling his head out of the water, his father yelled at him, "You could have killed your brother!"

Phillip tried to gasp air before his father pushed his head back under, but he was too busy coughing up water to take in air. His father pushed his head under the water and pulled him out four times before it ended.

Phillip woke with a start and was thankful he didn't have anyone sitting by his bed. He remembered the fear he experienced while his head was under water. He had never found the opportunity to explain to his father what had happened with Charles. He remembered thinking it was the last time his father would be able to punish him, because he was certain he was going to drown. He also remembered the disappointment when he woke up in his bed the next morning. Doctor Bell, his father's physician, stayed by his bed until he was able to assure his parents their son would live.

The last thing he remembered from his dream was his name. He now knew his name was Phillip.

He lay awake the rest of the night remembering his fear as the doctor told his parents he would live. He remembered berating himself for fighting his father to get his head out of the water. He wished his father had killed him. As the sun came up, he whispered aloud, "It would have been easier if he'd killed me."

Emma walked into his room for the first time in a week. He was sitting in a rocking chair across from the nurse, covered in a blanket and looking out the window at the scenery.

Emma knocked on the door to get their attention. "Do you mind if I come in?"

"Please join me," he said, pointing to another chair. He pushed his breakfast tray away.

She moved the chair closer to him and sat. At first, she also sat looking out the window but then broke the silence by saying, "You've been here for more than a month, and we still don't know your name."

He thought about telling her his name but decided to wait and see what she had planned. "What do you suggest we do about it?"

She made a show of concentrating hard. "We could give you a temporary name. What about George?"

He scrunched his nose up. "Doesn't feel right."

"Nathaniel."

"Do I look like a Nathaniel?" He drew the words out, showing his reluctance for the name.

"Hmm. No." She laughed as she said, "Romeo."

This brought a big smile to his withdrawn face. "Only if I have a Juliet by my side."

She giggled for a bit and then said, "Fine, if Romeo won't work, what about James?"

He shook his head, enjoying the flirtation. "Still doesn't feel right."

"We could call you William."

"Is this due to my love of Shakespeare?" he asked.

"You're right, it does not fit you," she said, tilting her head to examine him.

He handed her the book he had in his hands. "I've been reading *The Merchant of Venice*. What about Shylock?"

"I think the Duke of Venice matches your stamina much better than Shylock," she said in jest.

A sudden memory flashed though his mind—a picture of the formidable man he knew was his father when she said "the duke." It must have shown on his face because she stopped speaking about names and asked, "Are you ill again?"

"No, what about the name Phillip?" he asked, wondering what she would say.

"Phillip? It could work. It isn't ridiculous like Romeo or Shylock."

"What if I told you my name is Phillip?"

He watched as she considered his words. "Have you remembered your name?"

He nodded as though it was no big deal.

"Phillip! I'm so happy for you," Emma said with excitement. "When did you remember?"

"I had a dream last night. I'm certain my name is Phillip." He rubbed the side of his head.

"You are ill again!"

The nurse stood and walked over to him. "Let me help you back into bed."

"I'm well enough. Please let me stay here by the window."

The nurse forced him out of the chair, and Emma helped pull him over to the bed. He watched Emma walk out of the room as the nurse grabbed the bottle of laudanum.

"Please, I don't want the medication."

"Don't argue with me. I can see another headache is starting. Open your mouth."

He quickly fell back into a drugged sleep.

His first day out of bed found him slowly walking with a pair of crutches. The headache he experienced after the flirtation with Emma ended, and the nurse stopped administering the medication so he could wake from the haze.

Walking with crutches was a strenuous task, but he continued to go for walks, hoping to move from crutches to a cane in record time. The doctor told him not to expect to use a cane for at least another month due to the severity of the breaks.

Emma and Henry walked next to him, both of them ready to catch him if he fell. As time continued, small memories would come back as his mind healed. Many of them were positive, unlike the dreams he experienced under the laudanum. He remembered going to Eton and attending Oxford. He knew he had gone to London for the season every year since he was a boy.

"Is your leg doing well, or should we turn back?" Henry asked in concern.

"If you don't mind, I'd like to continue."

Emma looked worried as she responded, "Doctor Price will be displeased if you injure your leg again."

"I won't overextend myself." Phillip hoped his words were reassuring.

"Once we get to the bench, you're going to rest before returning to the house." Henry's tone left no room for argument, and Phillip agreed out of respect for his friends.

When they reached the bench, Henry took the crutches and set them to the side. "Will one of you tell me about your favorite memory?" Phillip asked. He didn't care which one responded, but he noticed they exchanged a curious glance.

Henry took a deep breath and reminisced about his first horse ride.

"My grandfather gifted me a horse for my birthday, so my father decided he would be the one to teach me how to ride. I remember loving the horse. I named him Topaz. My favorite memory is when I rode him for the first time." Henry spoke about the freedom while riding a horse. Phillip understood; he had a similar experience flow into his mind. Henry continued and spoke of watching nature fly by while the horse cantered and of the wind as it blew through his hair and clothing.

Emma caught Phillip off guard as she asked, "Do you remember the first time you rode a horse?"

In his mind Phillip saw the first horse his father had given him. "Yes, I was young. My father presented me with a horse." He stopped speaking as another memory flashed. The horse was a gift for his father throwing him in a dark closet for two days without food or water.

"Do you remember the horse's name?" Emma prodded as he let his memory take him away.

"Loxley."

"From the tale of Robin Hood?" she asked, surprised.

"Yes. My governess would entertain Edward and me at bedtime by telling us stories. Robin Hood was one of our favorites," he said as the memory continued to flow through his mind.

"Edward?" Both Henry and Emma asked in unison.

Again, without any thought he said, "My twin brother."

"You have a twin brother?" Henry asked, trying to prod more of a memory from him.

"Yes, I believe I do. The memory came back as we were speaking," he said with excitement.

Both Phillip and Emma were startled when Henry stood. "Please excuse me. I forgot I have a previous engagement." Looking back as he walked away, he said, "I will return to help you back into the house."

They watched as Henry left. He had purpose in his steps, which caused Phillip to believe he would be gone for a while.

"I apologize for my brother, Phillip."

He smiled, realizing he enjoyed it when she said his name. "It feels wonderful to have a few memories coming back."

"I believe it won't be long before you have your full memory, and then you will leave Springhill Abby," she said. He thought the smile on her face looked forced.

"Miss Emma—" he started as she cut him off.

"Please, call me Emma. There's no need to be so formal."

Nodding his head in acknowledgment, he continued, "Emma, I don't know what I would have done these past weeks without your kindness in reading to me and keeping my mind off the injuries."

"It's wonderful to have another person at Springhill Abby who enjoys literature as much as I do," she said as she ran her hands down her dress to smooth the bodice. He could see she was nervous.

A flutter went through him as he looked at her face.

She smiled at him as though she could see through into his thoughts and the struggle he was fighting. He couldn't start a relationship with her. It was unwise without his memory.

"We should go back inside," he said, pulling his crutches to each side so he could pull himself up.

"Should I get Henry?" she asked.

"No, I think I can make it."

Eleven

EMMA SAT IN THE DRAWING room sketching. Since her morning with Phillip, she'd stayed away from him. She was falling in love and didn't know what to do about it, mainly because he was still unsure of who he was. If he had a firm grasp on his memories, she wouldn't worry so much about losing her heart to him. As it was, she feared thinking there could be a possible future with him.

"I have something I need to say," her father said as he entered the room.

"When did you get back from London?" Henry asked, shaking their father's hand.

"I've only just arrived." He turned to Phillip, ignoring further questions. "If you'd like, we can speak in private. I have information regarding your identity."

"You've all been so wonderful to me. This journey isn't mine alone. Please, say what you've found."

Emma gave an inward cheer and thought about dancing the waltz as she wouldn't have to wait to get the information later.

"Lord Arundel," her father said. He paused as though he expected a response. "Does the title sound familiar?"

Emma kept her eyes on Phillip as her father's words sunk in. She saw recognition on his face.

"Yes." Phillip laughed as he shook his head in reverie. "Yes . . . I'm Arundel." He sounded surprised, as though his name should have been normal to him and he should have always known it. "I don't know why it was so lost in my mind."

"What else did you find out?" Emma asked. She tried to keep the reluctance out of her voice. The more he found out about himself, the more she worried she would lose him.

"You are the eldest son of the Duke of Ashby."

Emma let the words fade from her hearing as she feared Phillip's entire life was coming back to him. She wished she could go back to the time they'd shared in the garden to enjoy it more fully instead of being so nervous. She was about to leave the room when she heard Phillip.

"You would think my name would bring more memories back. I guess it will take more time."

"We know who you are, and as soon as Doctor Price allows you to travel, we can restore you to your family." Her mother's words brought comfort to Phillip but distress to Emma. She knew it was ridiculous to feel this way, but she didn't want him to regain his memory. It was selfish, but it was because she was in love with him.

Her heart further dropped when her father said, "If you write a letter, I'll have a rider deliver it for you."

As Phillip continued to use crutches, he didn't need as much assistance as he had in the beginning, and Emma found they could go farther than the rose garden. She took him for walks to the churchyard, cemetery, and a small stream. Each was close enough he could get to it and return after a bit of rest.

"Lord Arundel," she stated as she walked and he hobbled down a dirt road to the church yard. "You are doing much better with the crutches."

"I do feel like I have more freedom. Why are you calling me Lord Arundel?" he asked in annoyance as he pushed a rock out of the pathway with his good leg.

"I want to help you get used to your title again." She pointed to a boulder in the distance. "We will go as far as the large boulder today, and you can rest before we head back."

"I would prefer you call me Phillip," he said with a nod, indicating he saw the destination.

They approached the boulder, and she helped him position himself in a way he could rest his leg until they headed back.

"This is the perfect resting spot," he said with a warm smile.

She played with her fingers as they sat. She didn't know where to take the conversation.

"I was wondering if you have any Greek mythology in the library at Springhill Abby," he said.

She let out a breath of air she had not realized she was holding. "Yes, we do."

"I might like to read a few more books while I'm here if you think your father wouldn't mind."

"No, I don't think he would mind." She kicked herself for not saying something more intelligent. She could've remarked on her favorite Greek myth about Psyche and Cupid.

As he looked at her, she could see the same tense feeling in his face that she had in the pit of her stomach. She leaned toward him, letting him know she was willing to explore an intimate moment with him, but he stood and grabbed his crutches.

"We should go back," he said, putting the crutches under his arms.

She blushed as she watched him trying to avoid her. She put her hands over her cheeks to hide the evidence.

"Emma, I . . . I don't know who I am. I know my name, but I don't know much about myself. I don't want to give you false hopes or make promises I can't keep." He pulled her face up so she could see him. "I'm very fond of you." He looked into her eyes. They were a window into her soul betraying her every thought and feeling.

"Phillip, even though you don't know who you are, you can trust the way you feel about another person."

A thrill of excitement went through her as he leaned into her. Her hands were moist as she waited. Just before his lips touched hers, she closed her eyes. The kiss was perfect. She didn't realize it until he kissed her, but it was a feeling she'd been waiting to have her entire life. Her heart told her this was right. He touched her face as he held her lips with his. Heat flooded into her cheeks as he explored her lips, touching both separately. He deepened the kiss, which caused her toes to curl. Her arms strengthened as she pulled him closer to her by taking hold of his lapels.

She lost herself in the kiss until she remembered where they were standing. They were in public. They hadn't taken time to notice if anyone else was around, and he was kissing her longer than was appropriate.

Satisfied by his gentle touch, she almost let herself forget about propriety. Coming to her senses, she pulled away. "We should be more cautious." She hated the words as they came out.

He pulled away from her and nodded. She watched as he made his way back to the house. She stayed at the rock in the churchyard, fearing if she moved the magic of the moment would leave her.

Twelve

PHILLIP KNOCKED ON THE DOOR of Lord Anthony's den. He couldn't stop thinking about Emma and the kiss they'd shared. He was certain she was the first woman he'd ventured to kiss. Such a kiss would never leave a man's memory.

"Enter," Lord Anthony called.

"My Lord," Phillip said.

"This is a surprise. What can I do for you, Arundel?" Lord Anthony pointed to a chair. Phillip limped over to it. He was certain the limp he now had would be permanent. He still used the crutches so he wouldn't put too much weight on his leg as it healed.

"Thank you for seeing me, sir. I wanted to know if you'd heard from my family yet."

"I expect we will have an answer from them any day now. Doctor Price is still reluctant to let you travel, as he hasn't found a source for your headaches."

"The headaches have become less intense as I've healed." Phillip squirmed in his seat. He had a feeling he should wait until he knew more about himself, but he remembered Emma's words telling him he could trust his instincts, and decided to move forward with his request. "I would like to ask for Miss Emma's hand."

Lord Anthony's right eye raised in surprise. "It is inadvisable to enter into an engagement when you know so little about yourself. Have more of your memories returned?"

"Few memories have come back. But I cannot deny the love I have for Emma. When you told me my name, you told me I am not married."

"You are correct."

"Do you have an objection against my character?"

"No, you are an honorable young man." He stopped speaking, but Phillip thought there was something more he was going to say. Instead of speaking, Phillip waited, hoping Lord Anthony would continue. Instead of making the comment he suppressed, he stated, "I give you my blessing."

"Thank you, my lord." Phillip pulled himself up, excitement adding a hop in his hobble.

Deciding he should ask Emma to be his wife without further delay, Phillip grabbed his crutches and limped out of the house in search of her. It took a short walk along a path strewn with shrubs for him to find her sitting under a large oak tree. He hesitated before approaching, as he hadn't planned a way to ask for her hand.

"You are walking much better," Emma said, pulling him out of his thoughts.

"I have a slight limp, but over time I hope to be able to hide it," he said as he slowly found his way to sitting on the grass next to her. He noticed her sketch book lying on the ground and decided to change the conversation.

"Henry told me you enjoy drawing. Do you have any sketches I could view?"

He didn't know why she was blushing, but he loved the way she looked with her dark brown hair, green eyes, and pink cheeks. He stopped speaking as he lost himself in her face. Hoping her attention moved away from her sketch book, he reached for her drawings only to have her pull away.

"Is there a reason you don't want me to see your drawings? Henry told me you do landscapes."

She looked relieved when he mentioned the landscapes as though she expected him to say something different. "Yes, but they aren't any good."

"You're being modest," he said, holding his hand out in expectation. "Let me see the sketches, and I can give my opinion on your talent."

"I don't want your opinion," Emma said, moving the sketchpad further out of reach.

"Have I made you uncomfortable?"

"No, you haven't." She looked down at her hands. "I'm not ready to show you my sketches."

He looked at her and scooted around so they were facing each other. He touched her face and then ran his hand through her loose curls. *I'm making the right choice.* His heart pounded so hard he could hear it pulsing in his ears. She filled his thoughts during the waking hours, and he dreamt of her when he was sleeping.

He smiled at her and held her eyes with his before he leaned forward and kissed her. She fell into his arms, allowing him to kiss her lips, cheeks, and neck. He pulled back with a start. A gentleman would never compromise a woman such as Emma.

"Why did you pull away?" she asked in a dreamy voice, her eyes closed as she waited for him to kiss her again.

"We need to stop this insanity," he whispered. The feelings he had for her scared him. Although he still didn't have his memory back, he knew he'd never been in love before. This was a new experience for him, a frightening but wonderful experience.

She looked offended, so he placed both hands on her face to explain. "I shouldn't compromise you in this way."

"I've already told you I don't feel compromised, my lord."

She moved closer to him and kissed his cheek. He wanted to stop the response his body gave at her touch, but he couldn't pull away. Instead he gave in and kissed her.

They pulled apart and were staring into each other's eyes as he again asked, "May I see your sketches?"

She gave him a playful smile. "No, you may not."

Taking her flirting as a challenge, he reached over and grabbed for her sketchbook.

"I said no!" she chided as she moved the book further away from him by grabbing it and standing.

"You have an unfair advantage," he teased as he worked to pull himself off the ground. Keeping his injured leg from taking too much weight, he used the other with his hands to lift himself off the ground. He wasn't sure how this would help him with asking her to be his wife, but he'd figure it out.

"Unfair?" she said with a grin. "I think not. These are my sketches, after all."

With his crutches he moved forward, playing her game. Intrigued by her desire to keep the sketches secret, he wanted to see them now more than he did when he first sat down. He reached forward and just missed taking hold as she pulled away.

"A gentleman would respect my desire to keep these hidden," she said with a mischievous grin.

"Are you saying I'm not a gentleman?" he asked, moving closer.

"Oh, I believe you were raised to be one," she chimed, moving away again.

He laughed as he watched her back away. He knew the only way he was going to get the sketchpad was to surprise her. Instead of reaching for the pad, he put his arm around her waist and pulled her to him. He would've picked her up for the kiss since she was a half a head shorter than him, but he wasn't sure his one leg would hold both their weight.

He placed his lips on hers and took his time. He started on her bottom lip, causing the sketchpad to drop from her hand. He thought about ending the kiss so he could claim his victory by seeing the sketches but decided he was enjoying it too much to stop. He moved to her top lip and with deliberate slowness continued the kiss.

He heard her sigh. He smiled as he realized she was enjoying this as much as he was. He continued from her lips to her cheek. Lost in the moment, he moved down to her jaw line. A warning went off in his mind telling him he needed to stop, but holding her close to him was warm and comfortable and he didn't want to let go. He moved his hands up to her hair, which smelled like peppermint oil, and removed the pins holding it up. As her hair fell over his hand, he moved back to her lips and kissed her with more urgency.

"Are you aware you're in public?" Richard's rebuke pierced the air and put a stop to the moment.

Phillip pulled away and turned to see Anne and Richard on the path beside them. Richard, ever the vicar, looked disapproving. Anne had a knowing smile on her face.

He gently released Emma from his arm, and she moved away from him. He looked down at the sketches and saw they weren't landscapes as he had been led to believe. He saw his face looking back up at him.

Finding his voice, he looked at Emma to see she was blushing. She grabbed the pins from his hand and fumbled to put her hair back in place.

"I apologize. I was caught in the moment and shouldn't have let it go so long." He hesitated as he spoke, wanting to be precise with his words.

"No, you shouldn't have," Richard said, reproving both of them. "You shouldn't be alone anymore." Richard's voice rose with anger as he spoke.

Emma's hands covered her face as she attempted to cover the heat. Phillip watched as she looked down at her sketches. Her eyes went wide in embarrassment. She didn't speak as she bent down to pick them up.

"I'll help you," Anne said with the same knowing smile on her face.

Richard continued his hard glare. Phillip was embarrassed. He should have asked for her hand and left her with a chaste kiss on her cheek.

"I agree." Phillip turned back to watch as they picked the sketches off the ground. "We shouldn't be alone to make certain we don't cross a line."

Richard raised his eyebrows. "I believe you've already crossed it."

"Richard, you don't get an opinion," Emma said, standing with her sketches back in hand.

"Emma, go home. This is between the earl and me," Richard said as he continued to stare at Phillip.

Emma went to argue with her brother, but Phillip turned to her. "He is right. I crossed a line."

"It would be wrong if I didn't want—"

Anne grabbed Emma's arm and dragged her away.

Phillips actions had been unwise, and he regretted them. But he didn't regret the love he had for Emma. He waited until she was out of hearing range before speaking again.

"You look like you're ready to strangle me," he said to Richard, who continued to look at him with dislike.

"We brought you into our home and took care of you while you were ill, and this is how you repay us?"

Phillip closed his eyes. Another headache was starting. He was certain it was due to the stress of the moment. He didn't speak, because he knew he couldn't say anything to make Richard understand he didn't intend to hurt Emma.

"Do you realize if anyone other than Anne and I had come upon the two of you during such a display, my sister's reputation would be ruined?" His fists were clenched in anger.

"Yes, I realize this now," Phillip said, forcing his voice to sound repentant.

"Don't tell me the amnesia has blocked your sense of propriety."

"No, it hasn't. I realize what I did was wrong," he said, hoping the apology would end the conversation.

"You now realize this?" he mocked.

Phillip steadied himself for the blow he knew was coming. Richard's hands had been clenched since the kiss ended, and his anger continued to build. If he was hit in the face, he needed to make certain he was grounded enough so he didn't fall over and break his leg again.

"Richard?" Henry called, running down the path.

"What?" Richard growled at his brother.

Henry looked between them and said, "It's going to rain. We need to get back to the house."

"Do you know what's happened here?" Richard barked at his brother.

"Yes, both Anne and Emma have apprised me of the situation," Henry said with a smile. He looked over at Phillip and laughed. "Richard is a bit protective of our sisters."

Phillip didn't smile as he responded, "As he should be." He turned back to Richard. "I do apologize."

Richard didn't speak as he turned and made his way back down the path. Henry laughed again and moved his head to indicate they should follow.

They walked in silence, which was preferable for Phillip due to the headache. His vision was starting to blur, and his neck and upper back sent shooting pains into his head. Henry walked slowly so Phillip could keep up with him and spoke once the house was in sight.

"Emma has fancied you since she realized you know the sonnets by number. I'm certain she's happy you share her feelings," he said with a sideways glance.

"I meant her no disrespect," he said in remorse. "I also didn't mean any disrespect to your family."

"I know," he responded, "but reputations are fragile, and Richard is correct that her reputation would be destroyed while you wouldn't be affected."

Phillip stopped hobbling even though thunder rolled through the sky. He looked up as the first drops of rain started. Henry turned back. "I plan to ask for her hand. I'm not trifling with her heart. And Lord Anthony has given his blessing on the union." He closed his eyes against the sharp pains in his head. "I'm in love with her."

Henry raised his eyebrows in surprise. Phillip expected a response, but Henry didn't speak. Phillip took a deep breath and let it go. He didn't know what more to say.

"We should get out of this rain. You look pale," Henry said, moving closer to him.

"I think it's just this blasted situation," Phillip responded in annoyance. "The thought of hurting Emma and disrespecting your family is bothering me."

Henry pointed toward the house and they walked. Phillip's crutches sunk in the mud as he limped back to the house. Phillip went to his room to lie down. He didn't tell anyone about the headache and shooting pains. He hoped a nap would relieve him of the symptoms before supper. He needed to get out of his wet clothes, so he sat on the chair next to the window to remove his clothing. *I'll close my eyes for a minute and then get the wet clothes off,* he thought as he laid his head against the plush chair. *I should've stopped kissing her,* he berated himself as he continued to sit with his eyes closed.

He didn't realize he'd fallen asleep until the door opened and Richard said something about the evening meal. He stayed where he was without moving. His body shivered and his head pounded.

"What the devil?" Richard said as he touched Phillip's forehead. "You're burning up with fever."

He didn't want to be a bother. He wanted to go home to his family where they would care for him. But at the moment it wasn't possible. He heard Lady Amelia's and Lord Anthony's voices as though from a distance.

"Send for Doctor Price," Lady Amelia said as soft hands pressed against his forehead and face.

Thirteen

EMBARRASSMENT PLAGUED HER MIND AS Emma paced her bedchamber. Richard and Anne had walked in on what she would consider a very private moment, but Phillip had seen the sketches of his face. She wanted to argue with Richard and stay to defend herself and the kiss he interrupted, but Anne had pulled her toward the house.

She went over the day, reviewing her actions. She wondered if it had been smart to kiss a man with amnesia. She was in love with him. She couldn't explain the way he made her feel. She wanted to read poetry, sing songs of love, and dance in the rain whenever he was around. When he kissed her, she never wanted to be parted from him.

She was surprised when she went down for supper to find Phillip was suffering from another headache. He'd been in his room since returning. Due to her embarrassment over the situation, she'd stayed in her room sketching.

She walked into his room to see he was incoherent and jittery.

"Emma, bring blankets," her mother told her as she entered the room.

She ran to retrieve them, and her mind went back to the night he arrived at their home. She was sent for extra blankets then as well. She took the blankets back into the room and placed them on the bed. Richard removed Phillip's boots, as he'd kept them on after coming in from the outdoors.

"Emma, you shouldn't be in here," Richard said as he placed one boot on the floor.

"Leave me alone, Richard," she shot back at him. She wanted an apology from him for the way he behaved earlier.

"Will you take this argument into another room?" their father said as he went to pour laudanum into Phillip's mouth.

"Father, don't," Emma said walking forward. "He doesn't like the laudanum."

"Swallow," her father said as he leaned over Phillip and forced the liquid in his mouth. "It'll be better if he sleeps."

Emma watched as her father laid Phillip's head back on the pillows and her mother covered him with blankets.

"He received a letter from His Grace, Ashby, while he was out. I'll take a look at it as soon as the doctor arrives," her father responded, helping to spread the blankets over Phillip's body.

As they stood to leave him with a maid, Doctor Price and Nurse Brown entered the room. The family waited in the hall as the doctor examined Phillip. Emma closed her eyes as she sat on the chair. She knew Richard was staring at her, and she didn't want to see his disapproving gaze.

"Lord Anthony, I'm afraid the head injury is too severe. It is behaving as an infectious disease," Doctor Price said with a glance around the group.

"What should we do to relieve him of the pain?" her father asked.

"I would like to bleed him."

"Is he strong enough for a bleeding?" her mother asked, concern etched on her face.

"Doctor," Nurse Brown called from the room, "he's conscious."

Doctor Price turned from the hall and entered the room. Emma entered behind her parents and watched as the doctor sat on the bed next to Phillip.

"My lord, you have a high fever, which is causing an infection in your brain. I would like your permission to perform a bleeding."

Phillip didn't speak for a bit, and Emma wondered if he had gone back to sleep until he croaked, "If it will help."

"I believe it will," Doctor Price said, patting him on the shoulder.

The doctor turned to grab his bag when Phillip grabbed his arm. "I don't want any more laudanum." He closed his eyes for a moment and reopened them. "Please let me know when I can go home." The words came out more as a slur.

Hearing Phillip say he wanted to leave caused her to panic more than seeing him in a feverish state. If he left, she would never see him again. She looked up at the ceiling, hoping the tears wouldn't fall in front of everyone.

Doctor Price took Phillip's hand off of his arm and laid it back on the bed. "I will use laudanum only if it is necessary; you have my word."

The doctor moved off the bed and placed a basin under his elbow. The smell of blood permeated the air. She watched the doctor pierce the skin, and blood seeped out of his body into the bowl. Nurse Brown wiped the sweat from his face and neck. She saw him closing his eyes and thought he was going to sleep.

"Emma, I love you," he said as he dozed off.

She didn't dare look at her brothers or her sister as he said the words. He'd implied his feelings were deep and he enjoyed being with her as he'd kissed her. But this was the first time he had said those words. She could tell there was heat in her cheeks as her brothers broke out in smiles.

"You two are immature," she responded, continuing to look at the wall in front of her.

"He's drugged," Anne said, trying to hold in a laugh.

"He won't remember saying it," Richard said with a smile.

Emma turned to him. "So now it's funny?" she asked, glaring at him.

"Oh no, what I saw this afternoon was not and is still not amusing," he said in all seriousness, "but what he just said in there was."

She didn't look at her parents as they exited his room. Her mother pulled her into a hug. And her father looked pleased.

Embarrassed by the redness of her cheeks she added, "And I am certain Richard gave a full account of this morning to all of you. Yes, he kissed me." She pursed her lips together to think of what to say next. "I quite enjoyed it." She walked away before anyone could respond.

Emma sat next to Phillip with her sketchbook. He was unconscious due to the fever and the bleeding. "I'm so embarrassed. Phillip saw at least one of the sketches if not more," she said to Anne as tears ran down her face. "How do I get myself into these messes?"

"You spend too much time in books." Anne sighed. "Relationships in real life don't happen like Romeo and Juliet. They're messier like Arthur and Guinevere."

She considered telling her sister of the passionate kisses he'd given her but decided against it. The one Anne witnessed was enough to shame her. She didn't want her sister to think she would allow any man the liberty of kissing her.

"Emma, you need to be careful," Anne added as she sat on the bed.

"I know I should've stopped the kiss," she said, heat rising in her cheeks again, "but the softness of his lips and the way he kissed me . . ." She allowed her voice to take on a dreamy element as she touched her lips, remembering his kiss. "I've never experienced anything so wonderful," she said, coming back to the moment.

Anne rolled her eyes. "If you'll allow a man to kiss you and touch you in public, people are going to wonder what you will allow in private."

"Don't tell me you haven't ever kissed a man," Emma said, walking to the window and peering out at the night sky.

"Emma, what would have happened if we didn't interrupt you?" Anne asked with her eyebrows raised and a serious look on her face.

"We would've ended the kiss and he would've seen the sketches."

"Are you in earnest? Or are you telling yourself he would've respected you? Because from what I saw he was making his way down—"

Emma cut her off with a quick turn from the window. "He wouldn't have taken advantage of me." She turned. "I want to be alone."

Anne walked to the door. "Then you can't stay in here."

"Please just leave," Emma begged, walking to the overstuffed chair. She laid her head against it and curled her legs into her chest. She let the tears fall. Elation changed to shame as she thought of her actions.

75

Anne didn't leave. Instead she pulled her chair closer. She grabbed a brush from the side table and ran it through Emma's hair. "I'm sorry I hurt your feelings."

Emma didn't respond. She let her sister continue to brush her hair as she thought about her behavior. She'd let the flirting go on too long and it went too far. She had never allowed any other man to kiss her. She wondered why she was allowing Phillip to do so, and without even a promise of the relationship continuing after he left Springhill Abby.

"Do you think he will ask me to marry him?

"I hope he does." Anne continued to brush her hair, and Emma let her.

Fourteen

SPRINGHILL ABBY WAS SMALLER THAN Wentworth Hall by at least half, if not more. Edward hoped to find Phillip healing and ready to travel home, but when he and his father entered the sick room his heart sank.

The door was open, and he could hear a woman reading a book. When he entered the room, he saw a doctor, nurse, and three women. One woman was sitting on a chair reading; the others were sitting on the bed, one on each side wiping sweat from Phillip's neck and head with wet cloths.

"Your Grace," Lord Anthony said as they entered the room, "may I introduce my wife, Lady Amelia, daughters Emma and Anne, Doctor Price, and Nurse Brown?" Turning to the room at large he said, "The Duke of Ashby and Lord Edward."

He waited for the niceties to be followed, and then Edward could no longer hold back. He walked to his brother's bed as the daughter moved away. He took hold of the wet cloth and wiped the sweat from his brother's neck and chest.

"How long have you been bleeding him?" his father asked. The smell of blood and infection was enough to make Edward sick, but he held the vomit back.

"We've done an irregular schedule of bleeding for the past week." Doctor Price walked over and placed a bandage on Phillip's arm to stop the current bleeding. He removed the bowl of blood and handed it to Nurse Brown. "I hope we don't have to do another round. He's not strong enough."

Edward watched as his father took Lady Amelia's place on the opposite side of the bed. His father pulled Phillip into his arms and held him. Edward had never seen this side of Ashby. He always appeared to be a strong, impenetrable man who didn't let situations such as this affect him. But their family had been through too much over the past months to hold onto pride any longer.

He knew everyone left the room without having to look around. He wondered if he should also leave and let his father have time with Phillip alone. Edward still hadn't forgiven his father for hitting him while the constable questioned him. He knew he'd have to at some point, but he didn't care to put forth the effort. As he moved to leave, his father reached out and took his hand. Edward flinched. His father ignored the movement and instead said, "Stay."

❧

By the following morning, Phillip's condition was unchanged, and his father continued the vigil. Standing outside the door, Edward listened as his father softly spoke. This side of Ashby was new, and it strangely bothered him to know his father could be soft, kind, and gentle.

"I have not been the father you wanted," Ashby said to the unconscious form.

Thinking it might be better for him to leave and let his father finish this one-sided conversation, Edward turned to go, but stopped when he heard his father's confession.

"My father told me to make a man strong, you had to teach correct principles. I fear I have done the same to you. I did not know why my father hit me until he lay dying. I cannot apologize for what I have put you through, as I believe it is the only reason you have the strength to heal now."

Shaking his head in frustration, Edward left his father to his mixed-up excuses. Beating his oldest son as a way to encourage strength was backward. It did not make sense, and it would not change the current situation.

Edward wandered out to the patio and saw a pathway through the garden. Deciding it would give Ashby ample time to say what he needed, Edward perused the flowers along the pathway. He noticed most of the flowers were roses of all different colors.

"Lord Edward?"

Edward turned to see both Miss Parker and Miss Emma sitting on a bench. He gave a small bow in their direction. "Do you mind if I sit with you?"

"Please do, Lord Edward," Miss Parker said, pointing to the empty bench next to them. "Has there been a change in Arundel's condition?"

"I'm afraid not," Edward replied as he sat. "My father wanted time alone with him this morning."

"I'm sorry to hear this," Miss Parker said. He noticed she squeezed her sister's hand.

He wondered what they'd been discussing before his arrival. Searching for something to say he remarked, "This garden is beautiful. Do you spend much time out here?"

"Emma has spent a bit of time out here of late," Miss Parker said with a smirk.

"You have?" he asked, wondering why this was the response.

"Yes. The garden has been wonderful this year," she demurred, glaring toward her sister.

"Lord Arundel also enjoyed the garden this year," Miss Parker said as an aside.

"My brother?" he asked in surprise. Edward noticed a blush in Miss Parker's smile as she spoke. When she smiled her face lit up and her green eyes sparkled.

"Yes, he hasn't been this ill the entire time," Miss Parker responded. "Emma and Henry helped him walk out here as he healed from his initial injuries."

"I'm certain he enjoyed the time. When he is home, Phillip spends so much time outdoors his hair gets bleached by the sun," Edward commented. "It is one of the easier ways to tell us apart." He added the last as an aside to keep the conversation going.

"I hadn't noticed the difference," Miss Parker replied. "Emma, did you notice?"

"No," Emma said, her voice rising in pitch. He thought she looked a little guilty for the lie she was telling. He knew from her response she had noticed the difference in their hair.

Edward thought her reaction was strange but brushed it off as a misunderstanding of her intent. For a moment he wondered if she held feelings for his brother. But Phillip wouldn't have given her false hopes due to his engagement to Lady Olivia. They sat in silence for a few minutes before it was too tense and unbearable.

"We have a rose garden at Wentworth Hall similar to this. Has Phillip spoken about it?"

"No, he hasn't," Miss Emma responded. "Didn't Lord Arundel mention the amnesia?"

Nodding, he realized how stupid the question had been. "Yes, he did. I had hoped he would have a few memories, though."

"He never mentioned the garden or Wentworth Hall," Emma responded.

Again, an uncomfortable silence moved over the group. Perhaps it was strange for them to see he was identical to his brother. He stood not certain where to go with the conversation anymore, and knowing he'd interrupted them he decided he should leave.

"Forgive me for my intrusion." He gave his most courtly and flirtatious bow to both the Miss Parkers and left without a backward glance.

He heard Miss Parker speaking, although he knew she was trying to be quiet. "Do you think Phillip and Edward are as similar in personality as they are in looks?"

Miss Emma responded, "I doubt it. And is it strange? I don't think they look anything alike."

He quickened his pace, not wanting to appear as if he were eavesdropping on them. He did find it strange to hear Miss Emma say they didn't look alike. He and Phillip were identical. They were duplicates minus the scar. He shook his head in amusement and moved to the patio, where he saw Doctor Price speaking with the Parkers. The door to the patio was open, giving him the chance to overhear as he headed to the house.

"He is through the worst of the infection. He is on the mend," Doctor Price commented.

"This is wonderful to hear," Lady Amelia responded. He could see the sincerity in her posture and face. He made a mental note regarding the similarities of Lady Amelia and Anne. Anne was a younger version of her mother.

"Ashby would like to move Arundel to London before the end of the week. It won't be long before your lives will be back to normal."

"We will forever be thankful you found my brother," Edward said before either Lord or Lady Parker could respond. He didn't want to hear his brother had worn out his welcome.

"As are we," Lord Anthony said with a smile. "Lord Arundel is a welcome addition to our home. Life will not go back to normal with his absence."

"Thank you. I do appreciate your generosity to him and my father and me." As Edward walked into Phillip's bedchamber, he saw Ashby standing by the window. "May I come in?" he asked, hoping his father was ready for company.

He nodded and pointed toward Phillip. "He is still out. The doctor believes he is mending. We will leave for London as soon as Phillip is well enough."

Relief came a short time later as Phillip woke.

"Where did you come from?" Phillip asked.

"It's about time you came back to us," Edward said.

Taking a deep breath Phillip asked, "Am I still at Springhill Abby?"

"Yes, you've been too ill to move. Although, since you're awake, we can discuss moving you to Lancaster House in London."

"Sounds exhausting," Phillip said as he tried to pull himself into a sitting position.

Edward reached forward and pulled him up and situated the pillows behind Phillip for support. "How bad is the amnesia? You know who I am, right?"

Phillip looked over at his brother. "Wait, you aren't my reflection?"

"I'm asking a serious question here," Edward chided.

"I've had flashes and dreams, but I don't know what I'm missing." He smiled and shrugged his shoulders. "It is normal to have a nurse sitting with me, or Lord Anthony's youngest daughter Emma. What did I do to get you in here?"

"You'd prefer the nurse?"

"No, I'd prefer the daughter."

Edward laughed. "She is a beauty."

"Yes, I agree," he said. "Back to my question. What did I do to get you in here?"

He pointed to Phillip's arm where the bandage showed the bleeding. "You threatened to die, again."

"Hmm . . ." He closed his eyes for a moment, then asked, "Again?"

"Doctor Price and Lord Anthony have regaled us with the story of how you were found. You are fortunate to be alive." Edward stopped to take a deep breath before continuing. "Mother has been distraught, and Father is beside himself. He will be happy to know you're awake."

"When you write to them, will you tell Mother I love her?" Phillip sighed before finishing. "My relationship with Father, it's complicated, right?"

Edward gave him a questioning look but shrugged it off. "You can figure it out as you talk with him. I'll send him in if you'd like."

Surprised, Phillip raised his eyebrows and tried to get out of the bed. "Father is here?"

Forcing him to stay in the bed, Edward responded, "Yes, we are staying with you until you are able to leave. But if Father has it his way, we will leave tomorrow."

Edward turned his attention to the door as he heard a soft knock. Phillip's valet walked in with a toiletry kit, followed by a maid with a supper tray for Edward.

"You've been eating in here as well? Also, who is he?" Phillip asked, pointing toward the man.

"He's your valet, Thomas. It looks like you are missing a lot."

"You can take his plate back to the dining room," Phillip said. "He doesn't need to get crumbs in my bed."

Edward laughed and stood to leave the room. "It is good to have you on the mend. And let Thomas do his job."

Fifteen

PHILLIP WATCHED HIS BROTHER LEAVE. For so long he'd wondered who his family was and where they were. Were they looking for him? He'd had so many questions since waking at Springhill Abby. Now with his brother and father there to retrieve him, melancholy rose up in him. He didn't want to leave Emma.

It was strange having a valet, because he didn't know the man and he was uncomfortable around him. He watched as Thomas situated his items on the table. He noticed the shaving kit, and he reached up to touch his face. There were hairs on his chin, so he must not have been shaved while he was ill. Thomas was a short man with dark brown hair and brown eyes. He had a mole on his chin, which distracted Phillip for a moment as he noticed a hair sticking out of it. He wondered how he could have forgotten such a sight.

"How long have you been my valet?" Phillip asked as he stared at the hairy mole.

"Three years, my lord," Thomas said as he continued to empty the toiletry kit.

"How old are you?" he asked, knowing it was a rude question but not caring. This man was in his father's employ. He was paid well for the impertinent questions.

"I'm twenty-seven years old, my lord."

"Do you have a wife and children?"

"No. But my family lives in Derbyshire near Wentworth Hall, and I am able to visit them on my half-days."

Since he'd been at Springhill Abby, Phillip's needs had been seen to by the nurse, but he had managed to dress himself. It was odd allowing someone to help him. "I can dress myself. No need to help."

"My lord," Thomas said, "I must earn my keep."

"Aw, well . . ." He hesitated, realizing he had made the man uncomfortable. "Go ahead then."

Thomas nodded, looking a bit uncomfortable with the entire conversation. "You can stay right as you are, sir. I will take care of everything."

Thomas drew Phillip a bath, which he appreciated, until he hit the water. The water was hot. Phillip tumbled out of the tub and glared at his valet. "It could use some cold water to temper the heat."

"I apologize, my lord. I must have forgotten to pour it in." Thomas didn't look repentant, but he rushed over to a bucket of water. After making certain it was cold, Phillip allowed him to pour it in.

The bath was heavenly. Thomas added peppermint oil to the water, which made Phillip think of Emma and the last time he'd kissed her. The heat of the water let off steam and soothed his aching body. He lay back after washing himself and closed his eyes. Thomas emptied water out of the tub and refilled it with heated water as it cooled. Still, Phillip lingered in the bath.

Phillip watched as Thomas picked up the shaving soap. He spread it across Phillip's face. Thomas helped him position his head and then ran the razor to clear the hair and soap. Phillip flinched when Thomas cut his face.

"Have a care!" Phillip said, touching the spot. He pulled his hand away to see blood.

"I apologize, my lord. My hand slipped."

Phillip washed the blood off and allowed Thomas to continue. Phillip waited for Thomas to finish the shave. His face received two more cuts. He wondered if Thomas was always so careless while shaving him.

After soaking for a while, Phillip looked down at his hands and noticed they were shriveled. He smiled. The bath was relaxing, and he didn't care if his fingers looked like prunes.

"Are you going to get out of the bath, my lord?" Thomas asked, holding a towel.

"I wonder," Phillip said without moving to exit the tub, "have you always been so careless with my shave?"

"No, my lord." Thomas looked repentant, so Phillip let it go until Thomas brushed his injured leg, causing Phillip to collapse.

"Are you trying to injure me further?"

"No, my lord. I would never try to injure you."

"Please, just leave me to take care of myself." Phillip dressed and made his way back to the bed. He didn't want Thomas anywhere near his injured leg.

Sixteen

"FATHER," EDWARD SAID AS HE entered the dining hall, "Phillip is conscious. I told him you are here. He recognized me, of course. He didn't know Thomas. He is confused."

"Once we get him to London, I'm certain his memory will improve," the Duke of Ashby said with confidence. "We shall leave first thing tomorrow."

"Father, don't you think it would be best to allow him to recover strength before setting out for such a long trip?"

"No." Ashby wasn't one to argue with, so Edward let it go.

"I'll make certain he is ready to leave," Edward said without sitting down for dinner. He was thankful for the interruption, as he was nervous around his father. The sensation started after Ashby hit him. It was an experience he never wanted to have again.

"Your Grace," Thomas said, entering the dining room. "Lord Arundel is resting." Thomas looked like he wanted to say something more, but he stopped and waited for the duke to dismiss him.

"Do you have something more to say?" Ashby asked, looking over at the man.

He stammered, "My lord, Arundel . . . is not well," he said. He paused and was going to continue when Edward interrupted him.

"What do you mean? He was talking to me and seemed fine while I was in there."

"While preparing the bath, I forgot to add the cool water in and his leg was burned. I also brushed his injured leg and caused him great pain, It was an accident. Your Grace, I do apologize for my clumsiness."

"Did you reinjure his leg?" Ashby asked in frustration.

"The nurse said it should be fine. She will have the doctor confirm when he arrives."

"Fine." Ashby went back to his food as Thomas stood by the door. "Thomas, have Arundel ready to leave tomorrow after the doctor has checked his leg."

"Anything else, Thomas?" Edward asked.

"Yes, my lord," Thomas continued, "I accidentally cut his face."

Ashby pushed his chair back from the table. "What were you thinking?"

"It was an accident, Your Grace."

"Edward, your valet will attend Arundel until Thomas learns how to do his position again."

Thomas bowed to Ashby and went to follow him out when Edward asked, "Thomas, do not attend Phillip again without David."

Thomas turned back to the room. "I understand, my lord."

Edward shook his head. "I should have stayed and helped him instead."

"No, my lord, it is my position." He again stopped and looked uncomfortable.

Edward's eyes widened. "You should go and get your supper, Thomas. My brother won't need any more services for the night."

"Thank you, my lord." Thomas bowed and left the room in a rush.

With Lord Edward by himself, dinner was a different experience. Emma listened as he spoke about Phillip. He was animated. The stories he told were of a different person, and she wondered if Phillip could be the fun, energetic person his brother described.

"During our years at Eton, Phillip and I would skip courses and spend our days out in the countryside." Looking toward the door, Edward turned back and in a conspiratorial whisper said, "Don't tell Ashby! Anyway, we built a raft and hid it in a shed at night."

Emma interrupted his story. "Lord Arundel made it sound like you were the one who skipped classes."

Edward laughed. "Well, he does have amnesia . . ." He left the words hanging, and she joined him in laughing. "He skipped a few times, but there were times I left him behind because he didn't want to miss a lesson on Shakespeare or Greek Mythology . . . seriously . . . boring . . . lessons!"

Emma enjoyed Edward's energetic personality. Even though he made fun of Phillip's love of literature and learning, she knew he respected his brother. He didn't say the words, but it was in the way he spoke about Phillip.

Anne was a different person with Lord Edward in the house. Emma was surprised to see how animated her sister had become.

"We were going to sail down the Thames and head to the North Sea."

Henry looked up. "I wouldn't be surprised if the story is still told to this day at Eton of the twins who tried to escape."

Pleasure filled Lord Edward's face. "Well, we didn't make it very far."

"The story is so epic," Henry replied.

Emma noticed a flash of pain cross Lord Edward's face as the pleasure left. "You heard all of it?"

"I was at Eton the same time as you and Arundel." Shaking his head with regret he said, "I should have recognized him."

"It's been a long time since Eton. Where did you attend after?"

"Cambridge."

"Ah. Phillip and I were sent to Oxford."

Anne cut into their exchange. "Are you going to finish the story? What happened on your voyage?"

Lord Edward reanimated himself. "Phillip has a love of literature, so I convinced him Thames was the River Styx and we left on a voyage to become invulnerable. Our governess would tell us the myth of Achilles at bedtime, and at one point it was Phillip's favorite story. She told us about Achilles' mother and how she dipped him in the River Styx during his childhood and it made him indestructible, until they found his heel had not been dipped." He took a deep breath and continued. "I convinced Phillip all we needed to do was find the correct spot and swim in the River Styx to be just like Achilles."

"What happened?" Emma asked, curiosity building in her at this different side of Phillip.

"We pulled our raft to the bank when we decided we found the entrance to the underworld, and then we made a blood sacrifice to the Goddess of the River Styx."

"What do you mean by 'a blood sacrifice'?" Anne questioned. Emma was thankful she asked, because thoughts of killing an animal for this purpose made her ill.

"We took a knife and slit my pinkie finger." He turned his hand over and showed Anne the tiny scar where he'd slit his finger so many years ago.

"You both slit your fingers?" Emma asked, confused by his wording.

"We both slit our fingers. Phillip and I are identical, so we agreed it was wise to match scar for scar." He scrunched his face up a little. "He's beat me with scars. The doctor told us the one by his eye could've blinded him, so Phillip decided we didn't need identical scars. In case you are wondering, I was ready to match the scar."

He changed back to his storytelling voice and continued. "Once the blood sacrifice was made, I told him to swim in the River Styx. We both spent the rest of the day swimming and jumping into the river from an overhanging tree."

"So . . . you weren't trying to escape Eton?" Anne asked.

"Oh yes, we were going to continue into the North Sea and go where the water took us. We had food enough for a week."

"What went wrong?" Emma asked.

"Headmaster Ollerton contacted our father and mother. They were in London for the season and close by. Our father can be an intimidating man when he wants to be. He questioned the boys in our dormitory, and it wasn't long before they revealed our plans to sail into the North Sea. Our father and Headmaster Ollerton found us before nightfall."

"They took both of you back to Eton?" Emma asked due to Lord Edward's falter in finishing the story.

Lord Edward smiled. "It was a stupid idea, but we had fun while it lasted." In a side comment he said, "I just wish it had worked," and then added for explanation, "the dipping in the River Styx."

"What do you mean?" Anne asked. "Why do you wish it had worked?"

Edward laughed. "He wouldn't be in the situation he is now if he were invulnerable."

"I suppose," Anne replied, "but if it had worked, we never would've met him and you."

Emma was not the only one in her family to take a double look in her direction. Anne was flirting with Lord Edward.

"Very true, Miss Parker." He paused before continuing. "But we have an unfortunate issue with someone trying to kill my brother, and we have no idea who it is."

"In these situations, it is common to be the next person to inherit," Richard said in an offhanded but pointed comment.

Lord Edward laughed. "You're correct. And our constable thinks along the same lines. I don't want the title or inheritance. I'll receive more than enough when the time comes. Phillip has said many times he'll receive far more than he needs. All of my siblings feel the same way. We don't need the wealth my father has." He added with a sigh, "It is overwhelming." He continued after a moment of thought. "Phillip tried to join the Royal Navy a few years ago. He wrote our father a letter and told him to name me heir." He sighed and shrugged his shoulders. "He doesn't want to inherit the mess."

"Mess?" Henry asked.

"Wealth brings challenges you wouldn't think about. Take this situation—someone tried to kill him. I have no doubt it has to do with money. I just wish they would make the request instead of attempting murder," Edward said as though he'd given the situation a lot of thought.

"Are there any leads?" Henry asked, pushing his plate to the side so the footman would clear it.

"No, my father and I hope Phillip will be able to give us information. But after speaking with him tonight, I don't think he remembers anything about it." Disappointment showed in his words and expressions.

Everyone stood to go into the parlor for the evening. Emma sidled up against her sister to whisper, "Lord Edward?"

Anne looked guilty as she took her sister's arm and whispered back, "I don't know what you mean."

"You've warned me to guard my heart," Emma responded, "so I'm going to give you the same warning. We didn't know Phillip was an earl when I fell in love with him. You know his brother is titled, and you are falling for him."

"Does this mean you're going to forget your feelings for Phillip?" Anne whispered as they both sat on the couch.

"No, I'm not giving up. We are a perfect match, and I have a dowry of five thousand pounds to tempt him." Emma shrugged her shoulders.

Anne shook her head in the negative. "Five thousand pounds won't tempt an earl. He'll have women worth fifty thousand pounds or more tempting him."

"But those women don't hold his heart like I do."

"I hope you are right," Anne said. Emma knew she was going to say something else, but she stopped herself before continuing.

"Anne," her mother called across the room, "will you play for us tonight?"

Emma looked to her sister before she stood. "I suppose our mother is going to help you with your conquest."

Anne looked back at her. "She wants both her daughters married." The smile on her face and the bounce in her step made Emma laugh as she watched her sister go to the piano.

Seventeen

WEARING CLOTHING HE WAS TOLD was his was a little strange. Phillip had been wearing Henry's clothing since he woke. The clothing was comfortable and although a little large due to loss of weight, his one thought was how surreal it was to know these were his.

Phillip hobbled into the dining room for breakfast. He wanted to find a way to pull Emma aside before he left so he could ask for her hand. It wouldn't be as romantic as he'd hoped, but he needed to ask before leaving Springhill Abby. He took a seat, across from his father, and had a second to consider what he wanted to eat before Ashby spoke.

"Constable Adams will be here this morning. You should prepare to speak to him. We will leave for London soon after."

"London? So soon?" Phillip asked with a glance toward Emma. She had her head down and her eyes adverted.

"You've trespassed upon Lord Anthony and his family for far too long. It is time we gave them back their home."

"Your Grace," Lord Anthony said before anyone else could speak, "my family and I do not begrudge Lord Arundel the time he has spent here. We are happy to have been of service to him."

Phillip's heart filled with gratitude for Lord Anthony and the entire Parker family. He again looked at Emma, hoping to lock eyes with her to indicate he'd appreciate a private assignation with her.

"You are very generous, Lord Anthony." This time it was Edward who spoke. Ashby wouldn't have been so kind. "We are indebted to you for the care Phillip received."

"Yes," Ashby said, cutting any response from Lord Anthony off, "but it does not mean we will continue to trespass upon your kindness. Constable Adams will interview Phillip this morning, the good doctor will make a final visit, and then we will leave for London." Turning to Phillip he said, "Arundel, make certain you are ready to leave."

Phillip didn't speak. He nodded to let his father know he heard. The room was filled with the clinging of silverware against plates, but Phillip couldn't bring himself to eat. He feared this would be the last time he saw Emma, as they didn't have the same connections. Realizing Ashby expected some type of response, other than a head nod, he asked, "Do I know the constable?"

"Yes," Ashby reassured, "he has been in the village your entire life, and he worked in the stables at Wentworth Hall before taking the job as the constable."

Phillip gave Edward a questioning look as he made a sound of dislike. He turned and asked, "Do you not like the constable?"

"No, I don't. And I don't think he has any intention of finding the person responsible," Edward replied as he ate toast.

Ashby looked over to Edward. "Once the constable finds the correct person I will request a formal apology for you. But for now, you may make yourself scarce while he is here."

"What am I missing?" Phillip asked with concern.

Edward finished chewing his toast before he spoke. "I spent time in a jail cell this summer for murdering you."

Phillip looked to Ashby for confirmation of Edward's words and then back to his brother. His concern over the clothing being too large seemed frivolous now that he knew Edward had been incarcerated.

"I'm not sitting in the cell right now because father's solicitor convinced *Constable Adams* he couldn't hold me without your body," Edward finished.

"Why would the constable suspect you?" Anne asked with vehemence.

Henry answered the question for everyone. "If the elder is dead the younger becomes the heir."

Edward nodded. "Somehow my ring ended up out in the bushes as well. Whoever did this had access to the house."

"Is this why the constable is coming? He wants me to say it was Edward who tried to kill me?" Phillip wasn't happy about the prospect of visiting with the constable.

Ashby looked over and said, "It's a possibility. Adams was very unhappy I allowed Edward to accompany me here to retrieve you."

Phillip was about to apologize to his brother when the butler entered the room. "Lord Anthony, there is a constable here to see Lord Arundel."

"Thank you. Will you show him to the parlor?" Lord Anthony replied.

Edward looked over and said, "He's here for you."

Phillip took his crutches from Thomas and limped from the silent dining room. He couldn't imagine spending time in a jail cell. His mind raced with this information as he entered the parlor to see the constable. He moved to the couch and sat across from the man.

Phillip looked at the constable, trying to pull some memory of this man out of his brain. He was tired of the constant fog over his mind.

"My lord?"

"I apologize I wasn't listening," Phillip said.

"I asked if you can tell me why you left the garden party at Wentworth Hall." Constable Adams had a pad of paper and a pencil similar to what Emma used for sketching. The pencil made Phillip think of her sketches.

He tried to remember the garden party but instead remembered his horse Bassanio. It was a memory he had before. "I don't know why I left. But I know I was riding Bassanio."

Constable Adams didn't respond. He wrote on his pad.

"Is Bassanio back at Wentworth Hall?" he asked.

"Yes. Can you tell me anything about your ride?"

Phillip closed his eyes hoping to bring out a memory. He could see his horse standing by a stream. "I remember sitting by a stream."

"We found a tree where you rested for a while. A tracker was brought in to tell us what path you took. You were on your way home, until you veered off into the woods. Do you remember any of this?"

Frustrated, he concentrated on what he thought was a memory when he remembered the sound of a bullet. "Someone shot at me. I had a bullet in my arm. Doctor Price extracted it. I think I fell off the horse when I was shot."

"How did you end up at Springhill Abby?"

"Lord Anthony found me in a river."

"How did you end up in the river?"

Phillip looked out the window. He concentrated on the horse tethered in front of the house. He remembered the dark figure standing over him. "I was dragged to the river."

"Did you see your assailant?"

Phillip looked up at the constable. He shook his head. "My memories are blocked."

Constable Adams switched tactics without notice. "Tell me, how is your relationship with Lord Edward?"

"He's my twin brother. Some would call him my other half. He's doing everything he can to help me, and I am thankful to him." It might have been a bit of an exaggeration, because he couldn't remember anything about their relationship, but the words were easy to speak and made sense to him.

"Has he tried to injure you since he's been here at Springhill Abby?"

"Certainly not!" he replied, raising his voice. "The one person to cause me injury since being here is my valet. He didn't find a need to cool the hot bath water, he was clumsy with my injured leg, and he gave me a few cuts on my face while shaving. Perhaps he is the culprit." He didn't know why he accused Thomas, but the words flew out before he stopped himself.

Constable Adams looked at him for a long moment as though he was assessing the truth of Phillip's words. "If you remember anything, please let me know."

Phillip grabbed his crutches, thinking it would be nice to visit the rose garden. He wanted to find Edward, and he wanted to see Emma. As he exited, Ashby and Lord Anthony entered.

"How much was he able to remember?"

"He doesn't remember anything we didn't already know. Lord Anthony, I would like to speak with you."

Phillip didn't stop to listen in on the rest of the conversation. On the other side of the hall he heard a piano being played. He hobbled into the room and smiled when he saw Emma. He didn't know she could play the piano. Anne was the one who played at night. He sat on the couch, put his head back, and listened.

"When did you come in here?" Emma asked as she stopped playing.

"I didn't know you play."

"Anne is more talented than I," she said as she sat next to him. "Were you able to answer any of the constable's questions?"

"Yes, I remembered a few details but not enough to help the situation. I was hoping to get a chance to speak with you. My father is convinced we need to leave for London, and I—"

Emma cut him off. "Phillip, I want you to be well, but I pray the doctor finds a way to keep you here."

"If I can convince him to tell my father I cannot travel, I will do so," he said sincerely. When she smiled, his heart melted. He picked her hand up and kissed it. Emma leaned forward and he kissed her. As he pulled away he noted her pink cheeks. He didn't have to do much to get her to blush. Her eyes were still closed, so he leaned forward and kissed her again. Phillip pulled back as he heard voices in the hall.

"My lord." The butler entered and gave a quick bow. "Doctor Price is waiting for you in the parlor. His Grace is also in the parlor. He is insisting on staying in the room for your visit with the doctor."

Phillip cringed. He didn't want his father in the room, as he needed to convince the doctor to make an excuse for him to stay at Springhill Abby. He limped toward the parlor, trying to concoct a plan of action, but nothing came to him.

"Doctor Price, thank you for coming," he said when he entered the parlor. "My father is anxious to depart for London." He tried to sound nonchalant and unaffected by the prospect of leaving.

"I must admit this is concerning." Doctor Price turned to Ashby with a determined look on his face. "Lord Arundel has been ill. The head injury he received has been quite bothersome to him and has caused much distress. There is no telling what a trip to London will do. The roads are not smooth enough, and the journey could irritate his injuries, your Grace."

"What do you suggest, Doctor?" Ashby's tone was condescending.

"He should rest for another week. I can then assess his injuries and determine if he should remain or travel."

"Not acceptable. We are leaving in an hour."

"Your Grace. Please understand the jeopardy you are putting your son in by forcing him to leave."

Phillip watched as Ashby debated the doctor's statement. He couldn't remember most of his life, but what he could remember made him know his father was more self-absorbed than caring. He also knew Ashby was a bully and not likely to be convinced to stay when he didn't want to.

"We will stay until next week, if you deem it necessary."

Surprised by Ashby's decision, Phillip submitted to the exam. After the doctor finished, Phillip made his way back to his room with the new cane, as he'd graduated from crutches. The morning had been exhausting.

Eighteen

EDWARD NOTICED THE LOOK OF sympathy on Anne's face when she heard he was accused of killing his brother. She was beautiful and he enjoyed her pity for his predicament. He hadn't flirted with a woman since the day Phillip disappeared, and although he had a small amount of guilt for not being around when he was needed, his desire to know Anne now took over.

As Phillip left to speak to the constable, Edward finished breakfasting and walked out to the rose garden. He wanted to stay as far away from Constable Adams as possible. He didn't like the man.

Edward walked to the bench in the rose garden and found Emma and Anne sitting as they had the first time he'd been out there. "May I join you?"

"Please," Anne responded with a smile. Her beauty sent a jolt of excitement through him.

He wanted her to like him. "It's a beautiful morning," he said as he looked around. He thought about the statement and then cringed. *I'm discussing the weather. How charming.*

"We were considering a walk through the grounds. Lord Arundel enjoys walking with us. Would you like to join us as well?" Anne asked. Her blue eyes twinkled in the sunlight as she spoke.

"It would be my pleasure." Edward looked back at the house. "However, I don't know how long Phillip will be . . . and does he walk, or is it more of a hobble?"

He smiled as both women laughed at the pathetic joke. He didn't consider himself funny, but for some reason women laughed at his attempts of humor.

Emma stood, startling him. "I think I'll practice the piano. I haven't played in a while. Why don't you take a walk?"

Is my attraction to Anne so obvious? he wondered. "Would you like to walk with me?" he asked Anne.

"Yes, I would."

Edward held his arm out and led her from the garden. She pointed him toward a dirt path, and he followed her directions. The mere touch of her arm in his made him think the trauma of having Phillip nearly killed was worth it. He never would have met Miss Parker otherwise.

"I am surprised to see you are not preparing to leave. Has something changed?" Anne asked. He could see her curiosity had multiple levels to it. She didn't want him to leave. Or was he imagining her intentions because he didn't want to leave?

"I will procrastinate until necessary . . . or my valet will take care of my things. But even when we leave, we can meet in London for the season," Edward replied. Before she could respond, he had an idea. "Will you dance with me?"

"Now?"

He shook his head as he laughed. "No, Miss Parker, at the first dance of the London season."

Anne blushed, which enhanced her pale skin and dark brown hair. "I would be delighted to save a dance for you."

"Then we have to meet at the same ball to make this happen. Tell me, Miss Parker, where does your family reside during the season?"

"Piccadilly. Hertford House."

He nodded. "Should we agree to find each other at the first ball held at Almack's Assembly Hall?"

"I look forward to it," she said, looking up at him.

His height was a nuisance. He would've wanted her to be able to look into his eyes without craning her neck. "You will save me just *one* dance?"

"Are you requesting more than one?"

"What about two dances?" He was making a fool of himself, and yet he didn't care.

"I would be honored." Her voice took on a dreamy tone.

He turned to her and stopped walking. "I would ask for three dances, but you know society won't approve."

"I would give you three dances, my lord."

Edward let her words sink in. Three dances in a night was equal to posting the banns. Was she telling him she also had feelings for him? Was it possible to fall in love in a day? He closed the gap between them.

"May I kiss you?" *I can't believe I said those words,* he thought after he asked the question. He'd been looking at her deep blue eyes and had the urge to kiss her. *Is she shocked? Is she appalled?* The questions rang through his mind as he waited to hear her answer. *Is she offended? Will she slap me? I deserve to be slapped.* An eternity passed, although it was only seconds after he asked the question when she responded.

"Yes."

Nineteen

LISTENING TO ANNE ON THE piano put a longing into Phillip. It was almost as though he longed to sit at the bench and play. He imagined the notes and knew he could play. This was the first time since being at Springhill Abby he'd had the realization of a musical talent.

Henry, Richard, Edward, and Lord Anthony were in a serious game of cards. Lady Amelia worked on her embroidery. Phillip sat on the sofa next to his father, both reading books, both tense and ignoring each other, but he continued to sneak looks in Emma's direction as she sketched. The night seemed as though it would pass in silence.

Anne finished playing a song when Edward spoke up. "Phillip, I haven't heard you play since you were at Wentworth Hall."

Phillip peered over the top of the book. He didn't hide his annoyance with Edward. Although Doctor Price told them to help restore his memory, Phillip didn't have a need to perform for everyone. He almost pointed out he hadn't been at Wentworth Hall for quite some time but instead replied, "Miss Parker is a far superior musician than I." He looked over at Emma to see if she realized he used her same excuse for not playing.

"You do remember how to play?" Edward asked as he placed a card on the table and exchanged it for another one.

"Perhaps," he responded, going back to the book.

"I do agree with you regarding Miss Parker's talent. She is much better than you. If I remember right, you stumble across the keys as though you don't know how to carry a melody." Looking as though he didn't care if his brother favored them with a song, Edward continued, "Father, would you agree?"

"I'm enjoying a book, Edward. I don't need you to manipulate me into performing," Phillip remarked, cutting over any comment their father would make.

"And I'm enjoying cards. After thinking on it, I'd prefer you don't play. It could prove to be distracting."

Phillip shook his head and went back to reading the book.

Joining the conversation Anne supplied, "Lord Arundel, if you would like I have a selection of sheet music you could use."

Edward commented, "I believe he doesn't remember how to read music anymore. Not due to the amnesia. He just doesn't play very well. I haven't heard Mozart or Chopin since we were seven or eight. He's correct; he isn't very good at the instrument."

"Then what do you play?" Anne asked, ignoring Edward's flippant remark.

Phillip looked around the room. Every person except Ashby was focused on him. He glared at Edward, frustrated with the conversation. He turned to Anne and softened his face. "I—"

His response was interrupted by Edward. "You don't want to hear what he plays. It's terrible music of his composition."

"You're a composer?" Anne asked in surprise. "Have you written anything down?"

Phillip tried to answer her question but again was cut off. He lifted his hand motioning to Edward.

"He doesn't compose well enough for anyone to want to duplicate the sound."

While trying not to laugh at Edward, Anne asked, "Will you please favor us with a song?"

Edward jumped out of the chair and pulled Phillip to his feet. "You can't turn down a request from a lady. I'll help you to the piano." In a loud whisper so everyone could hear he asked, "Do you need me to press the pedals as you play?" Edward dragged Phillip to the piano. "You won't get your cane back until you play for us."

"Do you have a specific request?"

"Play and I will tell you if it fulfills my desire."

Phillip took the music sheets from Anne and looked through them. Edward grabbed the music. "You have always told me when you sit at a piano the notes fill your mind. So, let's see what comes."

"Go away!" Phillip said with a shake of his head.

He sat staring at the piano keys. Emotions assaulted him as he looked at the ivory and black keys. Phillip let out a sigh of relief when he saw the music in his mind. Fingers in place, he experienced the sensation of having the ivory keys as an extension of his body. He played the first chords he could imagine. The music flowed through him down to the piano. For the first time in a long time, he knew who he was. His memories might not be restored, but he knew music was his life. It was a liberating moment, and the joy came out through the piano and made him calm. As he played, he thought of Emma and knew this song was for her.

When he finished playing, he looked up to see the one person he wanted to please. Emma wiped tears away. Pleased with her response, he turned to the rest of the room and reached his hand out for Edward to bring the cane to him.

"You should play for Lady Olivia when we arrive at Lancaster House tomorrow," Ashby said. He spoke in the most normal tone as though Lady Olivia were a regular part of Phillip's life.

"Who is Lady Olivia?" Phillip asked as he scooted to the edge of the bench and waited for his cane.

The cards Edward held flew out of his hands with the question in the air. Ashby raised his eyebrows.

"She's your intended, Arundel."

"I'm sorry," he said looking to Ashby, "did I hear you correctly?"

Edward stood up and walked toward him. "The betrothal happened right before you went missing. I'm not surprised you don't remember."

Phillip shook his head in confusion. "I realize there is a lot I am still missing. But please help me with this one by giving it to me straight."

"Arundel," his father said in a calming voice. "We can discuss this further when we arrive in London."

"Do I even know this woman?" he asked as he looked between his father and brother. He wasn't going to let the conversation stall until London.

Edward laughed. "Yes, but you do not enjoy her company. Oh, and last time you spoke to her you made her so angry she stomped on your foot and kicked you in the shins."

"Amusing," Phillip responded.

"I seem to remember you gave the same response when we all laughed about it."

"Who laughed about it?" He didn't like the idea of being laughed at.

"Us . . . me and our siblings. You walked Olivia home from church the first week the banns were read—"

"The banns have been read?" Phillip's voice rose as his temper flared. He hit the keys on the piano, causing a jumble of noise.

"One week of banns." Edward turned to his father. "This isn't going well. I don't think we should have told him yet."

"Shouldn't have told me?" Phillip panicked. "When would be a good time to give me this information?" He wanted to be with Emma, and now wanted to rip his heart out.

"Arundel, this is something we can speak about once we get to Lancaster House," Ashby stood to leave the room.

"Hand me my cane," Phillip said to Edward.

Edward walked forward in shock, grabbed the cane, and moved over to the piano. "It's not wise to argue right now. Let Father calm down."

"Calm down?" Phillip yelled. "Don't I have a right to know?"

The Duke of Ashby took a deep breath before turning back to his sons. "Arundel, you will be compensated well for the marriage. She has a dowry of seventy thousand pounds, and she is required to give you an heir and a spare."

Phillip grabbed the cane from Edward as he said, "Oh . . . well . . . let me rejoice in my good fortune. And I have no doubt I will inherit more than seventy thousand pounds from you one day. I don't need the dowry."

Smirking, Edward remarked, "She's at least pleasant to look at, when she isn't scowling at you."

"Shut up, Edward!"

"Arundel!" Ashby yelled, losing his temper. "There's no more to discuss. You will marry Lady Olivia. The banns are set to be read this Sunday in London. You have four weeks to consign yourself to the marriage. It's your duty."

"Duty?" Phillip was distraught. He didn't dare look at Emma. He had so many plans, and now they were no longer a possibility. "Duty? You must be jesting."

"No, I'm not," his father yelled. "Your social standing doesn't allow for a love match. You will do your duty, and I want no further argument."

"Is the conversation over?" Phillip asked. "Wait," he said with a little bit of hope. "The title has been transferred to you. You have to marry Olivia now."

Edward gave a nervous laugh and used his hand to cover his heart. "I would do anything for you, Phillip, anything. But I have to draw a line at Olivia—"

"No! It doesn't change the engagement." Ashby sighed. He was tired. "You are the one engaged, not the title. And Edward doesn't have the title. Since we didn't have a body, it wasn't made official."

Richard cleared his throat as he left the gaming table. "I know it isn't my place to interject—"

"Then stay silent!" Ashby said, not sparing Richard a glance.

"Yet, I must. Arranged marriages are frowned upon in the church. Does the Vicar of your parish know this is a forced marriage?"

"This isn't an arranged marriage," Ashby disputed.

"It sounds like one to me," Phillip argued.

"I agree," Richard said. He stared Ashby down.

"You accepted the arrangement, Arundel. You cannot back out of it now."

Phillip looked over to Edward to see if there was any truth to the statement. Edward slowly shook his head in the negative.

"I did not!" Phillip contended.

Ashby sighed. "You were not happy about the engagement but consigned yourself to the union."

"Well, I'm not consigned to it now." Phillip stood in shock as his father left the room. He decided to ignore Edward's advice. He followed Ashby out of the room. He had to find a way out of the engagement.

"I don't want to marry Olivia." He heard the hysteria in his voice and also the derisive tone in which he said her name. Her name sounded disgusting on his lips.

"Norland and I made a bet. If I don't go through with my end of the deal, I lose my lands, wealth, and titles. I will lose everything except Wentworth Hall. If he doesn't go through with it, he will lose the same."

"Why did you enter into this bet? Aren't you putting a lot at stake?"

"It's a gamble," Ashby said. "Whoever pulls out first loses."

"Father." Phillip tried to speak with the most calming voice he could muster. "I love Emma. The thought of marrying someone else makes me ill."

"You'd prefer to lose our way of life? You want me to give everything except Wentworth Hall to Norland?"

"Certainly not! But I want to make my own choice in marriage." Every minute his father refused to relent he experienced a new level of panic, as though no matter what he did, he was going to lose.

"Go to bed, Arundel."

"No. Not until you acknowledge this engagement is a farce and release me from it. I have already asked Lord Anthony for permission to marry Emma."

"Retire for the evening. I won't say it again." Ashby's hand twitched. Phillip moved backward, but the furious need to get out of this engagement took over.

"I won't marry her."

Phillip watched as Ashby lost the temper he tried to control. His father's hand came up and collided with Phillip's face. Phillip turned back to him. He remembered the abuse all too well.

He knew it was dangerous, but he argued again. "I won't marry her."

Ashby's hand again came up and hit him in the same spot. Phillip didn't move backward. He stood firm and let his father hit him a third time. As Ashby's hand came up for a fourth time, Edward intervened and grabbed his father's arm.

Phillip glared at Ashby. He didn't look at Edward. He didn't thank his brother for the interference. He wasn't sure the strategy of letting his father hit him over and over would do any good, but it was better than cowering before him.

"What do I have to do to get out of the engagement?" Phillip asked, gaining control of his emotions.

"You can't get out of it." His father's voice was tight as though he was trying to stay calm, but failing at the same time. "Instead of fighting it, accept it."

"I'll give up my place as your heir."

"You've already tried this, many times, and I've told you it isn't possible." Ashby turned from him. "Go to bed. We will leave tomorrow morning."

"Father," Edward said in surprise, "the doctor said it could be too dangerous for Phillip to leave right now."

"I don't agree. And it is better we leave now, before Phillip makes Lord Anthony's daughter a promise he can't keep."

Disgusted with his father, Phillip turned to go inside but stopped. He didn't feel like he could enter the house again knowing he couldn't be with Emma. Phillip sat on the stairs leading up to the entrance of the house. He put his head in his hands. He'd lived his entire life in those few minutes.

Twenty

CRUSHED WAS ONE OF THE words Emma used to describe her emotions. Internal bleeding was another way to describe her pain. She tried to breathe normally as she listened to the argument between Phillip and his father. She didn't want to look around the room because she didn't want to see the pity on anyone's face.

She was thankful she had been sitting by the door and could make a silent exit when Ashby stated Phillip had agreed to the marriage. She retreated to her room, which overlooked the front of the house. She could hear the argument between Phillip and Ashby. When she heard Ashby hit Phillip, she jumped and ran to the window and watched as he stood and allowed his father to beat him.

Emma didn't hold the tears back. She couldn't imagine life without Phillip. She walked to her bed and fell onto it, letting her tears flow. Her door opened and she thought about telling whoever it was to go away, but she couldn't bring herself to stop crying.

The pins in her hair were removed, and the soothing motion of brush bristles flowed through her hair.

"You're going to get a headache," Anne said.

"My heart is broken."

"Go ahead and cry."

"I never want to see him again." She was interrupted in her thoughts as voices rose in the yard. Emma stopped sobbing and pointed to the window. Anne rushed over and opened it for her.

"You could have given him the news of the betrothal at another time," Lord Edward said to his father.

"Edward, I'm your father. You won't disrespect me," Ashby stated, anger causing his voice to rise.

"I mean you no disrespect," Edward said to his father, "but it is obvious Phillip isn't . . . himself. The amnesia is worse than we were led to believe, and he is falling in love with Miss Emma."

"It's not love. He has been ill, and she assisted him during this time. Also, she isn't the type of woman he tends to notice. A few days away from here, and he will forget about her."

"I disagree with you," Edward argued. "She is his match in every way. But you would prefer he pay attention to fair hair and less brains."

"I still think a few days away from here and he will forget about Miss Emma Parker," Ashby insisted.

They were silent for a time before Edward finished the conversation. "We need to take him home. He's lost here."

Ashby grunted, and they either fell silent or went into the house. All Emma knew was she could no longer hear their conversation below her window. She motioned for Anne to close the window, and lay back on her bed. She didn't let anymore tears fall. She stared at the wall as she repeated, "I never want to see him again."

The following morning when Phillip left, Emma stayed in the house. She walked in the hallway to a window looking over the yard where the carriage sat waiting for its passengers. She watched as Phillip hugged her mother, shook her father's hand, and both of her brother's hands. He kissed Anne's hand and then looked to the door. He was looking for her. But the betrayal and anger seething within her stopped her from running out to say farewell. She wouldn't wish him a safe journey. She wouldn't ever look at him again.

Even as she thought the words, she betrayed her resolve as she watched Phillip climb into the carriage. As far as she could see, he never looked back as the carriage drove away.

Twenty-one

PHILLIP STOOD IN THE YARD of Springhill Abby ready to leave and thankful Emma wasn't there to see him off. He wouldn't be able to leave if she came out. He had a moment of embarrassment for the bruise on his upper cheek but decided the Parkers had heard everything the night before and knew about the altercation.

"Arundel," his father called over to him, "it's time to leave."

Phillip nodded and tried not to feel devastated about leaving Emma. "Lord Anthony, I owe you my life."

"We were happy to have you here."

"I hoped Miss Emma would be here so I could speak to her." He hesitated and stepped a little closer. "If I had known about the engagement, I never would have . . ." His voice cut off and he didn't finish the statement.

"We understand, and I will speak with Emma," he responded, putting a hand on Phillip's shoulder.

Phillip shook hands with Henry and Richard. He was ashamed of his actions as he realized the reality of Richard's words the day he accosted him for his inappropriate behavior. "You were correct. Everything you said by the tree was right."

Richard put one hand on his shoulder. "It doesn't make me happy to be right."

Phillip moved over to Anne and kissed her hand. Lady Amelia pulled him into her embrace, and then he found his way to the carriage.

As he left Springhill Abby, Phillip sat with his head back against the seat and his eyes closed. He hoped his father and brother would converse with each other instead of with him. Depression settled in as he thought about the engagement, the continued amnesia, and his desire but inability to be with Emma.

As they neared Lancaster House, a sense of nervousness joined the other feelings he was fighting. When their father announced they had less than an hour, the tension in the carriage was unbearable, and Phillip's left leg bounced out of nervousness.

"Calm down, Arundel," their father said, putting a hand on his leg to stop the bouncing.

"What if my memory doesn't return?" he asked, running his hand along his leg as the bouncing began again. "I have no idea which sister is Marianne and which is Charlotte."

"The doctor believes a familiar place should bring everything back," Edward commented, placing a hand on his shoulder. "Also, everyone knows about the amnesia. No one is expecting you to remember everything all at one time." Edward paused before continuing. "Charlotte is blonde, and Marianne has auburn hair."

Phillip nodded, telling himself to remember which sister was which, then decided to argue for time. "Father, I know you said I have four weeks before the wedding. Can't you give me more time? Give me time to get some memories back, straighten my mind, and feel comfortable at home?"

Ashby closed his eyes and took a deep breath before responding. He was annoyed and didn't hide frustration well. "We will talk about it at another time."

When the carriage stopped in front of Lancaster House, the family was waiting just inside the gate. Edward took the cane as Ashby helped Phillip out. As soon as his good foot hit the ground, his mother pulled him into her arms and held him. Although a memory hadn't triggered when he saw the house, he knew his mother's arms, and he remembered the smell of eucalyptus oil in her hair. It was a relief to recognize her.

His sisters pulled him into their arms and chatted about trivial matters. Marianne packed all of his favorite books and brought them to Lancaster House for him to enjoy. Charlotte spoke of clothing and items he had in his bedchamber at Wentworth Hall. She brought the mementos for him to enjoy and trigger memories.

His sisters and their endless chatter made him nervous. Ashby must have noticed as he stated, "Ladies, let your brother breathe. He's overwhelmed."

Charles walked forward and embraced him as well. "I'll walk you to your room."

His mother walked forward and touched his face. "You look exhausted. You should rest before tea."

He missed tea and slept until supper. He stood in the parlor, waiting to go into the dining room with the family. He examined a few of the paintings on the wall. The landscapes caused a surge of pain as they made him think of Emma and her joy of sketching. He noticed a piano in the corner of the room and thought about playing while they waited for their parents.

"The Duke and Duchess of Norland and Lady Olivia," Hodgens announced to the room, pulling Phillip out of his thoughts.

He took a deep breath and looked toward the door to see his intended. Olivia walked in with her face set in a scowl. Her hair was pulled up under her bonnet. She removed it and threw her bonnet at Hodgens to reveal curly blonde hair pinned atop her head. *She would be beautiful if she didn't wear the scowl.*

"Arundel," she said as she pointed her glower in his direction, "welcome home." She didn't wait for a response. She walked across the room and sat in a chair next to Charlotte and Marianne.

"Thank you." He continued to look at her as she sat with his sisters.

She didn't speak to anyone else in the room, and no one spoke to either her or her parents until his parents arrived. Dinner was an uncomfortable affair for him, as he was forced to sit next to Olivia. This meant he was expected to speak with her. He didn't know what to say, and so they sat in silence throughout the meal and the rest of the evening. The scowl she wore in the door stayed with her through the evening and into the next morning.

They sat next to each other again during a tense breakfast. Every time Olivia looked at him she gave a nasty glare of disgust. Just as he was ready to leave the dining room, without a word in her direction, she spoke.

"Arundel," she said as she replaced her teacup on the plate, "I would like to speak with you, my parents, and your parents this morning."

He didn't speak but nodded in agreement.

"I have a feeling I know what this discussion will be," Norland said as he pushed his plate away and motioned for the footman to remove the dishes. "We may discuss here, if you are in agreement, Ashby."

Phillip looked over to see his father nod.

"Would you like us to leave?" Charlotte asked, looking to their parents.

"No, you may stay," Ashby replied, taking a sip of tea.

The room was still and silent for a full minute before Olivia began her prepared speech. "I don't mean any disrespect to the Duke and Duchess of Ashby, or to Arundel, but I am requesting to be released from the engagement."

Phillip looked from his parents to her parents, waiting for a response. His mother and father were both looking to Norland.

Norland gave his daughter a blank look of disappointment. "Is this request the best you can come up with? No, Olivia. You and Arundel will be married as soon as he is well. Your mother and I agreed last night to delay the reading of the banns due to his continued amnesia, but we won't delay long."

"Father, I beg of you, don't make me marry him. I'm in love with Lord Folly." A shrill cry escaped her mouth. She put her face in her hands and shook as though she were sobbing.

"Arundel?" Norland asked, seeking his opinion.

"Your Grace, I'm not one to stand in the way of true love. I'm more than willing to release your daughter from the engagement," he replied with amusement and a wave of his hand in her direction.

Everyone turned as Edward made a coughing noise and tea came out of his nose in an undignified manner. Charlotte poked him in the side, and Marianne and Charles both hid smiles behind the guise of wiping their mouths with a serviette.

"Perhaps my other children should leave the room if they are unable to control themselves," their father announced with a warning look in their direction.

"This engagement was based off of an ill-advised bet," Phillip continued. His words were bitter and angry, reflecting his emotions. "I would like to know the details of the bet."

Norland gave a lazy response. "Love fades over time, as does attraction. I believe you will find happiness in the future."

"Olivia, it is unfair of you to take your dowry from Arundel. He has been promised seventy thousand pounds for your hand," the Duchess of Norland said as she buttered her toast.

Phillip tried to sound obliging in his response. "Your Grace, I don't have a need for the dowry. Lord Folly and I have been friends since Oxford." Phillip stopped as he realized what he said. The memory of friendship came back without any effort on his part. He was elated at the thought of gaining another memory. He finished, "Folly is a good man, and the dowry will bring him more joy than it could ever bring me."

Edward interjected before anyone could speak. "You remember we know Folly?"

"Yes. Just now."

"Amazing," Edward said, his surprise evident. "The doctor said memories would come back, but I didn't think it would be so quick."

Olivia let out a sob, bringing the attention back to her. She kept her hands over her face as she whimpered.

"Darling," her mother said in an effort to stop the display, "your father and I are certain you will be happy once you are married to Arundel and installed at Wentworth Hall."

Before anyone could speak further, Olivia stood and threw her chair backward. The footman behind her caught the chair before it hit the ground. "I won't marry Arundel," she stated as she made a violent and thunderous exit from the dining room. The exit started with her screaming as she grabbed Phillip's cane and threw it at the side buffet, causing the food to fly off plates and crash to the floor. She continued her path of destruction through the room as she brushed her arms over the table and knocked over the teapot and teacups. As she made her final exit, she threw the door open and let it crash against the wall.

Footmen, maids, the housekeeper, and butler raced to clean up the destructive path she took as she continued down the hall. They heard items crashing to the floor as she continued to scream unintelligible words. Then the front door opened and slammed shut.

Phillip turned to look at Ashby. He was about to comment on the situation when his father beat him with the first response. "You're going to have an interesting life if she continues behaving as a child."

"Can we not come to an agreement to end the engagement?" Phillip asked, hopeful her display would help convince their parents.

"I'm more than willing to free Olivia from the contract, Norland. I have no desire to have my home disrupted by your daughter," Ashby said.

"Of course, you are, Ashby. And you will take my wealth along with your graciousness. I'll speak with my daughter about her duty," he said as he stood to leave. "Send me the bill for her demonstration." He looked to Phillip before leaving the table. "You will have your hands full. Rest well before it's official."

Before Phillip left the dining room, he turned to his father. "I don't understand. You already have everything you need. We aren't destitute. You're one of the wealthiest dukes in all of England. Why do you need his money?"

"You don't need to understand. You need to do your duty to your name and your family."

Phillip hated his father. He left the dining room and went to his bedchamber. Another headache threatened to start, and he decided to sleep it off.

Twenty-two

EMMA COULDN'T STOP THINKING ABOUT Phillip and the last hours they spent together. She'd been waiting for him to speak to her father and ask permission to marry her. He showed what she thought were feelings of love toward her, and she'd allowed him to kiss her multiple times. She'd not expected to hear he was already engaged. Emma stopped herself mid-thought and repeated the words, *I hate Arundel. I don't want to see him again.*

She was drawn back to the conversation when she heard Henry say, "It's best the Earl of Arundel is no longer with us."

"Why do you say this?" Anne asked.

"His extended presence in our home has already caused the women of London to start gossiping. If anyone finds out about the closeness he and Emma shared, she could be ruined just by word."

Emma was surprised by her mother's sudden outburst of anger as she defended the earl. "Phillip was a gracious guest in our home. How dare the gossips make it into something it wasn't? And when have you taken to listening to rumors?"

Looking chagrined, Henry responded, "Mother, we have much to be concerned about. We not only have our parents' generosity, but we also have two younger sisters who have spent a considerable amount of time in his presence."

Taking courage from his older brother, Richard continued, "What do you think people are going to say if he doesn't marry Lady Olivia Harrison?"

Emma looked over at her brother. "I would prefer we don't talk about Lady Olivia." She tried to stop the anger, but her words dripped with emotion.

"Your mother and I were impressed with both the earl and Lord Edward. Both were considerate and gracious while in our home," her father said.

"Perhaps this is true," Henry said in an effort to convey worry, "but you haven't heard the rumors people have spread regarding the Parker girls. We have our sisters' reputations to think about."

Emma looked up from her plate. "I had no idea extending generosity to a man who was injured and near death would ruin our reputations."

"Can you, in all honesty, say our family only extended generosity to him, Emma?" Richard asked. Richard and Anne had seen one of the kisses she shared with Phillip, and it had been the most passionate. She didn't know if they told the rest of the family of her inappropriate behavior, but her parents hadn't reproved her. "Anne and I saw the two of you, Emma."

"I know you did," she said, her voice rising in pitch.

"By the tree when you were sketching," he added, as if she had forgotten the day.

Her cheeks went red out of embarrassment and anger. "You had no right to eavesdrop on us."

"We weren't eavesdropping. But if it had been seen by anyone else, you would have a ruined reputation." He leaned toward her to make his point.

"I didn't know he was engaged. Had I known, I would never have spent time with him, and I wouldn't have kissed him nor allowed him to kiss me," she said in defense.

"It was inappropriate, Emma. I pray you would never allow another man to take such liberties until you are married." The preacher in her brother was coming out in every word he spoke.

"Liberties?" Emma squeaked. "What do you think we did?"

"I don't want to say in front of our parents. If you allow a man to touch you in public, what would you allow in private?"

"We weren't in public, and he touched my back."

"He also put his hands on your waist and undid your hair and ran his hands—"

"Both of you stop this behavior!" their father demanded, slamming his fist on the table. "Emma, your mother and I will speak to you regarding proper behavior before you attend any parties this season."

"I pray no one else saw you kissing," Richard continued, ignoring their father's request. "I've made inquiries since being in London. No one has information regarding the engagement."

"Is it London's best kept secret?" Emma said in fury, looking at her dinner plate.

"We also found," Henry said as he cut his meat, "Arundel hasn't been seen in public since arriving in London."

"What's the reason?" their father asked.

"His family tells everyone he is unwell," Richard said. "They don't expand on his condition. Whenever anyone asks why he isn't attending social gatherings, the excuse is he isn't well and will attend when he recovers. Any bets Ashby beat him and he's staying out of sight until the bruises heal?"

"A few people have speculated he isn't in London but has been taken to one of their country estates," Henry added, ignoring Richard's speculation of a beating.

Emma looked over. "His father said they were going to London."

"If he is unwell, a doctor hasn't been seen at Lancaster House," Henry replied, taking a bite of meat.

"The Duke of Ashby's position in Parliament puts his family in the sight lines of society. It's not an enviable position to be in," her mother stated, picking her teacup off the table and sipping a little.

"If you ask me, you're fortunate he didn't propose marriage to find out he couldn't follow through," Anne said.

"What do you mean?" Emma asked trying not to take offense but feeling very defensive of Phillip.

"From the behavior Richard and I saw, I can't even comprehend what you would have allowed if you thought you were engaged." Anne's words were a rebuke.

"I don't think it's fair for you to assume I've been ruined. I'm not the only Parker child who's engaged in passionate kissing." Emma shot toward her sister. "Do I need to remind you of Mr. Bennett? And Lord Edward. Did you kiss before he left?"

Anne's blush told the truth of the statement. "How do you know about Lord Edward kissing me?"

"You blushed too much when he said farewell. Do I also need to point out you lit up like a candlestick when Edward would enter a room—"

"This conversation is over!" their father shouted. In a calmer voice he added, "I hope Arundel has not taken ill again. It would be a pity if he had."

Emma was thankful the discussion ended as the butler walked into the dining room with a letter on a tray.

Anne brightened. "I hope it's our first invitation for the season."

Their father opened the letter and looked to his wife. "This is a surprise."

"Who's it from?" Anne asked, again not hiding her excitement.

"The Duke and Duchess of Ashby. From the conversation we just heard, I don't think either of my daughters should attend," he said, handing the invitation to his wife.

"If we do not go, all of society will talk," her mother said, handing the letter back.

Emma thought about Phillip as she dressed and readied for her first party of the season. She stopped herself mid-thought and repeated the words *I don't love him. I don't ever want to see him again* in her mind until she thought it was safe to think of another topic. She wondered if he would be at the party, then berated herself for thinking about him again. It seemed odd his family would host a party if all of their children weren't present. "Grr," she grunted, realizing her every thought went to Phillip. Society was already focused on Phillip due to the attempted murder during the summer. She didn't need him in her every thought. She looked in the mirror and gave up the fight on talking herself out of loving Phillip for the night.

She dressed with care, hoping he would notice she made an effort to dress for him. She picked her favorite navy-blue muslin dress because the dark colors made her feel pretty. As she walked into the entryway of Lancaster House, it was as though she were in a palace. The ceilings were high and covered in intricate patterns of plaster. The walls were covered in beautiful artwork, and the tables around the entry hall held vases of lilies. Emma followed her parents to greet their hosts while taking in the beauty of the room around her. The Duke and Duchess of Ashby stood at the foot of a staircase that led to the second floor of the house. To the right was a large room where people were dancing and chatting. To the left was another room with men playing cards.

Emma and her family moved closer to their hosts as each visitor greeted and moved off to one of the rooms.

"My dear, this is Lord Anthony and Lady Amelia," Ashby said to his wife. "May I present my wife, the Duchess Margaret of Ashby."

Emma saw her mother curtsy and her father bow as they greeted both the duke and duchess. She listened as Ashby introduced Lady Charlotte, Lady Marianne, and Lord Charles. He looked disapproving as he turned back. "Edward is around here somewhere."

"May we inquire after Lord Arundel?" her mother asked out of concern.

"Phillip has been unwell since arriving in London," Duchess Margaret responded. "He's in the library reading tonight."

"I pray it isn't anything serious," her mother replied out of genuine concern.

"He's still struggling with amnesia and worries society won't take his condition well," Ashby responded.

"Please convey our well wishes to him," her mother responded, taking hold of Duchess Margaret's hand and squeezing it for support.

"We are trying to convince him memories aren't as important as what he does with the rest of his life." She gave a sad smile. "He doesn't agree at this time. It has been a difficult three weeks for him. I think he preferred being at Springhill Abby."

Her mother didn't hesitate before saying, "When he was at Springhill Abby, he wanted to be with you. There were nights when I sat next to his bed trying to lend comfort as he was recovering and he would ask for his mother."

This information took the duchess off guard. She wiped tears from her eyes. "Thank you for your kind words."

"Miss Emma, would you dance the quadrille with me?" Lord Edward asked as she entered the ballroom.

She was surprised as he approached her instead of her sister. "Lord Edward, I would be delighted." She looked at Anne, who shrugged her shoulders. Emma walked with Edward to the dance floor.

With a knowing smile he said, "My brother is in the library."

"Your parents told us he wasn't coming down to the party. Is he well?"

"Well enough." They bowed to each other as the dance began.

As they joined arms and danced in a circle she asked, "Have you enjoyed your time in London?"

They separated as Emma moved diagonal on the floor, turned once with another woman, and came back to take his hand and perform another turn. "It has been an interesting season so far. Phillip is still struggling with memory loss, and Lady Olivia is still his intended, which has caused him a great deal of stress."

His words caused her to miss a step in the dance. "Can we please not discuss *her* or Phillip in the same sentence?"

She was thankful he nodded his agreement to stay away from the topic of Lady Olivia and Phillip. She had no desire to cry or sob while she was attending a ball at Lancaster House. The rest of the dance proceeded in silence.

They both bowed as the dance ended. He led her back to her family and thanked her for the dance. He then turned to Anne and asked her if she would join him for the next dance.

As the evening progressed, she both feared and hoped Phillip would come down to the party.

"Miss Emma?" Lady Marianne approached with an outstretched hand. Her sister Lady Charlotte was close behind her.

"Lady Marianne, it's nice to meet you and your family," Emma said, unsure of what this visit would entail. She looked to her parents, who both shrugged and her brothers who were amused by the attention.

"Edward is supposed to introduce your family to our acquaintances. Perhaps he'll start after he finishes dancing with Miss Parker," Lady Charlotte said.

Marianne pulled Emma aside. "Would you take a turn with me?"

"Certainly," Emma responded, unsure of her intent.

Marianne linked arms with her and led her out of the ballroom. "I'd like to give you a tour of our home."

Emma stopped walking. She knew where Marianne was taking her. "I'd prefer not to see him."

Marianne smiled. "He regrets not being able to speak with you before he left Springhill Abby. And a letter would be inappropriate given he can't court you."

"I regret it as well," she said, looking down at her hands.

Marianne urged, "You look as though you dressed with care tonight. Was it in hopes of seeing him?"

Emma nodded. She liked Marianne and could tell they would be friends if given the chance.

Marianne put her arm back through Emma's. "If you would prefer not to see him, I will show you every room except the library."

Emma smiled and made a split-second decision. "I would like to see the library."

Marianne squealed in delight. "I hoped I could convince you."

As they approached the door, Emma took a deep breath and again stopped. "Lady Marianne, I don't know if I can go through with my decision."

"Please, call me Marianne. I believe we are going to be good friends," she said as she stood outside the library with her. "He doesn't know I have concocted to bring you up here. He didn't request it of me. So . . . he won't be disappointed if we don't go in."

Emma stood taking a few deep breaths. "You can call me Emma. She smiled and pointed to the door. "I'm ready."

As they entered, Emma saw Phillip in a chair next to the fire with a book closed on his lap. He was sleeping. Either Marianne didn't notice, or she didn't care as she called out his name.

Startled, Phillip jumped out of the chair. The book dropped to the floor. "Emma?" His whisper reverberated through the room.

"Hello." Her voice took on a high pitch from nervousness.

He walked toward her and stopped, then looked to Marianne. "I didn't know the Parkers were coming."

"Would you have come to the party if you had known?" Marianne asked with a challenge in her voice.

"I don't know." He looked back to Emma and pointed to a chair. "Would you like to sit?"

She moved over to sit down. Marianne walked to the window. "I'll be over here when you're finished speaking."

He shook his head in exasperation and grumbled, "Sisters!"

Emma looked at him as he took his seat again and picked the book off the floor. "I see your leg has healed," she said, pointing at the right leg.

"Yes, I still have a limp, but I'm no longer in need of a cane," he responded.

Looking around the room she said, "This is an amazing library. It's much larger than the one at Springhill Abby."

"I could get lost in here and spend the rest of my life reading."

"We heard you were ill after arriving in London."

"It's the continued amnesia. But we use the excuse of being ill, because I don't want to go out into society without knowing who people are," he said without guile. Before she could speak again he said, "I didn't know about the engagement . . . I mean, I had to have known and my family tells me I did. But I didn't remember."

She tried to smile but was certain it came out as a tortured frown. "I understand."

"I wish I understood," he said, sitting back against the chair and running a hand through his sun-bleached hair.

"Emma, I wanted to mar—"

She cut him off, knowing he was going to say he wanted to marry her. She knew he did by the way he kissed her and because he told her he loved her. "Don't say it." She couldn't handle hearing the words. She refused to cry over him while at Lancaster House.

"I need to make certain you know I wasn't using you or trying to ruin you," he said leaning forward on the chair and reaching for her hand. "If I were free to make the decision, I would ask—"

Again she cut him off and pulled her hand out of his. "I already know." Her voice caught in her throat as she looked up at the ceiling and hoped the tears wouldn't fall. "I can't hear you say the words." She was thankful he understood as he gave up. She looked back at him and smiled. "We were never supposed to meet. It was by chance, and since our families don't run in the same social circles we won't have to see each other often and can now become former acquaintances."

She stood, ready to leave the room. She needed to get away from him before the tears fell. He stood and walked to her and put his hands on the side of her face.

"What are you doing?"

"I want to memorize you."

These were the type of words written in books by the hero. She dreamt of a man telling her he wanted to memorize her every feature, but she never thought one would actually say the words to her. She looked into his eyes as he held her face in his hands.

After looking at her for what seemed an eternity, he released her face and closed his eyes. "Emma, I'll figure out how to get out of this betrothal. If I do, will you marry me?"

The tears she'd held back all evening gathered in her eyes and threatened to release. She wanted to believe he could get out of it, but she didn't want to give herself false hopes. He ran his thumb along her cheek to wipe away the traitorous tears.

"I love you, Emma. Please tell me there's hope."

She knew it was a terrible desire, but she wanted him to kiss her. He wasn't free. He was another woman's man, and yet she wanted to steal him away. She didn't know much of anything about Lady Olivia, but she didn't like her. Instead she shook her head. "It's a false hope, my lord."

Phillip closed his eyes. He looked sad and depressed. "You once asked me if my name was Romeo."

"And you told me only if you had a Juliet."

"Please be my Juliet?"

"It's a story, my lord. It isn't real life."

"I can find a vicar who'd marry us. We could marry in secret."

Emma laughed as she shook her head. "My lord, it's a story. We would be a scandal and never escape the stigma."

"If anyone saw us right now, *scandal* would spread through the *ton*. We'd be forced to marry."

"Is this how you plan to get out of the engagement . . . ruin me?"

Phillip again wiped the tears on her cheeks. She had so many plans to keep the tears from falling and he'd ruined all of them.

I shouldn't have come in here, she said to herself as he continued to look into her eyes.

"Marianne, you should take her back to the party."

He was right. She needed to go back to reality. Before she walked away, she stood on her tiptoes and whispered, "I will always love you, my lord. But we don't live in the city of Verona." In a very daring and scandalous way, she kissed him on the cheek. She didn't look back to see his response. She had to leave the room before she agreed to run away with him.

"I didn't mean to cause either of you pain," Marianne said as she walked behind Emma.

He cleared his voice as he said, "You didn't. Thank you for your consideration." Emma looked back as she left the room. Phillip was sitting in the chair again but this time leaning forward with his head in his hands.

While she was mourning the relationship and what could have been, she never gave thought to how he was handling their separation. She realized this was as difficult for him as it was her. She didn't hear anything Marianne said as they walked back to the ballroom. She kept looking up at the ceiling and repeating the words *don't cry*.

"Emma, Lady Marianne," Richard said as they returned, "where have you been?"

"I took her on a tour of the house."

Richard looked at Emma and took her arm. "Will you join me in the next dance, sister?"

She nodded but didn't speak because she didn't trust her voice.

As was his duty, Edward spent time introducing the Parkers to everyone in the room. Each time he found another person he wanted to connect them with, he would bring them over and make introductions. Emma wondered how Phillip would respond about the different gentlemen asking her to dance. They also asked Anne to dance, but she could see the pleasure in her sister's face when Edward asked her to dance one more time.

"Lord Edward." A beautiful woman with blonde curly hair and wearing a gold and white dress made of fine silk approached. "Will you introduce me to your friends? I do believe I am the one person in this room you kept them from." Her voice was laced with disdain.

The tension was visible in Edward's posture as he looked at the woman. "Lady Olivia Harrison, this is—"

Emma wanted to run from the room as he introduced Phillip's betrothed. Instead she bowed her head and gave a small curtsy. Her mind wandered to speculation on how Phillip could have forgotten this beautiful woman. She realized how foolish she had been to spend extra time on her appearance. She compared the dark blue of her dress to the white and gold silk Olivia wore, and her dark brown hair to Olivia's light blonde hair. Emma chose to wear her hair in plaits pulled up around her head. Olivia's hair looked majestic with ringlets and a bun. Emma decided Olivia was regal and she was common.

"Miss Emma." Lady Olivia looked her over with smug disapproval. "I wonder if you would join me for a turn around the patio? I'm a bit warm, and you look as though you could use the air."

Without waiting for a response, Olivia linked arms with Emma to take her toward the exit.

"Lady Olivia," Edward said as he stepped in front of them. "I was just about to ask Miss Emma if she would join me in the next dance."

Olivia glared at Edward. "I thought you preferred her sister?"

Marianne put her arm through Emma's other arm. "Olivia, Emma and I were talking about taking a tour of the house."

Olivia gave a malevolent smile. "You've already given her the tour. I've been told the library was the main attraction. Now move away, Marianne."

Emma looked back at her family, Marianne, and Edward as Lady Olivia pulled her out to the patio. Olivia didn't speak, causing her to feel more nervous as they exited the house. She noticed the trees, benches, and shrubs in the garden and thought it would be the perfect place to relax and bring a book.

After their third turn around the patio, she asked, "Was there a reason you wanted to speak with me?"

"Yes. Arundel . . . you may call him Lord Arundel," she said as a way to show the separation in their social standing, "has lived a confining life. His parents tell him where to go, what to do, and who he will love."

Emma stayed silent as she listened to the woman talk. At one point she wanted to respond and tell Lady Olivia she had no desire to be with *Lord Arundel*, but the words wouldn't come from her mouth. No matter how hurt and angry she had been due to the marriage contract, her heart wouldn't allow her to lie. The more this woman threatened her and belittled her, the more she wanted to be with Phillip as though her goading was a challenge.

"Phillip and I are engaged. It is not something we speak about, due to the delicacy of society and the pressure of marriage. I also wanted to enjoy a few London seasons before marriage. I don't believe I should have to miss out on the parties and dances with my friends," Olivia bragged.

"I was under the impression neither of you knew about the engagement until last June," Emma replied. She put a sneer into her words to let Olivia know she wasn't easy to manipulate.

Olivia narrowed her eyes and smiled. "Fine, I will be honest with you."

"Please do, as you are wasting my time," Emma responded. These few moments with Olivia made Emma dislike her more than she had due to the hold she had on Phillip. Olivia's beauty didn't transfer to her personality.

"Convince Arundel to take you to Gretna Green. His memories are sparse, and he might not realize the societal implications of an elopement."

"He isn't daft, and neither am I."

"You fell in love with an engaged man. You aren't very intelligent."

"It would ruin my sister's chances at a match for me to elope."

Olivia stopped walking. The smile on her face was one of pleasure and conceit. "You have two choices. Get him to elope with you or see him marry me. If you choose the latter, I won't stop Arundel from taking a mistress. If he does decide to take you as one, stay out of my way."

"I have no intention of becoming a mistress." She spat the words at Olivia as she took a step away from her.

Olivia grabbed her arm so she couldn't leave without causing a scene. "Get him to elope with you, or I'll make certain everyone in society questions your virtue."

"Let go of me," Emma said as she tried to pull her arm from Olivia's grip.

"Olivia? Emma?" Phillip rushed out on the balcony, surprising Emma with his appearance. "What is going on?" He wasn't dressed for the party, as he hadn't planned to attend, but his appearance made Emma's heart race and ache.

Olivia laughed. "Arundel, you won't make an appearance for your mother, but you will for Miss Emma Parker?" Before she turned to leave, Olivia whispered, "Gretna Green!"

"What was she on about?" Phillip asked as Olivia pranced away from them.

"She wants me to convince you to elope."

Phillip nodded. "Did you tell her we don't live in Verona?"

Emma stood nervously next to him. A part of her wanted him to whisk her away to Gretna Green where elopements were legal, but it was selfish.

Phillip looked at her as they walked back into the ballroom. "Are you hurt?"

She wanted to speak the words *only my heart*, but instead she shook her head and swallowed the lump in her throat. "I'm well enough."

He escorted her back to her parents. She noticed the looks Phillip received as he walked through the room. Everyone had been told he was not well and would not attend the evening. His sudden appearance sent whispers through the room. His wardrobe at the party was also surprising, as he was not dressed for the evening.

"Lord Arundel," her father said as they approached, "it is wonderful to see you this evening."

"Thank you, Lord Anthony. Had I known your family was in attendance, I wouldn't have stayed away. I owe you a debt of gratitude."

"We heard you were unwell."

Phillip smiled as though he were schooling his words. "It's the blasted amnesia and some minor headaches. Nothing to be concerned over."

"What brought you to the party?" Emma asked.

"Marianne told me Olivia dragged you out to the patio. She is a vicious viper, and you shouldn't have to deal with her. Edward was supposed to keep her away."

"Arundel!"

Emma turned to see a man rushing up to their group. She'd seen him earlier but didn't know who he was. He was the same height as Phillip with auburn hair and freckles.

"Lord Folly," Phillip responded.

"I'm glad you remember me," Folly said. He put his hand on Phillip's arm. "Do you have a moment to talk?"

"Yes."

Folly looked around to see who was by them. Phillip turned. "Lord Folly, allow me to introduce you to Lord Anthony and his family."

Emma listened as he introduced everyone. She curtsied at the correct time, but she took notice of the panic in Lord Folly's mannerisms.

"Arundel," he said in a rush, "please tell me you have found a way to get out of this engagement."

Someone else hopes to end the union. Who is he and what is his interest? Emma questioned as she listened.

"I've tried. Both Ashby and Norland are greedy, and neither will allow us to end the farce."

Lord Folly looked as though he were trying to choose between crying or hitting someone. Instead he calmed himself. "Do you remember what I told you at Wentworth Hall?"

"Yes."

"Then you have to end the engagement."

"How do you suggest I do this?"

"Olivia suggested you take Miss Emma to Gretna Green."

Emma didn't feel the shock of the statement as she'd already processed the information. But her parents' reaction told her Gretna Green was not an option.

"Lord Folly," her father said in anger, "if you don't mind ruining a woman's reputation, then take Lady Olivia and elope. Don't expect my daughter to bring scandal to our family."

Emma didn't wait for anyone else to speak. She glared at Lord Folly. "My family means everything to me. I wouldn't ruin my sister's chances at a match. Lady Olivia doesn't have any sisters. Take her to Gretna Green."

Lord Folly looked distressed. "She won't go. She wants Arundel to make the move."

"She fears her father's retribution. She won't be responsible for her father losing his lands, titles, and wealth," Phillip said as he put his hand on Lord Folly's arm. "If I pull out of the engagement, I would cause my father the same loss. The consequences are higher than a ruined reputation."

Lord Folly looked ill and frustrated. He turned and left without another word.

Emma hadn't realized the serious nature of the situation. She put her hand on his arm as Edward approached. She wanted to tell him she understood, but she didn't understand. When she said those words in the library, she was lying.

Edward grabbed hold of Phillip's arm. "Lady Turnley saw you enter the room. She's asked Ashby to have you perform."

Phillip looked back at her family. "It was nice seeing you all again."

The ballroom seemed empty as she watched Phillip leave. Ashby entered, searching for Phillip as Lady Turnley pointed over to where he'd stood talking to her family.

"Edward, was Arundel in here?" Ashby asked.

"Yes. He took care of a situation regarding Lady Olivia and then left."

Ashby nodded. "The girl is a thorn in my side. He's going to have to teach her some manners once they are married."

Emma knew she shouldn't be surprised by Ashby's words. She knew Phillip's father was abusive, but she was certain Phillip wouldn't behave in such a manner. Emma danced with a few other men during the evening but was thankful when her family left Lancaster House. She decided if they received another invitation, she wouldn't attend.

Twenty-three

THE MORNING AFTER THE PARTY at Lancaster House, Edward sat across from his brother and watched him pick at his breakfast. Phillip was agitated and upset.

Edward had a small amount of guilt for his attraction to Anne. He wanted to spend time with her and get to know her. He just didn't know how to do it without parading it in Phillip's face.

"I danced with the Earl of Glendale," Charlotte said as she and Marianne spoke about the evening. "He is dreamy," she finished as she buttered her toast.

"You spent enough time flirting with him at the garden party last week," Marianne said before she took a drink. "If he didn't ask you to dance it would've been in vain."

They giggled and their father looked up from his newspaper. "Will you girls discuss dresses, dances, and men in lower tones?"

"Yes, Father." Both girls looked rebuked and quieted their conversation.

"I don't know why everyone in this house has to hold discussions in quiet tones around you, *Your Grace*," Olivia announced as she took a seat at the table.

Edward saw Phillip's head come up with Olivia's words. He looked over to his father to see the anger burning in his eyes.

"If you are going to eat in this room, you will behave yourself," the Duke of Norland announced from his spot at the table.

"Father, I will express myself however I feel," she said as she slammed her plate on the table.

Phillip stood and the footman rushed forward to grab his chair and pull it backward. Edward looked at his brother's plate as it was taken away. He'd picked at his food but hadn't eaten any of it. As he left the room Olivia started yelling his name, but Phillip didn't turn back. Edward finished his breakfast listening to Olivia as she argued with her father regarding her behavior.

Edward left the dining room annoyed with their house guests. He didn't understand why Norland and his family were staying at Lancaster House. They had their own home in London. They could stay there and come for visits when invited.

He walked toward the music in the parlor, knowing by the sound it was Phillip at the piano. He stood in the doorway until the song was over. The music expressed sadness and left Edward wanting at the end.

"The song was beautiful," he commented, walking into the room. "It's nice to hear you play, although the song didn't feel right."

"I'm sorry I'm not the person I used to be," Phillip quipped as he slammed his hand on the piano.

"Tell me what's going on."

Phillip looked over to his brother. "I have amnesia. Otherwise, I'm fine."

"Amnesia is a small part of it."

Phillip stood and walked to the door. He closed it so they wouldn't be overheard. "Last night I didn't want to attend the party because I don't know anyone. I don't know if I can do this."

"Do what?"

He spread his hands out to indicate everything around him. "This life. I'm not the same person anymore, and I don't know if I can be *the Earl of Arundel*." He said his title with disgust.

Edward crossed the room and put his hands on Phillip's shoulders. "You have been in London for three weeks. No one expects you to be *yourself* right now. But this isn't the only problem."

"I love Emma," Phillip said, giving up the fight.

Edward kept his hands on his shoulders. "Let her move past you. Otherwise it will hurt more if you continue to try and see her."

"Olivia suggested Emma and I elope. Leave for Gretna Green and bring scandal to both our families. And the worst part about it is, I asked Emma the same an hour before."

Edward tried to hide his surprise. Again, he noticed the difference in his brother of how he behaved toward Emma. "You are in love with her."

"I am not myself. It is like I am losing my mind."

Edward smiled in agreement. He understood the statement. Since he'd met Anne, he'd noticed the same passion in himself. But he didn't have the restrictions Phillip had. He could court Anne and make his intentions known. "Does Emma want to elope?"

"No. She wants a reputable marriage. And she has every right to expect one."

Phillip walked back to the piano and played another song. The anger and hurt flowed through the piece. Edward stayed to listen for a few more minutes before he could no longer handle listening to his brother pound on the piano. His playing was less smooth than in the past, and he missed keys as he played. The songs were rough and angry.

Edward left the house to take a walk and send flowers to Anne Parker. The night before, he asked her to dance as many times as he could without causing the gossips to wag their tongues. He enjoyed getting to know her, and he wanted to continue the relationship. He purchased a dozen red roses and wrote a card to Anne, trying not to sound ridiculous but hoping he conveyed his desire to court her. He was advancing the relationship much faster than he ever had before.

As he exited the flower shop, he saw Phillip on the opposite side of the street. Walking behind his brother, he noticed the limp. It wasn't as pronounced as it had been while he was healing, but it was still there. He thought about calling out but decided he would follow and see where Phillip was going. He realized Phillip was walking without a destination. They passed parks, shops, and houses, but Phillip never stopped.

As they entered the bridge, Edward wondered if Phillip was a little lost. The amnesia hadn't taken his general knowledge, so Edward wasn't certain if it made him forget directions. He decided to catch up to his brother when he saw an arm collide with Phillip's shoulder and pushed him into the street.

Edward ran as he saw Phillip try to catch his footing, but his arms flew backward. Right before a carriage hit, Edward pulled Phillip out of the way. He looked to find the person who pushed his brother. "Stop! He's running away!" Edward yelled, pointing.

"Are you injured?" Edward asked as he dragged Phillip back onto the walkway.

"No," he responded, trying to catch his breath. "I'm well."

"Did you see who pushed you?" Edward asked as he pulled Phillip into an embrace.

"No, I didn't see anyone." Moving back from his brother's embrace, Phillip said, "Tell me the truth about myself. What have I done to make someone want to kill me?"

"Stay here," Edward yelled as he ran after the man. He didn't know if anyone else was in pursuit, and he wanted to find the person responsible. He ran across the rest of the bridge, anxious as he looked around trying to locate the assailant. A sense of foreboding came over him as he searched the streets to find nothing. Just as he was ready to give up and go back, he saw a man peer around a corner.

Edward raced after him. By the time he rounded the corner, the man was gone. Edward slammed his fist against the building. He regretted it as he pulled his hand toward him to see he split the skin on his knuckles. He walked back to the bridge, giving up the search.

Phillip stood with a group of people gathered around him. People were chatting about the incident and the man they saw. Edward sighed as a constable stood to the side taking notes and questioning witnesses.

"Were you able to find him?" Phillip asked as Edward approached.

"No. I saw him peeking around a corner, but he escaped."

"What happened to your hand?" Phillip took Edward's hand in his to see the cuts.

"I hit a brick wall. I've learned too much from Ashby." Edward laughed a little. He added the last part for levity.

"You didn't answer me when I asked you if I am a terrible person."

Edward laughed. He was stressed from seeing his brother nearly run over by a carriage, but it was absurd to think Phillip would do something to cause another person to want to kill him. "You're a straight arrow. We'll figure out who's trying to kill you."

Edward experienced a moment of fear as the constable walked up to him and started questioning him. He had a flashback to the jail cell he'd sat in after Phillip's disappearance. He answered the questions with as much detail as possible. The assailant wore all black and had a hat. Edward didn't see the man's face. He was thankful when the constable offered them a ride in his carriage; he needed to get Phillip to Lancaster House.

As soon as they entered the house, Edward listened to the constable's retelling of the accident. Edward held onto Phillip as if letting go would cause his death.

"Phillip, did you see who pushed you?" Charles asked, helping him to a chair.

"No I didn't," Phillip said. Edward noticed he was shaken and looked to be in shock.

Edward walked over to him and shook his shoulders. "Snap out of it."

Phillip's eyes glazed as he tried to come to terms with nearly being killed. "I'm tired. I think I need to rest." He stood and left for his bedchamber.

Edward followed him from the room with his eyes. As soon as he was out of the room, confusion broke out.

"Edward, start from the beginning. What happened?" their father demanded, slamming his hand against the wall. "Who's behind this?"

"I saw Phillip taking a walk, and I followed him." He sat on the couch, exhausted from the day's events, and cradled the injured hand. As he explained what he witnessed, Charlotte cleaned and bandaged his hand. Helpless and powerless, he said, "Phillip was pushed into the street as a hansom cab neared. I grabbed him right before—" He shook his head and waited until he could speak without his voice cracking. "If I hadn't sped up, I would've watched my brother flattened by a carriage. I wouldn't have been able to do anything about it." Edward was certain his dreams would be tortured with replaying the scene. Overall their family was helpless when it came to protecting Phillip.

The constable spoke as Edward finished. "I would like to know how the assailant is able to tell the two of you apart. This is someone who knows your family. It's someone who can see the difference between you from a distance. If I came across both of you on the street, it'd be impossible for me to choose between you to know who Lord Arundel is."

Edward hadn't considered the detail until the constable said the words. He knew the person had to have access to the house at Wentworth Hall, because his ring ended up by the river. But he didn't know of anyone outside of their family who had the ability to recognize them from a distance. Most of the serving staff had an issue with telling them apart unless they'd been with the family for years.

"The assailant is intimate with your family." The constable stopped speaking to let the words sink in.

Edward needed to decompress. He took a walk through the garden, trying to pull anything from his memory of the arm or the person peeking around the corner. He now understood the frustration Phillip had with amnesia. Although Edward didn't have the same issue, it was difficult not to be able to pull details from his mind.

Edward occupied his time making a list of the people who were able to tell them apart. It was short, and he knew from those on it, it wasn't complete because all of the people on the list were trustworthy. As he sat down to dinner, he watched Phillip again picking at his food. Edward understood he was shaken after the near miss earlier, but he hadn't eaten breakfast or lunch and he still wasn't eating. Just when he was going to kick Phillip under the table, Olivia interrupted the silence with another tantrum.

She picked her plate up and threw it on the floor. Her glass flew across the room and shattered against the wall. "Father, why won't you listen to me?"

"Olivia, I've told you if you can't behave yourself you will eat your meals in your room," Norland responded.

Edward looked to Phillip to see a reaction and saw he was still playing with his food and was either lost in thoughts or was ignoring Olivia's outburst. He continued to focus on his plate until Olivia threw her spoon at Phillip's head.

"Are you listening to me?" she yelled.

Phillip rubbed the spot on his head. He looked over and glared at her. Without saying a word he stood and left the room. Again, he left without eating anything.

"Olivia, sit down or find your way to your room," Norland yelled as he knocked his glass over. The liquid spread across the table and began dripping on the floor before the footmen were able to clean the spill.

Edward thought the show was over until Olivia picked Marianne's plate off the table and threw it at her father.

"I don't want to be gambled away in a contract!" she yelled. She picked Charlotte's plate off the table and threw it at Norland. The footmen stopped trying to clean the room because the mess continued to build with each plate of food thrown.

"Olivia, go to your room!" Norland yelled again, thinking a demand would stop his daughter's tantrum.

Olivia threw her chair at one of the footmen. "Get out of my way!" she yelled at the servants standing around the room. She grabbed her mother's plate and threw it across the room, hitting Mr. Hodgens in the arm before she stormed out.

Edward looked to Ashby to see his reaction. It appeared as though his father had taken Phillip's approach to Olivia's outbursts. He sat eating his food, pretending he didn't have a guest covered with food and a mess in the dining room.

Twenty-four

ONE PART OF THE LONDON season Emma could do without was the exhaustion that came from constant visits, garden parties, and dances. At first the diversion of company was enjoyable, but after days of the same thing, it grew old. Emma listened to her sister and some of the other débutantes chatting about men they wanted to ensnare and was caught off guard by the mention of Phillip.

"The Earl of Arundel has been subdued this season," Miss Willis stated. Taking a sip of her lemonade, she gave a knowing look to one of the other girls. "We heard he has been ill."

"I heard he was out at Springhill Abby this summer," Miss Berry said, looking for gossip.

Neither Anne nor Emma offered information, but the women seemed to already know more than expected.

"Did you hear about the accident on London Bridge the other day?" Miss Willis asked, leaning forward as though this was the hottest topic in society. "Arundel was almost killed—"

"What?" Emma blurted out, not caring about the volume of her voice. She saw people turn to look at her due to her outburst, and her cheeks went pink from embarrassment.

Miss Willis smiled before she continued. "He was pushed in front of a hansom cab. Lord Edward pulled him out of the street right before the horse ran him down."

Emma turned from the group, frantic for information on Phillip's condition. She'd seen Lady Charlotte and Lady Marianne earlier, and she wanted to find them.

A search through the patio, greenhouse, and garden proved a waste. A sense of agitation built through each space as she considered the next room to check. When she entered the blue room, Marianne stood with a group of women.

Taking a deep breath to calm herself, she willed her feet to move at a regular pace so as not to bring attention to her frantic pounding heart. "Marianne" she said, nodding her head in a slight bow.

"Emma, it's nice to see you again." Marianne put her arm out and took hold of Emma's. "Will you walk in the garden with me?"

As they walked, Emma tried to think of a way to ask about Phillip, but every time she tried to form the words, she stopped herself.

"I know everyone is talking about the accident on London Bridge. Phillip is shaken but well in body. Edward pulled him out of the way before the horse ran him down."

Emma squeezed her eyes shut as they walked. "Did he see his assailant?"

"No. There were many witnesses, and Edward saw the back of the man. The constable is conducting an investigation."

"Marianne, will you be honest with me?" Emma asked, hoping she wouldn't make a fool of herself. She waited for the nod of agreement before continuing. "Is Lord Arundel well?"

Marianne smiled. "I think my brother wouldn't be happy to know you just used a title to refer to him. He doesn't speak much anymore," Marianne observed. "We are all worried about him. Edward watches him almost as though he's wondering where his twin brother has gone." Marianne took her hands and held them as a way to comfort her. "I wish it could turn out differently, because I would prefer to have you as a sister."

Emma nodded, not trusting herself to speak. She pointed to the door and walked away from Marianne.

Knowing another party, this time at Almack's Assembly Hall, was set for the evening, Emma told her mother she was leaving the garden party to rest. As she walked home, Emma decided she was going to dance and flirt with as many men as she could, and she would get over Phillip Watson.

She again dressed with care, this time with the effort to ensnare another man. She wouldn't reach for another earl; she could be happy with an untitled husband. But as she walked into the ballroom, she betrayed herself as she found she was searching for Phillip.

"Who are you looking for?" Anne asked, taking Emma's hand.

"I know it's ridiculous, but I want to see him and see he is well."

"I'll ask Edward about the accident on the bridge, but you should focus on dancing with other men."

Emma nodded; she'd keep her resolve. It didn't take long before she was asked to dance. Mr. Carrige asked her for the first dance of the evening. As she walked to the floor, she noted the bounce in his step.

"Mr. Carrige," she said as he took her hand and they bowed to each other at the start of the dance. "How have you enjoyed being in London?"

"It has been an enjoyable season," he said as they passed by each other, dancing alongside other couples. "I see Lord Edward is paying call to your sister. Are they courting?"

Emma didn't know if she should answer his question, so she decided to answer in a different way. "Lord Edward is a good friend of our family."

"As is Lord Arundel?" Mr. Carrige asked, stepping again to her side.

"Yes, he is." Emma found she was looking around the room, still searching for Phillip.

"Are the rumors true?"

"I don't listen to idol gossip, Mr. Carrige. So, I can't confirm rumors." She took her hand out of his and wished the dance would end.

"I heard he spent the entire summer at Springhill Abby," Mr. Carrige said, taking her hand again to help her spin around.

"He was at Springhill Abby." Emma didn't think the confirmation wouldn't cause any problems. She was thankful the dance ended so she could escape his presence.

As he left her with her family she turned to her brothers. "The reason I am asked to dance is to confirm rumors regarding *the Earl of Arundel.*"

Henry reached for her hand. "Dance with me and I won't ask anything about Arundel."

Henry escorted her to the floor. As he led her in a waltz around the room, she saw Phillip dancing. Her heart seemed to stop until she realized he was dancing with his sister.

"So much for taking my mind off of him." She used her eyes to point in Phillip's direction.

"Lord Edward said his parents are forcing him out of his self-imposed reclusion. If you continue to attend dances, you will end up seeing him."

"Is it terrible of me that sometimes I wish Father had never found him?"

"He would be dead. Would you prefer the alternative?" Henry was surprised by his sister's comment.

"I wouldn't have known him if Father hadn't found him. So, it wouldn't affect me." As she said the words, a pang of regret and longing hit her heart.

When the song ended, they turned to walk back to their family. She looked back and saw Phillip leading his sister from the floor. "Do you think he'll ask me to dance?"

The sound of a gunshot echoed through the room.

Emma screamed as she found her legs were going out from under her. Henry pulled her to the floor. The room was filled with pandemonium. Emma's eyes were still trained on Phillip as she'd been watching him exit the dance floor. A scream escaped her mouth when she saw his body jerk to the side and blood fly in the air.

Henry pulled her head into his shoulder and held her in a protective embrace as the commotion continued. "Is he dead?" she cried as he pulled her to the side of the room.

"Who?" Henry asked, letting her head come up, as there were no other gunshots in the room.

She pointed in the direction where she saw Phillip fall. She couldn't get the words out; she was stunned into silence and trying to catch her breath. People were now up and running for the exit.

"Emma, we are going," Henry said, trying to pull her with him.

"No." She pulled her arm from his, trying to make her way toward the crowd of people surrounding Phillip. She had to make certain he was alive. She wanted to believe her eyes were wrong and he wasn't the one on the ground.

Henry grabbed her around the waist. "Father and Mother will expect us to meet them at the carriage."

"I have to see if he is . . ." She couldn't let the words leave her mouth.

She fought to get out of Henry's arms as he pulled her toward the exit. They were nearly there when they were hit by another couple running from the room. Her head and back hit the wall. She opened her eyes and fought to catch her breath, feeling dizzy as she fell to the floor.

"Emma, can you stand?" Henry asked, trying to get her to focus. "Emma, answer me," he called to her. Turning from her he called, "Richard, I need help."

"I can stand," she said, letting him pull her off the ground. She looked back to the side of the room where she knew Phillip was lying. The crowd was still gathered around him, and chaos continued as Henry yanked on her arm again and dragged her from the room. He pushed her into the carriage where they waited for their parents and Anne.

Emma's mind was numb. She could feel tears trickling down her cheeks. She registered pain from having fallen to the ground during the rush to escape.

"Emma!" Henry had his hands on her shoulders and was trying to get her attention. "Are you injured?"

"It was Phillip," she said. "He was hit by the bullet. I . . . I saw the blood," she said as she stared at her brother with her glazed eyes.

"Emma, answer me. You fell down. Are you injured?" Henry asked again.

She didn't understand why he was asking her if she was injured. Yes, she fell down. But she was also sitting with him in the carriage. "Phillip is injured," she said again, trying to get him to realize what she'd witnessed.

Henry pulled her into his arms and held her as they waited for the rest of their family. She didn't understand his concern for her until she heard Henry say, "I think she's in shock."

Twenty-five

BEFORE THE GUNSHOT RANG THROUGH the room, Edward pulled Anne out to the patio for a tête-à-tête. Anne stood with her family, waiting for him to claim his dance. He'd done so without further delay. In the last flower arrangement he sent, he made it clear he wanted to court her; at least he hoped he had done so. His plan to take her on a carriage ride through Hyde Park had been delayed due to the accident on London Bridge. But it had been a few days and Phillip was recovered, so he planned to set a time with Anne for the ride.

If they hadn't been interrupted by the gunshot, he would have pulled her to a private corner to steal another kiss. He was good at kissing. He'd done it a lot. A new sense of guilt rushed over him as he realized he'd been engaged in a similar activity at Wentworth Hall and now at Almack's when his brother was attacked.

A loud noise pierced the night sky as he said the words, "Will you join me for a turnabout Hyde Park tomorrow?" Instinctively he pulled Anne to the ground as both glasses of punch flew from their hands and spilled down their fronts. He heard the glass break on the rock patio as he covered Anne with his body and protected her from the shot.

The dance hall was filled with confusion when he and Anne reentered. Who, if anyone, was hit by the bullet? When he realized others were running to get out of the room, Edward pulled Anne toward the exit. He saw Henry dragging Emma out the doors.

Edward pulled Anne through the room, then changed direction as he realized a group of people were gathering around his sisters.

Marianne and Charlotte were holding onto Charles, both with their heads on his shoulders.

"Is there a doctor here tonight?" Ashby called out to the group surrounding them.

"I'm a doctor," a man yelled as he tried to push through the crowd. "Will everyone please move away?" he demanded.

Edward saw a glimpse before the crowd gathered back around his family; Phillip was lying on the floor in a pool of blood. "No . . . no!" Edward heard himself crying out. He pushed through the crowed but was blocked by people gawking.

"Edward?" Lord Anthony pulled him into his arms as he released Anne from his protective embrace. "Edward, follow me. I will get you through the crowd."

He turned back to see Anne standing with her mother, her hand over her mouth in disbelief of what she'd seen. "Is he alive?" Edward asked, holding onto Lord Anthony as they fought the crowd.

"I don't know." Lord Anthony shoved through the last few people to reach the spot where Phillip lay covered in blood.

Edward went down on his knees, wanting to help but not knowing how. His eyes blurred with tears he blinked away so he could see the doctor holding a hand on Phillip's head. Edward took his jacket off and moved forward to use it as a bandage to help stop the bleeding.

"Edward, order our carriage to the back of the building. We'll take him out where there's less of a crowd," Ashby demanded as he took hold of the jacket Edward was using as a bandage.

Numb inside, Edward waited for the carriage. He ran back to inform his parents and found he needed to help carry his brother out. He held Phillip's head in his lap, wrapped in the jacket until they arrived home.

Edward carried Phillip's limp body up to the bedchamber and helped lay him on the bed. His mother and father took over and told him to leave the room.

"Marianne, are you injured?" Edward asked, noticing she had blood on her.

"No, I was with him when it happened," she said, walking over to Edward for an embrace.

He held Marianne as she cried on his shoulder. They stood in the hall with Charlotte and Charles waiting for the doctor and their parents to tell them Phillip's condition.

"Master Edward," Hodgens said as he entered the hallway with a tea tray, "the cook is planning to send dinner up as well."

"I don't think any of us are hungry," he said, looking to the others.

The door to Phillip's room opened as Hodgens placed the tea tray on the side table. Edward looked to Ashby's face, trying to see if his expression would give anything away.

"Hodgens, please take the tea down to the parlor," Ashby instructed. "Have the cook prepare a small supper."

"Yes, Your Grace."

"Father, please tell us his condition," Charles said, unable to wait any longer.

"The bullet grazed the side of his head." An audible sigh of relief filled the hallway. "The doctor dressed the wound and Phillip is sleeping."

"Has he been conscious?" Edward asked, running a hand through is hair.

"Yes, he woke up right after you left. He has a terrible headache, but he will be fine." A smile crossed their father's face as he continued. "The only good to come from this situation is Arundel's memory is back."

The following morning Edward woke exhausted from staying up late into the night. He spent time sitting by Phillip's bed while his parents spoke to the constable and while the nurse and doctor made arrangements for care. He stopped by Phillip's room on the way to breakfast. Phillip slept while a nurse tended the room. He decided not to wake his brother.

As he sat at the breakfast table, he realized this was the first morning since Lady Olivia and her parents arrived that she wasn't throwing a tantrum.

Edward saw displeasure on his father's face as he read the paper. "Is there something wrong, Father?"

"Society," he said in a huff. "There's no way an investigation can be done with the number of fools Almack's entertained last night."

"What does the paper say?"

"The constable has over a hundred different retellings of the story. Some people said it was a masked man. Others say he had ginger hair. One person said it was a Scotsman." Ashby sighed in disgust. "At this rate, we won't find the person responsible."

Edward nodded. He ate and found his way back to Phillip's room.

"You can come in," Phillip said as he lay supported by a mountain of pillows.

"How are you today?"

"I have a headache. The doctor said it will take time to get rid of it." Phillip gave him a questioning look before he asked, "Aren't you supposed to take Anne riding through Hyde Park today?"

"She'll understand if I don't."

"Go. At least one of us should be happy."

"Is it true? Do you have your memory back?"

"I think I do. If I didn't have a head wound, I'd be jumping for joy."

Edward smiled at his brother's humor. "Are you upset with me for courting Anne?"

"I'll admit I have moments of jealousy. But if it works out and you make a good match, I'll support you in your decision. But if you keep skipping trips to Hyde Park after scheduling them, she'll find another suitor."

Edward nodded, taking the hint. "I want to ask her to marry me."

Phillip's surprise registered in his face. "You've already decided?"

"Yes. I know it's fast, even for society. But I love her."

Edward watched as his brother struggled to say the words he promised moments before. Phillip closed his eyes as he said, "I am happy for you."

The words were difficult, and Edward couldn't stand there as his brother's face contorted with suppressed pain. "I'll let you have some time to process everything. I'll visit when I return."

"I'll be here."

As Edward closed the door on his brother, he regretted telling him so soon. Compelled by his feelings for Anne, he had rushed the conversation with Phillip. Phillip wasn't just recovering from a bullet wound but also a broken heart. Although Edward wanted to make his intentions clear regarding Anne, he should've considered his brother beforehand.

His plan was to speak with Lord Anthony before he took Anne for a ride. Reminding himself that he did not need to be nervous since he was equal in social station to her parents, Edward entered the house with as much confidence as his brain would allow. It was as though he'd be more comfortable running from the situation and hiding in a cave. Although he hadn't taken time to speak with Anne about an engagement, he knew they were a match, and he refused to leave words unspoken between them. If good were to come out of Phillip's injuries and accidents, it would be Edward learning to speak and say what was important.

"Please come in, Lord Edward," Lord Anthony said as he entered the room. Edward was surprised to see Lady Amelia and Emma waiting as well.

Emma walked forward. "Lord Edward, is Phillip well?"

He smiled and took her hands. "Yes. The bullet swiped the side of his head. He has a headache and a new scar, but he is well."

He could see relief on her face. "Are there any leads on who shot him?"

"Nothing concrete. If you look at the society section of the paper today, you will read that everyone saw something different. The London police are as confused as Constable Adams. Phillip is a generous person, so it doesn't make sense."

"Thank you," she said looking uncomfortable. She left the room before he could respond.

"Please sit down," Lord Anthony said, pointing to a chair. Lady Amelia patted his arm as she walked by and left the room.

"My daughter is heartbroken. I don't know how many times she will ask about Arundel, but if it becomes uncomfortable, please let me know."

Edward made a quick decision. He didn't know if Lord Anthony would give this information to Emma, but it needed to be said. "Phillip is also struggling. He doesn't ask about her because he doesn't have a choice. He has to let her go."

"She is trying to move on," Lord Anthony said, "but she has her days, and the shooting at Almack's was a disturbing situation."

"I understand," Edward said, hoping to get the conversation onto the daughter he was in love with. "My lord, I wanted to speak to you today regarding Anne. I would like to ask for her hand in marriage."

"Before I give an answer, I have a question for you." Lord Anthony handed Edward a drink. "If you and Anne marry, how will this affect your relationship with Arundel?"

"I spoke with Phillip before coming here today. He choked on the words, but he said he was happy for me. I know he wants the best for me." Edward took a drink before continuing. "Phillip always puts others first. It's one of his greatest strengths but also a weakness for him."

"How do you think it will affect Anne's relationship with Emma?" Lord Anthony asked.

Edward looked into Lord Anthony's eyes as he replied, "I know my brother well enough to know he wouldn't have fallen in love with a woman who would be any less gracious than he."

Lord Anthony smiled. "I hope you are correct for both of them. I do have one more item for you to think about. It's tradition for the families of an engaged couple to spend time together up to the day of the wedding and afterward. How are they going to handle being brother and sister for the rest of their lives?"

Edward looked down before asking, "Is your answer no?"

"No, it isn't. I know Anne would be very upset if I said no, so my answer is yes. But you need to understand this will be an uncomfortable situation for everyone."

"I understand, sir."

"Anne is waiting to go to Hyde Park with you. She is in the hall."

Edward stood and left the room to take Anne on the ride he promised her. He couldn't wait to discuss marriage with her.

Twenty-six

THE MORNING MEAL AT LANCASTER House consisted of meats, eggs, breads, toast, and tea. Phillip stared at the plate Thomas put in front of him, trying to decide what to eat. He hadn't had much of an appetite since waking at Springhill Abby, and now with the stress he was under he had stopped eating all together. But after this last attempt on his life, he decided he should regain strength, and eating was part of it.

He acknowledged Ashby with a nod and sat next to Edward. As the room filled with his sisters and Lady Olivia, the conversation turned to the topic of the marriage, banns, and setting a date.

"Ashby, it's time we spoke about announcing the engagement of Arundel and Olivia."

His father looked up from the letter he was reading. "I told you we were going to delay the announcement."

"Does this mean you are forfeiting, Ashby? We both made certain the other couldn't back out to protect our interest and family name. Arundel's memory is back, so there's no further need to delay."

"I would still like my solicitor to review the paperwork before an announcement is made."

"I'll agree to this arrangement if you promise your son will no longer have anything to do with Miss Emma Parker."

"Norland, you are a guest in my home. Don't make demands of me and my son."

"My daughter won't be made a fool of as he attends parties and spends time with Miss Parker."

"You don't have the right to tell me who I can and can't speak with," Phillip said as he looked at the food on his plate and again tried to convince himself to eat.

"All of London is speaking of your obsession with her," Olivia chimed into the conversation.

"I'm not obsessed with Emma."

"You can't keep your eyes off her, and she looks for you the minute she walks into a ballroom. The last dance at Almack's she kept looking at you as though she expected you to ask her to dance."

"Both of you stop," his mother said, ending the argument. "Phillip, until the solicitor gets back with your father, I believe it's best for everyone's reputation for you to keep your eyes off Miss Parker."

"Mother, I don't agree."

"I didn't ask you to agree with me." His mother turned to Olivia. "You will be respectful in our home. Do you not see the wound on his head? An attempt on his life was made at the party you are complaining about, and never once have you inquired about his health."

Surprised by his mother's rebuke to Olivia he asked, "When will the solicitor have an answer?"

His father sighed. "I'll send for him today."

"If you want her, then put her in the cottage at Wentworth Hall," Olivia said, ignoring the censure she received.

"Not all women have the same lack of self-control as you." As Phillip said the words, he heard his sisters gasp as though he had said something scandalous. Charles hid a laugh behind a cough, and Edward dropped his silverware, making it clang against his plate.

"If you ever speak to Miss Parker again, I will make certain she doesn't have a virtuous reputation."

"You would give her the reputation you deserve?" he said, standing and pushing the chair away. His hands were on the table as he leaned forward, ready for a fight. Since his memory returned, he was aching to fight with Olivia. He no longer wanted to sit back and listen to her tantrums.

"I don't understand you, Arundel. She is tolerable to look at, but I wouldn't consider her a beauty. Nor does she have the connections you will need for a position in Parliament."

"I have sufficient connections, and you can keep your opinions of Emma to yourself. The only beauty you have ever acknowledged is in your reflection."

"The only reason a woman would strap herself to you is for your title. Emma Parker doesn't care for you. She wants to marry a title," Olivia yelled as she picked her cup of tea off the table and threw it at him. He moved to the side and let the cup fly past him as tea splashed on the table and in the food of those sitting next to them. The cup hit the floor and shattered. "According to the marriage contract, I have to provide you with an heir and a spare. Two male children. I pray they are the first."

"Please don't concern yourself with fulfilling any portion of the reproduction items in the contract," Phillip said sarcastically. Pointing to his brother, he said, "Edward and Anne's firstborn son can become my heir."

Olivia picked her plate off the table; it was still full of eggs, meat, and bread. She threw the plate his way, causing food to fly in all directions. He caught the plate mid-air, and before he could stop himself he threw it back in her direction. He was thankful when she moved to the side and the plate broke against the floor.

"It is rare for a couple to have happiness in marriage. We both know what to expect with our marriage," she yelled at him.

"There isn't going to be a marriage," Phillip yelled back. "Father, I refuse to marry her."

"Enough!" Ashby shouted, stopping them mid-fight.

Phillip turned to look at his father and didn't see Olivia grab the teapot off the table. He was ready to yell back when the steaming pot hit him. It shattered and cut skin on the side of his face, leaving a red burn. Phillip wanted to throw her out of the house, but it had been Ashby's decision to invite Norland's family to stay with them.

Phillip's skin burned from the tea. He hated money. He hated gambling. He hated both dukes.

"Olivia, stop!" her mother yelled as she found more items on the table to throw in Phillip's direction. He ducked as he heard an uproar happening around him. Olivia had taken her parents' dishes and silverware and threw them at him.

"Olivia, stop throwing plates and cups at my son. He is already injured." His mother had to shout to be heard above the commotion. "Stop your daughter from her tantrum, Norland. They will destroy each other. Is this what you want for our children?"

Phillip turned as Thomas walked forward with a towel and helped him clean himself. Phillip shuddered as the towel rubbed against his burnt skin. He needed to lie down. "Please inform me when the solicitor arrives." He left the dining room to clean up and get as far away from Olivia as he could.

The solicitor arrived in the late afternoon as Phillip was getting ready for the ball at Lansdown House in Berkley Square. Lord and Lady Bennett were the hosts. Phillip looked at the side of his face. The burns had been covered in medication, and the cuts had been tended to by his valet. He touched where the bullet grazed and thought about making an excuse for the evening, but decided to go to the ball in case Emma attended. He knew he shouldn't plan to speak with her, but a view of her from across the ballroom wouldn't hurt anyone but himself.

He delayed heading to Ashby's den, trying to gather his thoughts. It was very possible the solicitor would tell them the contract was binding. If it was, he didn't know what he would do. He only knew he wasn't going to marry Lady Olivia.

"Arundel, thank you for joining us." His father's tone conveyed annoyance at having to wait.

"I apologize for the delay," he said as he found a seat near his mother.

The room was warm due to the fire in the grate. Phillip looked around in a desperate need to escape. The solicitor stood near the desk holding what Phillip could only assume was the marriage contract.

"Let's get this over with. What have you found in the contract?" Ashby said, glaring at Norland.

His father's solicitor put reading glasses on and looked over the paper. "The contract is legal and binding."

"I told you it was binding, Ashby," Norland said as he congratulated himself.

"You may stay silent, Norland," Ashby stated in annoyance.

"Banns will need to be posted this week," Norland said. "We should move forward. I have no intention of staying in London for the full season."

"How do you break it if it is binding?" Phillip asked, catching the inference in the solicitor's words. There could be hope yet.

"First, the contract can be broken if both parties agree to destroy all copies. This would require the marriage contract is a secret and hasn't been announced to society. Second, through death, as a regular marriage is also ended at death. If it is mutual, funds are not exchanged. If not mutual, the sum of all lands, monies, and titles will be paid to the injured party."

Phillip sat in a quiet anger for the rest of the meeting as Ashby and Norland asked questions. He kept hearing the words *binding, unbreakable, and all lands and titles* tossed around in the conversation. He didn't realize the solicitor had left until his father said his name. He didn't understand the greed and coveting his father and Norland had for the other's assets.

His attention was brought back to the conversation as he heard the confirmation. "The banns will be read over the next three weeks."

The evening seemed distant from Phillip as he walked through the room and spoke to people. He chose not to ask Olivia to dance. He stayed away from her for most of the evening and did all he could to avoid her family. She spent her time with Lord Folly and friends. As he tried to gather his thoughts and come to terms with the marriage contract, he looked across the room to see Edward speaking with Anne and Emma. In a rash decision, he found the desire to anger Olivia.

"Miss Parker, Miss Emma, it's nice to see you both," he said as he kissed both of their hands. He noticed the smile on Anne's face and concern on Emma's. Looking at Emma he asked, "How are you?"

"I'm well." She leaned her head to the side in an effort to see the wound on his head. "Does it still hurt?"

"No, I had a headache, but now it is a distant memory." He forced a smile. He could see she didn't believe him as she continued to look at him with concern. They locked eyes, and a rush of emotions assaulted him. He realized he shouldn't have approached her. It would've been easier to stay away.

"Does the constable have any leads on who did this?" Anne asked, breaking his eye lock with Emma.

"No," Phillip answered as he turned to look at Anne.

Phillip turned back to Emma. "Will you join me for the next dance?"

"Of course," she squeaked, giving him her arm.

He saw the look Edward gave, and he knew what he was thinking. He didn't look at Edward as he guided Emma to the dance floor, or as they stood next to each other in the dance line waiting for the music to begin.

Emma curtsied and he bowed to start the dance. At first, they both remained silent until he noticed Olivia watching him.

"Have you been well?" he asked as he took Emma's hand for the first turn.

"I have."

"Are you angry with me?" he asked as he took her for the second turn.

"I am."

"Why?"

"Because I love you, and it is forbidden for me to feel this way about you . . . You aren't mine to love."

"Emma, I know I don't have a right to ask you, but can we pretend we live in Verona?" Without saying the words, he was asking her to elope with him. They didn't have to go to Gretna Green. They could find a vicar in London and purchase a special license.

"Where would we live?"

"We could sail to the States."

"What about our families? What about Edward? You can't live such a distance from your twin."

Phillip knew she was right. He and Edward were linked for life, and a separation would be too hard on both of them. "We could convince Anne and Edward to go with us."

He watched as Emma shook her head. "Your offer is tempting. But neither one of us could leave our family indefinitely."

To think he had tempted her enough to make her think about the offer was thrilling, until he realized she'd turned him down—again. Deciding he needed to apologize, he chanced talking to her one more time.

"May I speak with you? Have a conversation with you in private?"

"No. You may not," she said as the dance ended and she walked away.

The coldness from Emma ripped a hole in his heart. He was finished with society for the evening. Phillip left the party and walked toward Lancaster House. His parents would be furious with his decision to leave, especially without an escort and on foot. The person attempting to kill him could sneak up in the dark and succeed. But Phillip needed a small rebellion, and a part of him hoped the assailant would succeed after Emma's second refusal to marry him. He knew he couldn't be angry with her because he wasn't offering her the lavish wedding she deserved, but he loved her. He was offering her a life of love.

The cool evening air helped bring calm into his mind. He was angry with his father. He was angry with Olivia's parents, and he was angry with Edward because he was free to choose a wife who happened to be Anne Parker.

As he arrived home, he wished he was back wandering the streets. Instead he spent the rest of the evening in his father's library. Books had always been an escape for him, and he desired the release. He picked through a few and found Shakespeare's sonnets. He closed his eyes and rested his head against the bookshelf as he thought of Emma reading to him. He would never be able to pick the sonnets up again without thinking of her. He left the sonnets alone and found a book of short stories. He was almost finished reading when he heard his family return from the party.

"Where is he?" Olivia yelled as she entered the house.

"I don't know, my lady," Hodgens responded. Phillip knew Hodgens was aware of his current position because he had brought a tea tray minutes before. Phillip appreciated the lie on his behalf.

"Arundel!" she yelled as she walked through the house, throwing doors open in her latest tantrum.

He waited. Perhaps she wouldn't find him. He hoped she would give up and head to her room and leave the fight for another time. His hopes were dashed when she threw the door to the library open and picked the first book she found off the shelf and threw it in his direction.

"How dare you embarrass me in front of all of society!"

He was too exhausted to engage in the fight, but he couldn't stop himself from responding, "You spend your time with Lord Folly, and you expect me to watch you flirt and throw yourself at him?"

"This won't continue, Arundel. I won't allow you to be seen in society with the trollop."

He wouldn't stay silent any longer. Her accusations against Emma were unfounded and vicious. He wouldn't allow Olivia to destroy the woman he was in love with, even if he wasn't able to marry her.

"You will stop speaking of Emma in this way."

He dodged another book as she yelled, "I loathe you."

"I'm not fond of you either."

He watched as she tore through his father's library, throwing ink bottles, pen knives, pens, and books. She wasn't aiming for him in particular. Her main desire was to destroy the room.

"Olivia, you will stop this behavior," Norland announced as he walked in the room.

"Father, I won't have him parading around with other women now that we are engaged. He may have mistresses, but he shouldn't be allowed to be seen with them in public."

"Emma is not a mistress, nor will she ever be one," he yelled at her, "and you are still parading around with Lord Folly. Everyone in society is talking about you and Folly and what you have done."

"Don't speak to me!" Olivia yelled at him. "Don't defend the hussy."

"You have no right to speak of her in this way," he yelled, knowing he would regret losing his temper with her. But in the moment he didn't care. "You will refrain from your lewd comments."

He noticed his parents standing in the doorway and wondered how his father would respond. He'd been surprised by the lack of temper Ashby had displayed during her previous tantrums. He wondered if this was now the time his resolve would break.

"Phillip," his mother said with concern, "your father and I will speak with you in the morning." Turning to Olivia she coldly stated, "You will start behaving like a lady in our home."

Olivia's mother grabbed her arm and dragged her from the library. He watched her go and didn't expect his mother's final comment.

"You should at least try, Phillip. She is as stuck in the contract as you are."

He didn't look at his parents as he left the room. He tried to sleep, but he couldn't stop his mind from racing. He tried to read, but he couldn't concentrate on the words. He had a difficult time sleeping, so he stared at the celling all night.

"What were you thinking when you left the party last night? You could have been killed. You could have been abducted." Both his parents were furious with him. He knew he deserved the censure, but he had a small amount of satisfaction with his decision to rebel if for one night.

"I'm sorry I caused you to worry."

"Promise you won't go out alone?" his mother asked. He realized he couldn't hold back on the promise as he saw the worry lines near her eyes. He loved his mother and would do anything she asked.

A silence fell over the room after he made the promise. He hoped they were finished until his father spoke.

"Do you think I loved your mother when we married?"

Phillip looked over at his mother. Her face was stone as her husband spoke.

"I assumed you have been happy together."

"You are correct. We have been happy. When your mother and I married I had a girl I wanted to be with, just as you do. Mari was a maid at Wentworth Hall. My father spoke to me about duty and honor. He told me that taking a woman of a different social standing and putting her in our world would destroy her, so I married your mother. Mari stayed at Wentworth Hall for a few years after our marriage, and then my father sent her away."

"Son," his mother said, cutting her husband off before he could continue. "Women of my social standing have to accept they will be in a loveless marriage. Chances at happiness aren't available due to the connections you have to make. It is the same for men."

"Then why put on a show of débutantes coming out in society? Why do people go to the expense of a London season if marriage isn't to be of one's choosing?" he asked in defense.

"Arundel," his father said almost as though he were defeated, "I cannot end the contract without losing everything we have."

"You realize this marriage will be a nightmare?"

"We can see this," his father responded, "but you were once cordial to each other."

"Cordial doesn't mean 'please gamble our futures by forcing us to marry.' I discovered what I could have with Emma Parker. I can't ignore my feelings," Phillip responded.

Ashby sat in a plush armchair, his fingers pressed together in front of his face in deep thought. "You are acting like a child."

He could see his father had run out of patience, but instead of losing his temper he continued to act reflective over the situation.

"Edward has made a connection and is planning a marriage himself."

"I'm aware."

"Miss Anne Parker will be your new sister." His father paused to let the words sink in.

Edward being married to Anne would make Emma a part of the family; it would make her a sister. He had many thoughts that he chose not to voice.

"I'm happy for them."

He stood before he said anything he would regret and walked to the door. The conversation had gone better than he imagined, until Ashby pulled him around by his arm and slammed him against the bookshelf. This was the father he remembered so well.

"You will behave yourself during the upcoming dinner parties, garden parties, and activities associated with the engagement announcements." To illustrate, he released and slammed Phillip into the bookshelf again. "The banns will be read over the next three weeks, for both you and Edward." Releasing his

158

grip he finished, "You will behave in a manner conducive to your station."

"May I leave?"

Ashby's eyes shone with an anger Phillip knew well. It would be futile to argue or to push his father further, so he stood staring at the bookshelf across from him.

"Make certain you behave, Arundel. Society loves gossip, and it would be a mistake to air our family affairs."

He turned to look at his father. "You won't need to worry about me, as long as you keep Lady Olivia's tongue in her mouth." Before walking out the door he decided he had to make one more comment. "Society is already talking about Olivia and Lord Folly. If you don't want a scandal, you should start there."

Twenty-seven

A MORNING TURN AROUND THE garden with her mother still hadn't calmed Emma's nerves. She was thankful when her family left the party the evening before because she didn't want to see Phillip's family any longer, but the news of her sister's engagement to Lord Edward had renewed her dread of seeing Phillip again.

"Why did you and Father agree to an engagement between Lord Edward and Anne?" She wiped the tears away as she asked the question.

"Your sister is happy with her decision. Your father and I want to support her."

"There are other men she could marry."

"Would you have your sister turn the one she loves away? Emma, this is her fourth season. She is no longer a young débutante, and Lord Edward's proposal was most welcome."

"If he loves me, why won't he defy his father?" This was the crux of her hurt and anger. She didn't understand why Phillip was going through with the marriage contract.

"Status and titles are a burden. Be thankful you aren't titled."

"Why does it have to be difficult? He loves me—I'm certain of this."

"He'll find happiness in fulfilling his role and duty. Phillip will be a duke one day. The Duke of Ashby has a great deal of influence and wealth. This is the duty his father has burdened him with."

"I don't think duty should control the heart."

"Prepare yourself," her mother said as they walked from the garden. "You will see him tonight. We are invited to Lancaster House for a dinner party."

Emma spent the day thinking of excuses as to why she couldn't go to the dinner party. But when the time came, she dressed with care knowing she was going to see Phillip. She wanted to look her best so she wouldn't feel uncomfortable in front of his family, fiancée, and him.

Her family was one of the last to arrive. When she walked into the room she noticed Phillip stood by the doors leading out to the patio. She forgot to breathe as she gazed at him with his dirty blond hair offset by the brown of his dinner jacket.

"Miss Emma." Lady Olivia's silky voice caused her to shudder. Olivia took her arm and pulled her to the side of the room. In a whisper she said, "He is my betrothed. Keep your eyes, hands, and lips off, unless you plan to run off to Gretna Green with him."

Before she could answer, the butler announced dinner was ready, and everyone lined up to file into the dining room. She watched as Lady Olivia grabbed Phillip's arm and they walked into dinner together.

"Emma," Henry said, holding an arm out for her, "I'll escort you into dinner."

"Thank you." She took his arm and moved into the room to sit at the opposite end of the table. "I don't know why it still hurts so much."

He squeezed her hand. "It will hurt for a while yet."

The room was busy with conversation, but she focused on Phillip. When the engagement announcement was made by the Duke of Ashby everyone clapped. The smile she saw on Phillip's face was forced.

On top of the information regarding the engagement, all of London was whispering about Lady Olivia's outbursts at dinner and in the library. The serving staff at Lancaster House spread the gossip each day before morning tea. A visible tension fell over the room as Lady Olivia spoke. Her voice was high-pitched and loud.

"I don't know what his valet was thinking—a brown jacket for our engagement party. I picked a green jacket. I'm going to have to dismiss him."

Duchess Cecily looked surprised by her statement. "I don't see a problem with the jacket. It's very appropriate for the party."

Emma looked to Phillip to see if he'd heard the conversation. His face was passive as he ate. The surprise came when she saw the Duchess of Ashby put her hand on Phillip's arm. She wondered if it was to keep him calm or to extend support. Emma didn't know if he had noticed her even once during the evening, and the care she took to dress now seemed foolish.

"The green brings out the blond in his hair. I don't like the brown streaks. I despise brown hair," Olivia said with a smug glare down the table at Emma.

Duchess Cecily looked over at Phillip in confusion and responded, "His hair is rather light even with the brown jacket."

"Arundel and I plan to spend our time in London. With all of the diversions here, there isn't reason to go out to the country. He is to inherit Norfolk house in St. James Square."

Duchess Cecily gave a quiet response, but it was obvious Olivia made the comment for Phillip because she continued to stare his way, expecting him to respond. He focused on his food while he cut the meat and appeared to be deaf to her comments.

"Of course, Norfolk house will come after our wedding tour."

Emma looked over to her sister and Edward. They sat across from each other, the same as Phillip and Olivia. They had tense looks on their faces, not knowing what to expect from the loud conversation. It was soon very obvious everyone in the Watson family was focused on Phillip. His sisters and younger brother stopped eating to listen.

"Oh yes, he no longer has amnesia. We can thank the person who tried to kill him for the renewal of his mind," Olivia said. "I'm not worried about the attempts on his life. I think he needs another bump on the head to forget this last summer. He might be here in body, but he is not the earl he used to be." She glared down the table at Emma.

Emma exchanged an amused look with her parents. The room at large was uncomfortable.

"You would have to ask the Parkers what they did to him. He has become very quiet and withdrawn," she said, taking a bite of her bread.

His quiet constraint had become visible, as he also was no longer eating but was holding his silverware mid-movement. Emma saw Lady Ashby exchange a look with him, and then after closing his eyes and taking a deep breath he went back to eating.

Emma wanted to drag Olivia from the room so she could tell her how wonderful her life would be when she married Phillip. Emma was the one in line for a loveless life as she realized she would never love another man the way she loved Phillip.

"If I have anything to say about it, he will spend less time in the library and more time engaging in other pursuits. Reading is such a bore. I like to see a man engage in activities such as . . . fencing," she said after a short pause, as though she pulled the activity out of the air.

"You don't enjoy reading, Lady Olivia?" Duchess Cecily asked.

"No, it is a waste of time. Only *blue stockings* spend their days in the library." Olivia again sent a smirk in Emma's direction. She didn't know how Olivia knew so much about her, but she wanted to wipe the smirk off her face.

The conversation was absurd, but everything she said was another way to goad both Emma and Phillip to anger. Guests around the table commented on her rudeness and immaturity as she continued. Olivia complained about the plainness of Lancaster House and the preparation of the food. The common opinion flowing through the room was that the marriage would be canceled before the banns were read the following Sunday. Thinking Phillip's deafness would continue throughout the night, Emma was shocked when she heard Olivia address him.

"Arundel" she said in a high-pitched, sweet tone.

The chatter in the room died down as she continued to say his name. After the third time he looked up.

"Did you have something you would like to say?" The forced smile that didn't reach his eyes would have stopped Emma from speaking, but it didn't stop Olivia.

"Did you not hear me? I have been calling your name."

"No, I didn't hear you, as the pitch of your voice is too high for human ears."

If anyone had been speaking, they shut their mouth with Phillip's response in the air. A few utensils fell to the table. The silent shock was too loud not to notice.

Olivia's face turned bright red as she stared at Phillip. She didn't speak; her smile was one of success. Emma's mouth dropped open as Phillip glared at Olivia and finished raising the fork to his mouth.

Emma looked over to Anne to see her hand over her mouth in surprise. Lord Edward's head in his hands and shaking shoulders were an indication he was trying to hide laughter. Lady Marianne, Lady Charlotte, and Lord Charles were watching Phillip, waiting for his next move.

With Phillip eating, guests went back to uncomfortable conversation. Covert glances thrown in Phillip's direction told Emma everyone was waiting for Olivia to continue goading him to anger. As Emma went back to eating, she was shocked as Olivia stood and threw her spoon at Phillip.

"I loathe you."

Phillip didn't respond. He removed the extra spoon from his plate and continued to eat; this time a small amount of baked potato was on his fork. Emma experienced shock and joy at witnessing one of Olivia's tantrums. Of course, poor Phillip had to endure the shame of her outburst, but it was a sight to witness.

"I told you I wanted you to wear the green jacket," she yelled as her fork and knife flew through the air. He moved to the side and allowed the silverware to fly past his head.

"And I told you I'm old enough to make decisions on clothing," he said as he continued to eat.

Olivia picked her plate of food up from the table and threw it in his direction. Food flew across the room and hit the guests. The plate shattered as it hit the woman sitting on Phillip's right. Phillip turned and apologized. He removed the broken pieces of glass as Olivia's teacup flew across the table and hit him in the head.

Emma startled as the Duke of Ashby and the Duke of Norland began yelling at each other. She worried for Phillip. He was stuck with Olivia, and if her behavior were any indication of her psyche, the woman was insane.

Ashby yelled, "Norland, I told you to get your daughter under control!"

"She wouldn't behave this way if he would stop making *clever* comments," Norland responded.

Emma looked back to Phillip and saw blood on the side of his face. Thomas was next to him with a wet cloth, cleaning the blood and food. As Ashby and Norland continued to argue over the situation, Olivia grabbed her glass and threw it at Phillip. He wasn't expecting it, and he flinched as it shattered on the table and cut his hand.

"I refuse to marry you." Olivia's words were the only sound in the room for a full minute. Emma watched as Olivia and Phillip stared at each other with absolute hatred.

"Don't worry, Olivia, I have no intention of marrying you." Phillip used a serviette to wipe the blood off his hand.

"Yes . . . you . . . will!" Norland's words were accompanied by throwing his chair against the wall. Turning to Ashby he said, "I will purchase a special license, and they will be married tomorrow."

"Arundel," Ashby yelled, "you will consign yourself to your duty."

"Forgive me, Father," Phillip said in anger, "but arranged marriage never gave anyone in this room marital bliss."

"Phillip, please—" Duchess Ashby pleaded with her son.

"Sorry, Mother," Phillip said, looking chagrined.

Ashby and Norland yelled at each other, debating the propriety of a special license. The room was in complete chaos. Footmen were racing to clear dishes and silverware from the table so Olivia couldn't throw anything else.

"I don't want my family business thrown out to society as a topic of conversation!" Ashby slammed a hand on the table.

"Your son is the problem," Norland yelled back at him.

"Your daughter is immature and vile," Ashby yelled, pointing to Olivia. "I told you to get her under control for this dinner."

"If your son would stop goading my daughter to anger, she wouldn't behave this way!" Norland grabbed Olivia's arm. "You will go to your room and not emerge until you are ready to apologize."

"I want her out of my house," Ashby yelled, pointing at Olivia. "She will learn to behave or she is not welcome."

Norland grabbed Olivia's arm and pulled her from the room. Emma was elated as she saw Olivia leaving in shame. She looked down the table and pity consumed her for Phillip as he made apologies to the people around him. The valet put a salve on Phillip's hand and was wrapping it as the evening exploded with Norland returning to fight with Ashby.

Emma left the dining room with her family. She looked back at Phillip to see him one last time for the night. She saw him glance toward her and knew this situation would only get worse. Edward and Anne's marriage would be a source of pain for both her and Phillip forever.

Twenty-eight

"Phillip?" Edward, Charlotte, Charles, and Marianne walked into his room with a book.

He stood next to the window, watching as people left. "Don't tell me the minister who was at the party is ready to marry us tonight."

"Everyone is leaving," Edward replied. "Father kicked Lady Olivia and her parents out of the house."

He closed his eyes, sick over his behavior. "I shouldn't have commented on her shrill voice. Edward, I'm sorry I ruined your night. I'll apologize to Anne as well."

He was surprised to hear his siblings laughing. "Phillip, this is going to be the best party of the season. People will talk about it for years to come. This will be the top story in the society column tomorrow." Edward patted him on the shoulder to let him know he wasn't angry.

"Are you referring to Olivia's tantrum or my rude comment?"

"Both," Charles responded.

The room filled with laughter as they recounted the guests' reactions at Olivia's tantrums. Phillip listened to the various comments and thought of how lonely and sad his life would be without his family.

"Lady Grange is certain there won't be a wedding," Marianne commented.

"Lord Grange said he thought his wife was a nightmare, but he is certain you have a worse fate than he does," Charles added.

"If it's any consolation, Emma Parker was concerned for you," Charlotte commented.

"It's better I don't know what her reaction was. It hurts too much to think about her." Looking around for something to say, he noticed the book in Charlotte's hand. "What are you reading? Anything I would enjoy?" he asked, hopeful to keep the conversation light.

"It's a book of Shakespeare's tragedies and comedies. I brought it from your library at Wentworth Hall. I hope you don't mind," Charlotte responded.

"Will you read to me?"

"We should each take parts," Charlotte said as she searched through the book, found a story, and read.

She chose Romeo and Juliet on purpose. The story was excruciating to hear as he thought of Emma. Charles read Romeo's parts and Marianne read Juliet. Edward and Charlotte took the other parts and allowed him to sit and relax with his eyes closed.

He listened as Marianne read with emotion the scene where Juliet drank a sleeping draught. The despair and emotion of the scene made him wonder what Shakespeare could have done different with the characters. He wrote it as a tragedy, but with a few changes Romeo and Juliet could have survived and they never would have had to use the poison. The story could've gone from tragedy to comedy.

"Phillip? Is something wrong?" Marianne asked. She stopped reading Juliet's lament. He hadn't realized he had made a noise.

"I was pondering over Romeo and Juliet and the tragedy of separating two people who are in love." The comparison to his life was too realistic for him. He needed to share his feelings, but he didn't know what to say.

"If the characters had lived, do you think they would have been happy leaving their families and hiding from everyone they knew?" Edward asked, joining into the analysis.

"They could've been," Charlotte responded, closing the book but keeping a finger in it to mark the spot. "They lived in a city where their families were killing each other. It wouldn't be pleasant."

"I think they wouldn't be happy," Marianne said, giving the first argument in the negative. "After a while they would miss their family and friends. It could tear them apart."

"I've missed these conversations," Charlotte said, grabbing Phillip's hand. She sat in the window seat next to his chair. "You used to come up with these types of observations while reading all the time."

"Please tell me this is what we all think a simple conversation regarding literature." Edward took the book from Charlotte and closed it.

"What else would it be?" Charlotte asked in confusion.

"It is just an observation of literature. I asked Emma to elope and she said no. I will be stuck with an insane wife for life."

Over the following days, Phillip avoided Olivia as much as he could. He attended church with the family and listened as the banns were read. He attended the dinner parties his parents required of him, and he behaved the way Ashby expected.

At a party held by Lord and Lady Jellico, Phillip saw Emma and her family across the room. He stayed at a distance so she didn't feel threatened. He also kept his distance from Lady Olivia, avoiding all conversation regarding the wedding. He was going through the motions of life without experiencing it. Could he continue to do so forever?

The second week of the vicar reading the banns, he wanted to declare his objection when he heard the words, "If any of you know cause or just impediment why these persons should not be joined together in holy matrimony, ye are to declare it. This is for the second time asking." He dared a glance at Olivia and saw her looking at him as well. They locked eyes, daring the other to object.

"I object," a deep male voice called out.

A low murmur went through the room. Phillip, along with everyone else, turned to see who was objecting and which couple they were objecting to.

"Will the objector please come forward?" the vicar said, looking around the room.

Phillip held his breath as a man he didn't recognize walked to the front of the chapel. The man was older. He looked worn and tired.

"What is your objection?" the vicar asked.

The man didn't speak. He moved to the front of the room and handed the vicar a piece of parchment. Phillip didn't dare hope the objection was for him. There were many couples, including Edward and Anne, who had also had the banns read.

The vicar nodded to the man. "Is this accurate?"

"I was paid to deliver the information to you."

The vicar looked back at the congregation. "The Earl of Arundel and Lady Olivia Harrison will meet with me after the services."

With this announcement Phillip's expectations rose. Whatever the information was, could it be enough to end the engagement?

The services seemed to last longer than usual due to the build-up behind the objection. The vicar spoke about honesty in relationships. Phillip wondered if he heard about the problems in his and Olivia's relationship and the marriage contract due to the advice he was preaching. But if anyone was being honest in a relationship, it was them.

Phillip waited along with Olivia and their parents for the vicar to finish speaking with the congregation as they left. He saw the Parkers waiting near Edward and Anne, and he locked eyes with Emma. Desire flooded his heart. Would the objection be enough to end the madness?

Phillip exchanged a look with Olivia as the vicar approached. He motioned his hand to let her know she could go first.

"What is the objection?" Norland asked before anyone could sit in the chairs the vicar set out.

"The objection is against Lord Arundel. Evidence shows he was wed to Miss Emma Parker in Gretna Green this last week."

"This is a clear case of defamation," Ashby yelled, crumbling the paper and throwing it on the floor. "Someone is trying to destroy my son's reputation."

Phillip turned to Olivia. "Did you do this? You threatened to spread rumors about Emma. Are you trying to destroy her?"

Olivia didn't speak. She looked to her parents for their responses.

"I didn't go to Gretna Green. I admit I asked Emma to run away with me, but she said no." If they could void the engagement, it would be most welcome. But he wasn't about to ruin Emma's reputation when she guarded it so well.

"Norland," Ashby yelled, "are you behind the forgery?"

"An absurd allegation, Ashby. I would never. I'm an honorable man. I can see your son's hand in it. We all know he doesn't want to marry my daughter." Norland waved his hand in Phillip's direction as he made the accusation.

"I have Phillip well watched, since the latest attempts on his life. He didn't take Emma Parker to Gretna Green," Ashby yelled.

"What do we do now?" Phillip asked, hoping to bring sanity back to the conversation. He tried not to overreact due to his father's confession of having him watched. It was almost as though he was being tended by a governess again.

The vicar put a hand on both dukes' shoulders, "Until the allegation can be proven false, the engagement can't go forward."

"How did this person prove it took place?" Ashby roared.

"He provided a marriage license," the vicar revealed.

"Where is the license?" Ashby demanded, holding his hand out and expecting the paper to be given to him.

"Your Grace," the vicar said in a calming voice, "this is something you, the duchess, and your son should discus in private."

"No, it isn't," Ashby said, ready to throw a punch at Norland. "I want to know who purchased the forgery."

Phillip knew his father was angry, because Norland was now going to execute the part of the contract which stated his lands, money, and titles were to be handed over.

"I don't know who did this," Norland yelled, "but your son is backing out of the contract so I win."

Phillip took a deep breath before he spoke. He wanted to sound calm. "Emma and I are not married. You can't take my father's lands, titles, and monies because this is a forgery. My suggestion is you both agree to end this charade and allow Olivia to marry Lord Folly and I will marry Emma." Phillip hoped his words would have an impact on the greedy men before him.

"I'll have my solicitor draw up the paperwork tomorrow, Ashby."

"I will find out who did this, and if you or your daughter are behind it, so help me, I'll destroy you." Ashby walked away without another word.

The vicar looked over. "They will not be allowed to marry with this marriage license between Lord Arundel and Miss Emma Parker." He nodded to Olivia. "You are legally released from the engagement, but Lord Arundel is married to Miss Parker."

The words were cheap and distasteful. Emma didn't deserve the censure she would receive from the forged marriage license. The weight of the gamble pushed him down until he wasn't certain if he could lift his legs to walk.

It took everything within him to walk out into the church yard. He didn't want to face Emma. He didn't know if he could bear to see her reaction to the forgery. Would she be angry? Would she hate him? This would destroy any chance of a match for her.

"What happened? Who objected?" Edward asked as he and Anne approached.

"The vicar didn't say who made the objection." He couldn't stop the bile from rising in his throat, as he would have to tell Emma.

"What is the objection?" Edward asked in concern. "Father looked angry."

Phillip again tried to say the words, but he looked at Anne and couldn't bring himself to tell her about the horrible reputation her sister now had.

"Phillip, you're scaring me." Edward looked past him and walked to their mother to get answers. Phillip turned and watched as his mother said the words. Although he was too far away to hear, he knew what she said by the movement of her mouth.

Edward walked back to him and asked, "How angry is Father?"

"Norland is preparing the paperwork tomorrow. Everything will be gone if he can't prove it's a forgery."

Phillip saw his mother out of the corner of his eye. She walked over to Lord Anthony and Lady Amelia. Phillip couldn't watch. He didn't want to see Emma's reaction.

"This isn't your fault. Someone is playing a risky game here. When Ashby finds out who it is, he's going to destroy them." Edward's words were filled with passion, which was comforting. But all the passion in the world wouldn't do Phillip or Emma any good until they knew who forged the license.

Phillip cringed as he heard the reaction from Emma. Her life was forever changed the day her father took an injured stranger into their home. He swallowed the bile as it crept up his throat.

He opened his eyes to see Edward was still standing with him, but Anne had moved over to her family. "How devastated is Emma?" Phillip asked not daring to look at her.

Edward shook his head. "It's best you don't know."

Twenty-nine

EMMA LAY ON THE SOFA, curled up in her mother's arms and crying. Her reputation was destroyed. All of London would be aware of the so-called elopement before afternoon tea finished. She'd spent so much time thinking about how to get Phillip out of the engagement, she didn't expect someone to do it for them. She didn't expect the person to be heartless and ruin her reputation in the process.

By virtue of societal expectations, her entire family would share the burden of her shame. It didn't matter if it was a lie. It didn't matter that they had more than enough people to say it wasn't valid. The problem was that the evidence of a marriage certificate was produced.

Emma's mother ran her fingers through her hair, speaking calmly. She kept telling her everything would be all right. Ashby would find out where the forged document came from so he didn't lose all of his worldly possessions. The words didn't comfort her. She was devastated.

Emma stopped crying when a headache developed. She remembered the devastated look on Phillip's face as he spoke to Edward. He didn't want to be married to her. "I thought he loved me," Emma cried to her mother.

"Why do you think he doesn't?" Anne asked. Emma hadn't realized her sister was in the room.

"He was upset."

"You're upset. Does this mean you don't love him?"

"I do love him. I'm upset because my reputation has been destroyed. I'm Hester Prynne. I might as well wear a scarlet letter on my dress."

"I think this is taking your dramatic notions a bit far," her mother said as she attempted to sooth Emma's pain.

"No, it isn't," Emma sobbed. She thought about the book she recently read by the American, Nathaniel Hawthorne. The romantic themes she saw in it were now distasteful to her as she compared herself to the main character. She thought it would be a favorite of hers and wanted to share it with Phillip. But now she saw herself in the character and wondered what scaffold of shame she would be thrown upon to bear the burden of the forgery.

"You're being ridiculous," Anne said, downplaying the significance of the situation. "Phillip couldn't even say the words. It made him sick to think of what this has done to you. He didn't look at you because he didn't want to see your reaction. When he asked me to marry him, Edward told me Phillip is still in love with you. Edward is afraid our marriage will be the end of his close relationship with his brother."

Emma couldn't feel sorry for Edward. She couldn't feel sorry for Anne. She had spent the last month detesting her sister in secret while putting on a happy appearance for everyone. The façade would have to end at some point, but Emma continued to hide her feelings because she loved her sister.

She spent the following days hiding in her room. She refused to attend any social events. Her parents understood her reason for staying hidden. She didn't want to go through the shame and humiliation by herself, but she couldn't expect Phillip to come to Hertford House. It would throw the gossips too much ammunition.

When she emerged from her room, Emma sat in the drawing room, sketching the piano in the corner. She glanced at Edward and Anne sitting on the sofa in a private tête-à-tête. They were happy. Riddled with guilt over her anger at the couple, she peeked over to see the smile on her sister's face. Anne was in love. Anne had never been so happy, and it showed in her posture. Her self-esteem had changed this season. She was confident.

Emma watched as Edward held her sister's hands. They were to be married in a fortnight at Wentworth Hall. The banns had to be read one more time, and then they would depart for Derbyshire.

"Edward?" Henry asked as he strode into the room. Emma looked up, hoping no one noticed she was staring. "Do you know why your brother is speaking with my parents?"

Emma's heart raced. Was Phillip at Hertford House? She looked down at the dress she wore to remember it was her purple day dress. She lifted her fingers and cringed to see the stains of lead from her sketching. She touched her hair and pulled the loose pieces back into the pins.

"Phillip is here?" Edward asked in surprise.

"No . . . it's Charles. I was wondering if he was sent with information regarding the . . ." Henry hesitated and looked over at Emma before he finished speaking. "Information regarding the forged marriage license."

Edward shook his head. "No. As of this morning my father is still searching for the culprits. Norland is racing to prepare the documents to take everything my father has."

Henry turned as though miffed. "Why is he here?"

"I don't know."

Crestfallen to find out it wasn't Phillip, Emma went back to her sketch. She didn't need to worry about the lead smeared on her fingers and hands. She listened as the others made conjectures regarding the visit.

Emma ran her finger over the line she drew to smear the lead on the paper for shading. She was trying to get the effect of the sun on the piano as she heard her name.

"Emma? Your mother and I would like to speak with you." Her father stood in the doorway.

Weary of what was happening, Emma placed her sketchpad on the sofa and followed her father. If the visit were about the forged license, Edward would have known about it. She tried to think of any other possibility for Charles's visit, but nothing came to mind. She entered the morning room to see Charles standing. He was waiting with her mother.

"Lord Charles." She curtsied.

"Emma, please sit down." Her father pointed to a chair. He waited for her to sit before he spoke. "Lord Charles made an offer of marriage for you."

Emma wasn't certain she heard her father right. *Why would Charles make an offer of marriage?* The words flew through her mind, and the explanation for his reasoning didn't come. She realized everyone was looking at her.

"I'm sorry, I think I misheard you."

Her father gave an indulgent and understanding smile. "He has made an offer of marriage."

Charles cleared his throat. "Miss Emma, I'm the only one in my family who has the freedom to restore your reputation. Phillip can't do it, as he will be forced to marry Olivia once the forgery is confirmed. Edward can't because he is engaged to Anne. After me, we are out of options. I think in time we will find happiness together."

Emma couldn't think. Her mind raced with questions she didn't have answers to. She asked the first one to came to her mind. "Does Phillip know you're here?"

Charles looked down at his hands. "No. I'll tell him once I have your answer."

"Did your father tell you to do this?"

Charles didn't meet her eyes. "Yes."

Emma nodded her head. She knew Ashby had to be behind the proposal. She couldn't bring herself to look at anyone in the room. "Have you given him your approval?" She posed the question to her parents. She knew they'd been searching for a way to restore her reputation. They'd spoken about making a match with a few of the men who'd danced and paid call to her during the season. She never expected this.

She closed her eyes as her father responded. "Yes, we think it's best."

"I do not mean to sound ungrateful, but I would prefer to be a spinster." She stood and left the room without another word.

Thirty

COMMOTION CAUSED PHILLIP TO LOOK up from the book he was reading. It had been at least an hour since Ashby lost his temper, and it was time for another rampage. He wondered what could have happened to cause the outburst. Phillip exited the library with the intent of finding out what the issue was without entering the fray.

When he realized Edward was the one yelling, he walked into the parlor. Edward and Charles were fighting. He hadn't seen a fight between his brothers for years.

"How could you, Charles? Do you realize what you have done?" Edward yelled. He looked distraught.

Phillip walked forward and put his hand on Edward's arm. "What's happened?"

"You don't want to know," Edward snarled. His anger was pointed at Charles, so Phillip didn't take offense.

"He's going to find out," Charlotte said from across the room. She sat with her embroidery while she watched the argument. "It's best he finds out from one of you."

Charles looked ashamed as he admitted, "I paid a call to Lord Anthony this morning . . . I asked for Emma's hand in marriage."

Phillip's breath caught in his throat as though he'd been punched in the gut. He looked to Edward to see if he heard right and saw the truth of it on his face. "What?" Phillip couldn't think of what to ask. His mind raced with the implications. He knew he would have to watch as Emma married someone else. He didn't expect it to be Charles.

"Phillip, you have to understand this is the best way to repair her reputation. Once the forgery is revealed, you'll be married to Olivia. Emma will be stuck with the repercussions of a ruined reputation."

Phillip heard the words. He knew Charles was correct about most, if not all, of what he said, but he couldn't stop thinking of the implications. If Charles and Emma married, she would live in the same house as he did, unless he never saw Charles again.

He found his voice as he asked, "Did she accept?"

Charles fidgeted. He looked as though he were waiting for Phillip to attack him. "She was in shock, but she turned my offer down."

Phillip nodded and left the room. Once he was in the hall he panicked and noticed his lungs were constricted from the weight of the implications. He couldn't breathe. He rushed to the back of the house, went out through the servant's door, and entered the stables. He hadn't thought about riding since he arrived in London. He needed to think, and a dusty old library wasn't the right place.

Phillip looked at the horses, trying to decide which one to take when he noticed Bassanio. He walked over to his horse. He didn't remember anyone mentioning Bassanio being brought to London. Without another thought he saddled the horse and left. His mind raced with places he could go. His father owned estates throughout England. He could hide away at any of them and spend the season brooding in misfortune. But it would be too easy to find him at any of the estates close by.

He thought about leaving England and heading to the States. He'd heard a lot of positive information about Boston and New York. He could start over, remove Emma from his mind. As the thought *remove Emma* passed through his mind, he knew it was the last thing he wanted to do. He wanted to be with her.

For a wild moment, he thought about going to Hertford House to convince Emma to go to Gretna Green with him. *It would take a day or so to get there, but we could elope* and . . . and the thought ended. He was angry because of the person who made up the forged marriage license. He couldn't take Emma to Gretna Green, and he wouldn't ask her again because he loved her too much to bring shame on her. She'd already turned him down for an elopement at the church in London.

As Phillip calmed down, he sighed. *My parents are going to be angry,* he thought. He shook his head. They'd yelled at him once for leaving without an escort or protection. He'd promised not to take off again, although in his defense, an attempt on his life hadn't been made for quite some time.

Phillip rode out of London. His mind continued to repeat the words Charles said. *She said no.* He screamed in his head, *She said no! Charles never should have asked for her hand.* In anger, Phillip decided if Charles and Emma did marry, he would make certain the home Charles inherited was the one on the Isle of Skye in Scotland. It was far enough away he would never have to see either of them again. He wouldn't have to see their children. He wouldn't have to see Emma. *I would ban Charles from Wentworth Hall.*

Phillip's anger drained from him as he rode. He knew Charles was right. Emma would need someone to repair her reputation. The best way to do it was through a marriage and a boost in station. Due to the burden of title and inheritance, he couldn't rescue Emma's reputation. Charles was the only one in his family who could. He should be thanking him for the generous offer.

As the anger left him, he realized he'd left the house without a winter coat. It was chilly for October, and the sun was going down. He rode to an inn, checked to make certain he had a money purse, and entered to stay for the night. He would decide what to do in the morning.

Thirty-one

EDWARD UNDERSTOOD WHY PHILLIP LEFT. What he didn't understand was why he didn't return. After going missing over the summer, how could Phillip do this to their family again? Edward didn't handle the situation with Charles and the proposal well. He shouldn't have made a scene. He should've been more delicate, knowing it would upset Phillip.

He paced through the drawing room as he listened to their father speaking with the London police. His anxiety grew as he thought the killer might have succeeded this time. His brother could be dead. Edward didn't feel anything. He didn't feel connected to Phillip like he once had. He hadn't realized the connection was gone until Phillip didn't come home. *Does this mean he is dead*? Edward contemplated as he paced back and forth.

His relationship with Phillip changed once Edward started focusing on time with Anne. He and Phillip were growing apart. He never thought it could happen.

"Ashby, send letters to all of the estates. Ask the stewards if he is staying at one of them." His mother was trying to hold herself together by thinking of all the places Phillip could be. She didn't want to think he was dead.

"What about Norfolk House?" Edward asked. Norfolk House was in London a few blocks from where they currently resided. "I'll ride over to see if he is there."

"I already checked," Ashby said. "They haven't seen him."

"Aren't you having him followed?" Charles asked.

"He agreed not to leave the house. I didn't have him watched within the house."

"Your Grace," the officer said as he readied to leave, "I will send Lord Arundel's description out to surrounding areas via telegraph tonight. We should have responses by morning."

Edward left the room, unable to listen to anything else the officer said. He walked to the library to find Charles sitting in front of the fire.

"May I join you?" Edward asked, not wanting to interrupt Charles's thoughts.

"It wasn't my idea, Edward." Charles looked as though he'd been torturing himself since the argument.

"I should've known Father put you up to it."

"I know Phillip is upset, but how can he do this to Mother again? How can he do this to our family?"

Edward shook his head. "I don't understand it either."

"I'll send a letter to Miss Emma and her parents. I'll apologize for the offer in the morning."

"Be thankful she refused you. Otherwise, Phillip would've made certain the house you'd inherit is the one in Scotland." Edward smiled as he said the words, hoping Charles realized he was joking.

"You speak in jest, but I think you're right." Charles leaned forward and put his head in his hands. "I messed this up."

"Ashby messed it up." Edward knew where the blame should lie. His father had messed up more than enough this season in hopes of gaining more wealth. Instead he was on the verge of losing all of it.

Edward paced the house the entire night, waiting for Phillip to come home or for the police to drag him home. He nearly cried when Phillip walked in the door.

"Where have you been?" their mother sobbed as she pulled him into her arms.

"I owe you all an apology." Phillip looked as though he meant the words, although now that he was home Edward wanted to make him suffer as they had while he was gone.

"Do you know how worried we have been?" Edward yelled. He sounded like their father. "You could've been killed. You could have been floating in the Thames for all we knew."

Phillip looked repentant, but it didn't stop Edward from his rant.

"We all know you're upset, but you didn't have to punish us. Do you realize your actions affect every single person in this home?"

Edward stopped yelling and turned away from Phillip to see the surprised expressions on everyone's faces. He'd never lost his temper like this. It was a new experience. He didn't like this part of himself. He wanted to be the fun-loving, charismatic jokester he'd always been. Far too often of late he'd seen Ashby emerging in him, and he needed to change before he turned into his father.

Phillip pulled away from their mother and looked at Edward. "I'm sorry. I was angry, and before I knew it I was outside of London and it was night. I stopped at an inn."

"Well, we are all happy you had a comfortable night's rest," Edward continued to rant. "The rest of us have been pacing the house wondering when the police would come and tell us they found your dead body." He stopped and looked at his family. "Is anyone else going to join me in reprimanding him?"

Edward took a deep breath of regret as their father cleared his throat. He could see Phillip was waiting for the punishment. They were all waiting. The anger drained out of him as their father grabbed Phillip and shook him while he yelled. The words were lost to Edward as he watched Ashby beat Phillip for the irresponsible behavior.

Edward took a step back and realized he needed to control his temper; otherwise he could end up like his father. Ashby was already angry and desperate due to the debacle with Norland. Phillip's decision to leave the house without protection from the person trying to kill him was more than enough to throw their father over the edge.

When their father left the room, Phillip stumbled out. Edward followed him up the stairs and helped him with his bloody nose.

Phillip gave a derisive laugh as he said, "Are you still going to yell at me?"

"No. I'm not angry with you anymore. I am ashamed of my behavior." He vowed he would never turn into his father, and if he saw any sign of it, he would change course.

Edward decided he wanted to see Anne. He needed to find out what Emma was thinking, and he needed to be away from his family. As he arrived at Hertford House he was thankful they didn't know anything about the night's events. He walked into the drawing room to see Anne at the piano and Emma on the sofa sketching.

"Edward!" Anne always looked happy to see him. He spent every moment he could with her, and it made him a better person to do so. "I hoped you would come this morning."

"I had a busy night." He didn't want to worry Anne, so he would omit the events of the previous evening.

Thirty-two

THE BEST PART OF HIS relationship with his father was once Phillip received the beating, Ashby didn't harp on him over the mistake. But he feared his father. When Hodgens passed the message to him letting him know he was expected in the den, Phillip's anxiety hit the ceiling.

He slowly walked to the den, holding an arm over his stomach as if it would help stop the pain from the beating. He wondered why he was summoned. He paused outside the door, thinking of excuses he could use to get out of the meeting. He could feign an illness. He could claim a headache; it seemed to work for women when they wanted to get out of a social engagement.

"Come in, Arundel," his father said before Phillip knocked on the door.

Phillip entered to see his parents and the Duke and Duchess of Norland. He looked around the room and found Olivia in an overstuffed chair by the window. As he looked at the occupants, he wished he had faked the headache.

"Arundel, my investigation is complete. My solicitor found the culprits of the forged wedding license."

This information piqued his interest. Although he would love to be married to Emma, he now understood why it couldn't be in Gretna Green. "Who?"

"Lady Olivia and Lord Folly concocted the plan together." Ashby looked jubilant as he said the words.

Phillip didn't have to ask why; he knew why they did it. He just didn't understand the purpose of destroying Emma. She was innocent. He wanted to tell Olivia what he thought of her, but he couldn't bring himself to do it. Ashby would say something awful in this situation, and Phillip was not his father. His father would rage and yell. He would hit walls and slam the desk. Instead Phillip sat on a chair to hear his fate. He wondered if he was a coward but decided it took strength to stay human when treated so diabolically.

"Now this mess is cleared up, we can continue with plans for the wedding," Ashby announced, "unless your daughter is backing out of the contract, Norland?"

"She isn't backing out. She is apologetic for her actions. She will offer Miss Parker an apology today."

Phillip looked up at the mention of Emma. His head came up too quickly and caused the room to spin. He wondered how long the effects of the beating would stay with him. This was one situation he wasn't going to sit back and accept an apology over. "What does she expect Emma to do now that her reputation has been tarnished?"

"I think you should marry her and save her reputation," Olivia said, speaking to Phillip for perhaps the second or third time since they were thrown into this engagement.

"I would gladly do so, if your father would leave my father's estate and titles alone."

"Not an option, boy." Norland's amused smile showed his greed. "If you back out, I will take everything."

"Arundel," Ashby said with a lazy drawl, "Miss Parker's reputation will be secured in a marriage. She has refused Charles, but I committed to Lord Anthony I would find her a suitable match."

"Is there anything more?" Phillip asked, turning away.

"You and Olivia will be married at the same time as your brother and his intended. We will obtain a special license to skip the banns."

Phillip needed to be alone. He didn't trust himself to speak. He didn't excuse himself. He slowly stood and walked to the door.

"Arundel?" Phillip turned as Olivia said his name. "May I speak with you?"

"Not right now." He didn't trust himself to stay calm.

"It won't take long," Olivia insisted.

Phillip let out an angry sigh and relented. He turned back to hear what she had to say, but she looked nervously at her parents and motioned to the door. "In private, please?"

"Don't leave the house, Arundel." Ashby's tone communicated the dangerous consequences if he did. Phillip nodded and left the room. He didn't need any more bruises.

He cringed and held back the surprise when Olivia grabbed his arm and pulled him to the parlor. Her grip irritated the bruises on his arm. She looked around to make certain they were alone and then closed the door. Phillip walked over to open it because he didn't want to be alone with her, but she put her hand on the doorknob.

"What do you want?" He could've been nicer, but he wasn't in a generous mood.

"I've done everything I can to get out of the engagement. I can't do it alone. I need your help."

Phillip didn't know what inspired him. Perhaps it was the word *alone*, but he realized a way they could get out of the engagement. They had to work together. If they both walked away from the engagement, neither one of their fathers could take the other's wealth. "It was foolish of you and Folly to obtain a forgery."

"I cannot apologize enough for my actions." She hesitated as though she were considering her next statement. Olivia closed her eyes as she said, "Folly and I plan to leave for the States. I no longer care about my reputation."

"What do you need from me?"

"Money." She blushed as the word flew from her mouth. "My allowance has been suspended, and Folly's father is bankrupt."

"I will give you everything I have."

Olivia laughed. "We don't need everything you have, Arundel. Just enough to run away."

It was a strange moment, almost surreal as he laughed with her. He never thought he'd find a way to become friendly or even civil with her. "For now, we should pretend to consign ourselves to the fate of marriage. Stop arguing and fighting."

"Do you not think our fathers would be suspicious of us?"

"No, they want us to get along. They would be happy if we stopped fighting. It would make them both feel secure."

Olivia nodded her agreement. "Therefore, give them a false sense of security with their wealth."

"Exactly!" Phillip said with a smile. "Olivia, I'm not going to let you run away. We'll get out of this engagement together and take responsibility together." He waited for her to agree before he let her leave.

Phillip and Olivia agreed to be charming and talkative the entire evening.

"You look happy tonight. Have you lost your mind?" Edward asked with a curious yet amused look on his face.

"I've decided I can spend the rest of my life being angry, or I can learn to be happy in my circumstances."

"I'm glad you've realized this."

Phillip's heart stopped as he saw Emma approach. He had to conceal anger and pain. His future with her was at stake.

Phillip turned away as Olivia approached. He noticed her beauty but acknowledged she would never be as beautiful as Emma. He could consider Olivia a friend.

"Olivia, would you like a drink?"

"Thank you."

He saw the surprise on everyone's faces as he and Olivia spoke cordially with each other. Neither one did anything to provoke the other. He returned with a glass of punch and handed it to her.

"What have you been talking about?" Phillip asked so he could join the conversation.

"We are wondering what's going on with you."

Phillip and Olivia looked at each other and smiled. "We are preparing for our upcoming nuptials."

Olivia gave a sweet smile. "We will spend the rest of our lives together. We should be kind and get along."

Phillip held an arm out as dinner was announced. Olivia took it and gave him a charming smile. He led her from the stunned group into the dining room and helped her with her chair. He made certain his mother had them seated together so they could continue the charade.

Phillip noticed Ashby and Norland were watching them. He and Olivia continued the happy deception throughout the meal.

When the women left the men to their entertainment, Edward and Charles crossed the room and pushed him in a corner.

"Speak. Now," Edward demanded. "What is going on with you?"

"I don't know what you mean."

"You've been lovesick and moping around here for months. You and Olivia now look like a happy couple. Edward spoke as though he were trying to explain a simple situation to someone who'd gone insane.

"I can't continue to be lovesick. This isn't a novel, and I've been told I don't live in Verona."

"Now you sound like Ashby," Charles said. "Emma is distraught."

"I don't want to hurt Emma." No matter how secretive he had to be, he didn't want Emma to become even more of a casualty of this mess. In a moment of weakness, he admitted, "I will always love Emma." He gave a nervous laugh as though he were barely holding it together. "I'll have to pretend to be happy for the rest of my life."

Charles looked down at his hands. "I'm sorry."

Phillip nodded. "Let me get through the next week, and I'll let you know how I'm going to handle the rest of my life." He looked around. He wanted to escape to the library but remembered the promise he made to Olivia. He had to last the night.

When he walked into the drawing room with the rest of the women, Phillip joined Olivia and spent the evening with her. They chatted with guests and acted as though they were happy about the wedding. When he made it to his bedchamber, he was exhausted from the deception. He continued to have pain in his stomach, which caused him to wretch into the chamber pot. He was convinced the pain from the last beating would last a while yet.

Thirty-three

EMMA LOOKED OUT THE WINDOW of the carriage as Wentworth Hall came into view. The size of the home was overwhelming. She thought the home looked sad covered in snow and an overcast sky. Or, perhaps it was her perception of the home because she was dying inside and could hear herself screaming internally. The screaming was loud; Emma was surprised everyone in the carriage couldn't hear the sound.

She decided on the trip from London she wasn't going to marry. She would go home to Springhill Abby after the double wedding and become a spinster. She hadn't told her family yet, as her father and Ashby were plotting a marriage for her. She was waiting for the right moment.

The last week watching Phillip with Olivia put a hole in her heart she knew would never heal. She watched as they danced at Almack's. She watched as they spent every moment together. Charles and Edward were convinced Phillip had lost his mind.

Emma shivered as the carriage door opened and cold air rushed in. Charles and Edward met the carriage and helped Emma and Anne out. She appreciated the attentiveness and kindness to her.

Emma found her way to her room and spent the rest of the day by herself. She wandered around the house looking at paintings, family portraits, and the architecture. She stayed out of the family rooms but was told there was a library in the east wing, and she wanted to explore. The empty halls were eerie as she walked by herself. The dark halls looked like they weren't used unless the house was full of guests.

Guests would start arriving in large numbers the following day, as there were four days left before the weddings. She was about to give up the search for the library and go back to her room when she heard Phillip's voice. She didn't want to eavesdrop, but she was curious.

Emma walked forward and noticed she was standing outside Phillip's room. She was surprised when she heard Lady Olivia's voice. Emma put a hand over her mouth as she let out a soft gasp. She turned and ran down the hall. She didn't understand what they were doing. She could only imagine what was happening.

Thirty-four

PHILLIP HELPED OLIVIA MOUNT A mare. He led both the mare and Bassanio out of the barn before he mounted. He and Olivia planned to put on a show of familiarizing themselves before the wedding, and so they set out for a ride. Phillip looked at Olivia as he readied to leave the yard. "Lord Folly is already installed at the cottage. We will meet him there."

It took a half-hour before they found Folly. He was waiting near the crossroads.

"We need to hurry," Folly said as he mounted his horse.

"It will take a few hours to ride to Gretna Green," Phillip said as he considered staying behind. The plan was he would accompany them for propriety, but it seemed ridiculous since they were eloping. He'd woken with a stomachache and hadn't been able to shake it. Each time the horse cantered, it shook his body and caused pain. "I should stay at the cottage while you go."

"Arundel," Olivia said with a start, "you have to come with us. What if someone finds out you are at the cottage? George and I will be found out and the plan will fail."

He sighed. She was correct. He nodded agreement and followed. He rode in silence. For hours the movement of the horse sent pain through his side. He put an arm over his stomach and leaned into the pain, as it was the best way to stop an ache.

After hours of riding, he witnessed the marriage of Olivia and Folly in a blacksmith's shop. They stood behind an anvil and were united by the priest through a handfasting. Phillip paid the man as soon as the hammer hit the anvil. He paid for a meal and two rooms at the local inn and waited while Folly and Olivia sealed their marriage. Phillip thought about eating but decided he'd be sick if he did. Instead he drank a bit of water and slept while he waited.

The scandal to ensue would be delightful to watch, he thought, as they rode back to Wentworth Hall. Olivia and Folly were married, and he was now a free man. They just had to inform their parents of their actions.

"Everything will work the way it should," Olivia said as he helped her dismount in the barn. Folly was hiding back at the cottage.

"I don't know how we are supposed to tell our parents," he said as he led both horses to their stalls.

"We will tell them tomorrow during the morning meal. As long as we stick together, all will be fine. We both did this. We are both to blame for the ending of the engagement." Olivia spoke the words, but her face showed her fear.

When he joined the dinner party, Phillip wished he'd stayed in his bedchamber to rest. The trip to Gretna Green took too much out of him. He'd never had pain from a beating last for more than a day or two. He walked toward Emma to speak with her and stopped when he saw the look on her face. He inched closer, wondering what she was thinking.

Emma didn't look angry. If he could put a word to the glare she gave him, it would be disgust. Phillip had to find out what the problem was. He decided to talk to her about the library.

"Have you had a chance to visit the libraries here?"

Emma scowled, "No."

"Have I done something to make you upset with me?"

"Yes."

"Will you tell me what I've done?"

Emma looked uncomfortable. She blushed and he experienced joy at seeing her cheeks turn pink.

"Why are you smiling?"

"I haven't seen you blush like this since we were at Springhill Abby."

"Don't speak about it."

He stopped smiling as he realized she was furious with him.

"Tell me what I've done to make you angry."

"I saw you and Lady Olivia in the east wing this morning." She whispered to not be overheard.

"You saw a conversation, Emma. We needed a place where we wouldn't be overheard."

"I don't want to hear your reasons. You'll be married to her this week. Whatever you did or didn't do will be covered up once you are married." She turned from him. "I do not think I ever loved you."

Phillip saw hatred in her eyes. Or at least he thought it was hatred. Her green eyes flared in the candlelight. He knew it would be a matter of hours before she understood. At least he hoped she would understand when morning came and all was revealed. But hearing her denial of loving him hurt. He knew she didn't mean it, but feeling as ill as he did, it was hard not to internalize her words.

Phillip went to his bedchamber after speaking with Emma. He couldn't bring himself to stay in the drawing room with her looking at him with so much hatred. When Thomas came by to help him undress for the night, he accepted the water Thomas brought and then sent him away. Phillip drank the water, hoping it would calm his stomach. He was nervous. Instead of receiving a calming effect, Phillip found himself bent over the chamber pot. When he finished vomiting, he slipped from his room and made his way to the west exit. Folly met him there.

Phillip led Folly up to the second floor and tapped on Olivia's door. Folly slipped into the room, and Phillip turned to leave. He saw movement from the corner of his eye and cringed as he saw he'd waken Emma, whose room happened to be next to Olivia's. He wanted to explain to her, but she scowled at him and went back in before he could speak.

When Phillip entered the dining room the following morning, he stumbled in the doorway. He was tired. *I need to sleep more,* he thought. He tortured himself by gazing at Emma to see her snub him. She didn't spare a glance in his direction. It would take time, but he would mend the parts of their relationship he had broken.

He sat at the table and allowed Thomas to bring his plate. He had taken one bite of the ill-tasting eggs when Olivia's maid came running into the dining room. "Your Grace," she shouted to Norland and his wife, "my lady, Olivia. It's . . . it's . . . terrible."

Phillip attempted to keep a straight face. Folly promised he'd leave by the side door before morning so Phillip and Olivia could explain her elopement to Norland. From the bumbling lady's maid, he realized everything hadn't gone as planned.

"What are you going on about, girl?" Norland yelled.

"My lady has . . . has . . . " The poor girl couldn't get the words out as her face turned scarlet. Olivia burst into the room followed by Lord Folly.

Phillip noticed the panicked look she sent his way. He knew he had to play his part well no matter how sick he was feeling.

"What is *he* doing here?" Norland shouted flying out of his chair.

Phillip didn't dare look at Emma. He didn't want to hope she'd give him anything but a glare.

"Father—"

Phillip stood with great effort. His stomach was in knots. "Your Grace," he said, looking at Norland, "yesterday afternoon, Olivia and I met Lord Folly by the crossroads and they were married in Gretna Green. As you can see from the situation this morning, they not only participated in a handfasting, but they consummated their marriage."

Norland looked at Phillip. "What is your part in this?"

Phillip reached into his pocket and extracted the marriage certificate. "I paid the anvil priest, I paid for an afternoon lodging in Gretna Green, and I witnessed their union."

Norland snatched the license from his hand. Phillip was elated as he heard Norland's muffled reading of the form.

Norland turned on Phillip. "You've ruined my daughter!"

"No, Father," Olivia said, entering further into the dining room. "I ruined myself by going to Gretna Green. I was part of the plan. If you want to put blame somewhere, put it on yourself and Ashby."

Norland spluttered unintelligible words as he stood in shock.

Ashby burst into laughter as Phillip knew he would. "I win, Norland. I win! Get ready to hand over everything."

Phillip knew Ashby would lose his temper, but he put a finger up to finish the rest of the speech. "Olivia and I realized last week if we stopped working against each other and started working together we could outwit Norland and Ashby. Neither of you win. Norland keeps his wealth, and Ashby keeps his."

Ashby glared at him. "What do you mean, boy?"

Phillip prepared himself for his father's reaction. He steadied himself as he waited for the blow. When it didn't come, he continued, "Olivia and Folly came up with the idea to run away. I never would've suggested it due to the fragility of reputations. But I financed the entire endeavor. Instead of agreeing to let them run off to the States or the continent, I convinced them to accept responsibility and come back here after the elopement. Folly and Olivia can live off her dowry, and I have agreed to help them if necessary."

Ashby stood at the head of the table, seething. Phillip hadn't ever seen his father brought to this much anger. He had a moment where he feared strangulation, but the moment passed as Ashby looked around the room. Phillip was thankful he chose to give the information in front of the group with people other than his family.

"You and Olivia planned this together?" Ashby asked, his voice shaking with rage.

"Olivia and I realized if we were still fighting, no one would believe we wanted to get to know each other. Fighting was clouding our judgment. So, we agreed to reconcile for the short term. You and Norland focused on other matters of business and quit worrying about losing the bet.

"We planned during dinners, in the drawing room, and while we danced at Almack's. It happened in front of your faces." Phillip took a deep breath and continued, "I know you are angry with me right now. And I don't blame you. But I would ask next time you plan to gamble away your wealth, please leave me out of the bet. Also, for the sake of my mother, please use more discretion."

Phillip didn't feel conceited. He didn't speak with condescension. He spoke the facts and waited for Ashby's response. He guessed his father was holding back his hand due to the guests in their home.

Norland turned to his wife. "I'll kill them both for ruining my daughter."

"Calm down, Father," Olivia said as she kept her distance from her father's reach. "I never had any intention of marrying Arundel. My plan was to marry George. You were too stubborn to listen to me."

Phillip looked to his father. "I'm ready for my punishment whenever you're ready." If he were honest with himself, he wasn't ready for the punishment, but he thought he would give Ashby something to think about before he strangled him.

Ashby seethed in silent anger. "You've made it so I cannot collect my winnings."

"Neither of you win, Father."

"As of right now, you are no longer my heir," Ashby spat as he ran a hand through his hair.

Phillip thought about staying silent, but he decided to throw the anger back. "If I had known this was all I had to do to be disinherited, I would have accompanied Folly and Olivia to Gretna Green last spring. It would have been preferable to being shot, dragged down a hill, and thrown in a river to die."

"Ashby." Phillip turned to his mother. She'd never stood between them during a fight. This was a new side of her. "Do not say something you will regret."

"I have no regret in naming Edward as my heir."

Phillip raised his eyebrows and patted Edward on the back. "Good luck! The burden of being Ashby's heir is one I wouldn't wish on anyone."

"Arundel!" Ashby yelled as he walked from the room.

Phillip turned around with a smile. He was far too amused to let his father off on disinheriting him. He'd wished for those words since he'd come to the understanding of what it meant to be Ashby's heir. "He's talking to you, Edward."

"You bloody well know I'm not speaking to him." Ashby's face was bright red with anger. Phillip knew they hadn't seen the explosion yet.

Phillip closed his eyes against the pain in his stomach. "I think we've said everything there is to say, Father."

The room spun as he made his exit. Phillip woke on the ground. He didn't know if he'd tripped or passed out, but when he tried to sit up the room was spinning. He lay back down and closed his eyes.

"Hodgens," Ashby said a little too close to Phillip for comfort. He flinched as he heard Ashby's voice. "Send for Doctor Bell."

"Can you sit up?" Edward asked.

Phillip wanted to shake his head, but he couldn't without nausea threatening to come up with the movement. "I'm too dizzy."

"When was the last time you ate a full meal?"

Phillip rolled to his side and pulled himself onto his hands and knees. "Will you help me to my bedchamber?"

He was surprised when Ashby pulled him up. "We will talk later, Arundel."

Phillip let out a careful breath, trying not to vomit. Instead his legs went out from under him, and his father caught him as he again passed out.

Thirty-five

THE HOUSE WAS FULL OF guests for the wedding, yet it was eerily quiet as people spoke in whispers. Edward couldn't go anywhere in the house without looks of sympathy following him in each room. As he searched for Anne, he thought about the previous days. Phillip had collapsed during the morning meal three days earlier. Since then, Edward hadn't found a moment free of worry. He spent most of his time standing or sitting in Phillip's room, waiting for his brother to wake.

"Edward," Anne said as he entered, "has the doctor given a diagnosis?"

He let out a sigh of frustration. "Phillip hasn't regained consciousness. He's hidden a severe loss of weight, and his valet isn't much help. Thomas claims there hasn't been any signs of illness. He has turned into the worst servant we have."

"You should stay calm," Anne said in an effort to comfort him.

Edward nodded. Her calming influence was why he'd searched her out. "I came to ask you if we could postpone the wedding a few days. At least until he wakes up?"

Anne looked sad, but she agreed without hesitation. "It doesn't seem right to marry without Phillip present."

"Thank you. I am sorry to ask. I'll let the guests know. I don't think anyone will be surprised."

He'd sat next to her for a short minute when Charles entered. "Constable Adams is here."

"Perfect!" he drawled voice dripping with sarcasm.

"Why is the constable here?" Anne asked, taking hold of his hand in a protective grip.

"He requested everyone who was in the dining room when Phillip collapsed to be in attendance." Charles looked meaningfully around the room. "We are gathering in the library. Mother refuses to go far from his bedchamber."

Anne held tightly to his arm as they walked. He appreciated her protectiveness. He wasn't going to allow Adams to accuse him of injuring his brother again. Phillip was ill. There was no reason for the constable to put his ore in.

For the first time since he'd found the Parkers, he noticed Emma. She looked as though she hadn't slept and had been in tears. He thought about speaking to her but couldn't find the words.

"Please, everyone be seated," Constable Adams said as they entered the library. Edward looked at the piano in the corner and turned from it. He thought about telling Adams he wasn't to give orders at Wentworth Hall, but he didn't when he saw Ashby already seated.

"Constable," Doctor Bell said with concern, "I have a patient to care for. Please make this quick."

"Don't worry, Doctor. I believe my investigation will help your patient." Adams walked around the room, looking at each person in turn. He looked in the eyes of each servant and then every other person. He stopped in front of Olivia and Folly and looked at them for a long moment before moving forward. When he reached Edward, although shorter than him, the constable glared up into Edward's face in an intimidating, expressionless stare.

"Do you have something to say, Constable?"

"Yes, I do." Adams turned to face the group of people he'd gathered. "The person responsible for Lord Arundel's condition is in this room. No one is leaving until a confession is made."

"If you are referring to Edward," Ashby said in a bored tone, "you are looking in the wrong direction."

"I'm not referring to Lord Edward. I owe him an apology." Adams waited for the talking to subside and then held out two photographs. "I have a likeness of Lord Arundel and Lord Edward. I would like each of you to mark on a sheet of paper who the likeness titled A is and who B is."

As Edward looked at the photos, he remembered the words the constable in London said after the accident on the bridge. He made the observation of not being able to see a difference between the twins. Edward smiled as he looked at both photographs. They were both of him. Neither one was his brother.

Adams collected the answers and read through each. "Miss Emma, how were you able to see both likenesses were Lord Edward?"

"What purpose does it serve to ask Emma this question? Our family was not acquainted with the Watsons before I brought Lord Arundel home." Lord Anthony stood in front of Emma in a protective stance. "She is not responsible for the attempts on his life."

"I apologize, Lord Anthony. You have a valid point." Adams searched through the papers and landed on another one with the correct answer. "Thomas, please tell me how you knew neither likeness was Lord Arundel."

"I am Lord Arundel's valet. It makes sense I should see a difference in them."

"No more than Lord Edward's valet, yet David answered incorrect. So, tell me how you knew the answer."

Thomas looked smug as he replied, "Phillip carries the burden of being Ashby's heir on his shoulders. Edward's posture is not impeded."

"Thomas, you are the only one outside the family who knew Lord Arundel before the first attempt on his life who can tell him apart from Lord Edward from a distance. Why do you want him dead?"

It took a moment for the words to register among everyone in the room, but once understanding dawned it took everything Edward had not to strangle the man. As if she knew what he was thinking, Anne held tightly to his arm. She would be a force for good in his life. She would be the reason he didn't turn into Ashby.

"I don't want him dead." Thomas spoke as though the attempts on Phillip's life hadn't happened. "I want to take my rightful place as heir, and I cannot take my place if it is filled with my younger brother."

"What the deuce?" Edward tried to pull away from Anne, but she held tight keeping him from reacting with a temper. "Brother?"

"Tell them, Father!" Thomas said, looking to Ashby for validation. "Tell them how you took advantage of my mother, who worked here at Wentworth Hall as a scullery maid, and when you found out she was carrying your child you gave her money and sent her away."

"You and I will speak in private about this," Ashby said, folding his arms to show he wasn't open to the discussion.

Edward looked between his father and Thomas. If he were honest with himself, there was a resemblance between them, but it couldn't be true. "I don't think this is a conversation for closed doors, Father."

"I agree. I want to know if Thomas is telling the truth," Charles said, pushing his way over to Edward as though standing next to him was a way to team up against Ashby.

Before Ashby could respond, the nurse attending Phillip entered the room and cleared her throat. "Doctor, I need to speak with you."

Edward turned back to Ashby as though nothing else mattered. "What is the truth? Is Thomas our brother?"

"Yes, I'm your brother, and I deserve an inheritance. I am the eldest. I am the Earl of Arundel."

"Phillip is the earl," Charles said. Edward put his arm out to stop Charles from attacking Thomas. It wouldn't help anyone for a fight to start.

Edward looked to their father for the truth. Ashby didn't hesitate with punishing Thomas. He walked forward, hands fisted, and hit Thomas in the jaw.

"Well, I suppose we should start our relationship with abuse. It seems to be the way you demonstrate your feelings for Phillip," Thomas said as he rubbed his chin.

"What do you want from me, boy?"

"I want an apology and an inheritance. My mother begged you to make me your ward. You didn't have to reveal parentage, but instead you made me a servant."

"I didn't have to take you in. I could have thrown you out of my house. I gave you a place to live and a way to earn your way in life. I didn't have to train you as a valet. I could have put you in the barn."

"I am your son! You should have cared for me."

Ignoring this last statement, Ashby continued, "As for the inheritance you are requesting, let me give you a bit of the education you would have received at Oxford had I seen fit to send you there. You are baseborn. Illegitimate. By law, you don't inherit anything."

"Please allow me to interrupt," Doctor Bell said as he reentered the room. With a compassionate tone the doctor finished, "Lord Arundel is no longer with us."

A numbness covered Edward's brain as he processed the words. Just moments before he'd thought finding out he had an illegitimate brother would be the worst to happen. He wasn't certain if he was breathing, but he knew he wasn't the only one sobbing. Edward clung onto Anne as he tried to process the loss.

"I am now Lord Arundel," Thomas said without shame or guilt. "If you choose to name Edward your heir, he'll meet the same end."

"Do not threaten me!" Ashby said with a tight yet controlled anger.

"Thomas," Doctor Bell continued, "will you please tell me what you gave him? From what I saw it was ingested."

Thomas laughed. Edward looked up to see the pleasure in his cold, dark eyes. "I wish I could have told him what I used. He would have appreciated it. But I'll let you know for Miss Emma's pleasure. I wasted time chasing him through the woods. Shooting a moving target was a mistake. Pushing him in front of a moving carriage was easier, but still messy. I was desperate when I tried to kill him at Almack's. I thought about killing him the night Charles offered for Emma, but I enjoyed his pain too much to put him out of misery. No, this was the best course of action. If I'd done it this way last spring, I'd be heir and have a valet now."

Edward looked to Emma, who was crying into her mother's arms. She wasn't listening to anything Thomas said.

"I spent too much time listening to Phillip plan how he was going to ask for Emma's hand in marriage. So, I took a page out of his book. I decided to use the same method to get him out of my way."

Emma's head came up. Edward was certain she hadn't been listening. He was surprised when she spoke. "What do you mean by using the same method?"

"Shakespeare!" Thomas smirked. "Do you know what poison Shakespeare intended in *Romeo and Juliet*?"

Emma shook her head. "Phillip wouldn't have given me poison."

"No, you stupid chit! I won't tell you what he had planned. It'd be wasted on you."

Doctor Bell interrupted Emma's reply. "What poison did you use?"

"Atropa belladonna. I started giving it to him a month ago." Thomas was speaking as though he couldn't stop. He wanted everyone to know of his brilliance. "I'd put a drop or two in his food and drink. At first, he was just tired. But when I increased the dose, the symptoms increased: hallucinations, stomach pain, vomiting."

"Thank you," Doctor Bell said as he moved toward the door. "Ashby, I'll need you to send a runner to the apothecary. Arundel will need the antidote if he is to recover."

"What?" Edward asked, pulling out of his numb sorrow.

"I am sorry to have caused you all so much distress. It wouldn't have worked so well if the reaction wasn't genuine. Lord Arundel lives."

"Constable," Ashby said as he glared at Thomas, "you have a job to do as well."

"Father," Thomas said in distress, "you wouldn't allow me to be put in jail or the workhouse? Think about what society will say!"

"Do not call me Father. I do not claim you. As far as society is concerned, they'll see a whelp claiming parentage without any proof."

"I have proof! My mother's diary tells everything."

"The writings of a spurned scullery maid."

Edward left the room, ignoring Thomas's plight. He didn't think the man deserved compassion. He wanted to spend his time with Phillip. He vowed to stay by Phillip's side until he woke.

By late morning the doctor administered the antidote. Edward kept vigil, along with Emma and his family. It was hard not to be worried, as Phillip was pale, thin, and lifeless. He hadn't moved since he'd collapsed in the dining room.

"All of you need to give him time to recover," Ashby said as he entered the room. "The nurse is here to attend him. Edward, you and Anne need to consider your nuptials. We have a house full of people waiting for the ceremony."

"I would like to wait for Phillip to be in attendance. Perhaps he and Emma could join Anne and I." He smiled over at Emma. "I happen to know what he had planned for a proposal. I'd help him with it once he recovers. I'm glad Thomas didn't divulge the plan."

"We still have the mess with Norland to consider, and Arundel's recovery will be a while yet."

"What's to consider? Olivia and Folly are married."

"No need to worry about it."

As Ashby left, Edward looked back to Emma. "Phillip isn't going to give up. He's going to fight Ashby until he wins."

Thirty-six

With fresh water and the lack of poison in his food, Phillip improved. His eyes were a bit blurry, making it so he couldn't read as he wanted. The poison also caused his limbs to go stiff. His fingers didn't work as well as they once did, which deprived him of the piano. The final three passions he had in life—literature, education, and music—were taken from him by a half-brother.

Once it was determined he would live, life went back to normal at Wentworth Hall. Phillip had been left out of the conversations regarding Thomas. Every time he asked, he was told not to worry. The Parkers and all of the other guests left, which made it so the house was quiet for his recovery.

Needing a diversion, Phillip sat in the library at the piano, trying to play. He exercised his fingers each day, but they were stiff and the music wouldn't flow as it once did. Phillip found himself pounding on the keys in frustration more often than not.

"The music sounds off," Edward said, walking into the room.

"My fingers are still too stiff to play right," Phillip responded in frustration.

He could see Edward didn't know what to say, so he turned back to the piano and then turned to the window. His family understood his frustrations and tried to help him with the exercises he was given. Edward took one of his hands and started moving the fingers for him. He massaged one hand, then the other.

"Your fingers will start working again. Doctor Bell said your eyesight will clear as well . . . over time. You must get more rest. If Mother finds you in here, she'll drag you back herself."

"I thought a diversion from my bedchamber would be nice," Phillip said, allowing Edward to pull him to his feet.

"Who did you convince to help you out here?"

"Hodgens. He brought my afternoon tea, and I convinced him to let me eat in here."

"I think the staff will do anything for you right now, even if it defies Mother and Ashby."

Phillip smiled as his brother walked with him into the hall. He had to lean on others for assistance and he moved slowly, but he was standing and walking. He refused to use the wheelchair the doctor provided. He was worried if he stopped trying to walk his legs would stiffen and never work again.

"I know I shouldn't take advantage of their concern for my well-being, but when I can convince someone to help, I will," he said without guile.

Edward helped him back into bed. "It won't be long until you will be able to walk without help. Until then, you need to be patient."

Phillip decided to agree instead of argue. On top of being supportive, his family was also nurturing him too much. "Edward, tell me what's going on with Thomas."

"You shouldn't worry about him."

"Yet I'm worried. He's our brother."

"Half-brother."

"Edward, what does Ashby have planned for him?"

Edward looked down. "Ashby put him on a ship to Barbados."

"I guess it's better than the workhouse."

"You shouldn't worry about it. You need to rest."

Phillip nodded. He wanted solitude. It was strange. When he was alone, he wanted company. When he was with others, he wanted seclusion. "I'll rest now," he said in response.

Edward gave him a look to let him know he didn't believe a word of it, but he left anyway. As soon as he was gone, Phillip pulled himself out of bed and used the table to stand. Over the past week, he had spent time trying to get his body working again. Since his family was worried about over exertion, when they weren't around, he would use the tables, bed, and walls to hold himself up as he exercised around his room.

He made it to the window and sat in the overstuffed chair. Although his vision was blurred, he looked out the window to see the trees. During his recovery the grounds around Wentworth Hall had moved from a frozen scene to lush green vegetation.

He was ready to go back to the bed when he heard a carriage driving up to the house. He changed directions and found his way over to the bell cord. He waited a few minutes before Mrs. Fraser, the housekeeper, rushed into his bedchamber.

"My lord, do you need help?" she asked.

"Who does the carriage belong to?" he asked, pointing out the window.

"The Duke and Duchess of Norland have arrived from London," she responded as she took hold of his arm. "You need rest, my lord. Let me help you back to your bed."

He nodded and allowed her to guide him. "Do you know why they are here?" he asked. Last he'd heard, Olivia still evaded her parents.

"I was told His Grace—your father—summoned them."

"Do you know why?" It was a well-known fact the serving staff was more knowledgeable about the comings and goings of the families they served than the family themselves.

"I'm unaware of the reason, Lord Arundel." She pulled the blankets over him and poured a glass of water. "I do know His Grace doesn't want you to worry about the visit. He doesn't want you to stress."

Phillip drank the water and handed the glass back to her. "Do you know what Mrs. Brooger has prepared for dinner tonight?"

Mrs. Fraser's face broke into a large grin. "It's wonderful to hear you have your appetite back. I believe she's prepared venison, potatoes, and vegetables, but for dessert she has made you a berry pie."

"She knows how to get me to eat," he said with a smile.

"My dear boy, she's trying to fatten you up." She again straightened his blankets. "Now, get some rest so you can mend."

Phillip wanted to rest, but his mind filtered through possibilities for the visit. He wanted to know what Norland was doing at Wentworth Hall. Phillip pulled himself out of bed and found his way to the drawing room. He stopped every few feet to rest, especially during the descent on the stairs. He could hear the conversation as he neared the room.

"Olivia and Folly are settled with his family in Bath," Norland informed whoever was in the room.

When Phillip entered, Edward stood and rushed to him. "What are you doing?"

"This sounds like a conversation I should be a part of," he said, putting his arm around his brother and leaning against him for support.

"Don't worry yourself, Arundel," Ashby said, walking over to help him instead of allowing Edward.

"You didn't tell us he was still ill." Norland gave him an uncomfortable look.

Phillip raised his eyebrows. His family told him he looked better each day. They must be flattering him.

"I can't believe you made it down here on your own." Edward pointed to a spot on the couch.

Phillip waited until he was sitting before he asked, "Is Olivia well?"

Norland looked angry. He schooled his tone before speaking. "She's happy and increasing."

"I'm happy for Lord and Lady Folly," Phillip said, using the titles to remind Norland his daughter was married and no longer available to hold him to an engagement.

"Olivia is married, so Phillip should be free to marry as he wishes," Anne said from across the room. She was sitting next to Charlotte and Marianne, working on needlepoint. This was the first time Phillip had been in one of the main rooms since he'd been ill. He thought all the Parkers had left.

Ashby nodded. "Norland, we can discuss the gamble in my den."

Edward pulled Phillip to his feet to take him back to his bed-chamber. As they slowly walked, Phillip asked, "Ashby's patience with me has been exceedingly lax while I've healed. It is out of character for him."

Edward nodded as though he were trying to find a way to respond. As they started up the stairs, he spoke. "Nearly losing his heir has caused great reflection in our father. I do not know if it will last, but for now, he is learning to control his temper."

"I have always wondered why he chose to hurt me." It was a statement he'd never dared speak out loud for fear of his father overhearing and using it to an advantage.

"Generations of abuse passed down by Grandfather Ashby," Edward said with a sideways glance in his direction.

Phillip wasn't sure he'd escaped the anger of his father, but for now, he'd be thankful to heal without the added stress.

As they neared his bedchamber, Phillip asked, "Edward, did you and Anne marry?"

He hadn't thought about the wedding during his illness. His heart fell as Edward responded, "We were married in December. It's been three months."

"Why didn't you tell me?" One of the biggest issues Phillip had was a mixed-up perception of the time while he was poisoned. He remembered hallucinations and the pain, but he didn't remember much about his actions during the time.

"You were too ill." Edward left the statement there. He didn't elaborate.

"Are you happy?"

"Yes. Anne is a wonderful woman. I will always be thankful I met her."

Phillip nodded. "How is . . . Emma?"

Edward smiled as he helped Phillip into bed. "She's well. She asks about you in every letter she writes."

"Do you think she'll forgive me for the anguish I caused her?"

"Stop blaming yourself. She knows you didn't have a choice."

Phillip continued to think about Emma long after Edward left. He hoped they could fix the relationship. He was still in love with her.

Thirty-seven

EDWARD WATCHED HIS BROTHER AS he walked into the parlor. Phillip no longer needed physical assistance. After months of recovery, he was walking by himself, but the family still found the need to keep a close watch on him in case his legs gave out. The doctor wanted him to use a cane, but Phillip refused to use one just as he had refused the wheelchair.

"Phillip, darling, sit next to me," their mother said, patting a spot on the couch. He obliged her. Edward moved to sit next to Anne while they listened to Marianne on the piano.

"Marianne, why don't you allow Phillip to play for us this evening?" their mother commented, patting his leg to get him to move to the piano.

"Mother, I would prefer to listen to Marianne tonight," Phillip responded. Edward knew Phillip was nervous about playing because he hadn't played for their family since they were in London.

"Nonsense," she said, refusing to take no for an answer. "The best way to recover is to start performing daily tasks you once had joy in." As a side note she added, "Except riding! I don't want you on a horse for at least another month."

"If we keep waiting, it will be a full year before you allow me to do anything outside. My hair is darker than it's ever been," Phillip said to their mother.

Edward waited for her to argue but was surprised to see Phillip had moved to the piano. Edward put his arm around Anne as he listened to his brother play. The piano sounded as it always did when Phillip played. He ran his hands over the keys with a fluid movement. The music evoked feelings of warmth and love. Edward had a sudden realization life would, over time, go back to normal.

"Mother," Marianne said as Phillip finished playing the piece. "Are we going to London this season?"

It was hard to believe the season started in less than a month.

"Yes, we are, although I want Phillip to wait until the spring session of Parliament before he travels."

Edward was surprised when Phillip argued, "I'd prefer not to go to London this season."

Emma was expecting Phillip to be in London. Edward exchanged a look with Anne before asking, "Is there a reason you want to stay sequestered at Wentworth Hall?"

"I think I caused enough scandal last year. It's best I stay out of the spotlight for a while." Phillip moved from the piano. "I can find diversions here to keep me entertained while you prance around London."

"Prance!" Marianne said with a laugh. "I don't believe I know how to. Will you please demonstrate?"

Phillip sat next to their youngest sister and pulled on her locks of curls to tease her.

"No one will remember the scandals of last season. Miss Prim is the newest scandal to hit the *ton*. Everyone is talking about her," Marianne said as an aside.

Edward thought about mentioning Emma but decided to wait until they were alone so the entire family didn't weigh in on the subject. He was ready to change the conversation when Charlotte spoke. She didn't have the same reservations Edward did.

"What about Emma?"

Phillip didn't flinch. Edward was certain he expected the question. "She'll be better off without me."

"How can you think such a thing?" Anne asked in defense of her sister.

Phillip pulled a paper out of his pocket. "This is why she would be better off. I have caused her too much pain."

Anne rushed across the room and snatched the paper from his hands. She swatted Phillip on the shoulder. "You don't understand women, do you?" She turned and walked back to Edward. "Why am I surprised? He's your brother. Of course he doesn't understand women."

Edward laughed, amused as he watched his wife. "Emma is in love with you, Phillip. She doesn't care about the gossip of society. Why don't you send her a letter?"

Edward shook his head as Phillip grumbled. "We aren't engaged. It'd be another scandal for me to write to her."

"This news clipping is old. It's from last year. No one will remember the fake marriage."

"Anne, have you forgotten about it?" Phillip asked.

"Of course, I haven't. She's my sister. But Marianne is correct. Miss Prim has caused much more of a scandal than you and Emma."

"So, you think I should write to your sister as well?"

Anne's voice took on a tone of intrigue. "Far too forward, Lord Arundel."

Phillip shook his head. With a jest he said, "Thank you, my lady."

Edward wrapped his arms again around his wife and listened as Charlotte took a spot at the piano and played for them. He was content. "I am thankful I don't have to worry about the marriage market any longer."

Anne smiled as she turned to him. "Wait until we have daughters, my lord."

Thirty-eight

As her family arrived at Almack's Assembly Hall for the first ball of the season, Emma had a sense of dread when she saw Edward and Anne across the room, with everyone in Edward's family except Phillip. She'd told herself many times over the course of the previous year to fall out of love with Phillip, but the problem was she couldn't. She was more in love with him this season than she was the last. But did he love her? He hadn't made any attempt to contact her since he'd healed.

Phillip had been very ill. She'd known he'd almost died from the poison. But Anne had told her he would be able to reenter society. She wanted him to fight for her. She wanted him to declare his undying love for her, similar to what all of her beloved characters from Shakespeare's works would do. Romeo stood outside Juliet's window and called up to his love to show how devoted he was. *Am I expecting too much?* she wondered as she scanned the rest of the room to see if Phillip was in attendance.

Every time she thought about *Romeo and Juliet*, she thought about the poison and how Phillip could have died. She still hadn't reconciled the fear she'd had when she realized he might never wake. It took days for him to open his eyes after the final dose of poison. Emma turned as someone touched her arm.

"Miss Parker." Disappointment plagued her as Mr. Bennett stood before her. She had danced with him many times the previous season and was surprised he approached now. "Will you join me for the quadrille?"

"I'd be delighted."

Emma took his arm and allowed him to lead her to the floor. She was stiff and graceless as she danced with Mr. Bennett. He wasn't his usual charming self, which added to the displeasure she had with the dance.

"Mr. Bennett?" she asked as he joined hands with her. "Is there a reason you look uncomfortable?"

"I'm sorry, Miss Parker. You don't deserve my rudeness. I've just had a disappointing conversation and I am letting it seep into our dance. Please forgive me."

"It isn't a problem." They separated and then came back together through the steps of the dance. "Will you allow me to help you with the disappointment?"

"No . . . no . . . it isn't something a woman should need to worry about."

She didn't speak again, waiting for Mr. Bennett to start a conversation. He stayed silent through the rest of the dance and led her back to the side of the room. "It's been a pleasure." He bowed before walking away from her.

What a strange encounter with Mr. Bennett, Emma thought as she looked around the room. She noticed Marianne and Charlotte walking out to the floor with partners, and a pang of longing accompanied her thoughts. She wanted to see Phillip.

"Penny for your thoughts?" Lieutenant Brady said as he approached.

Emma thought for a moment, trying to think of an excuse for staring off into the crowd. "I was admiring the number of new styles this season." She gave a sigh of relief when Brady accepted her excuse. "How is your family, Lieutenant Brady?"

"Very well. Thank you for your kind inquiry." He smiled as though she were the only woman in the room. "Would you do me the favor of dancing with me?"

Emma smiled her agreement and allowed him to lead her to the floor. She plastered a smile on her face as they danced. She had to keep reminding herself to listen as he spoke.

"Have you tried Parmesan ice cream?"

"No, sir, I must admit I haven't had the pleasure."

Emma looked over at Anne as Brady turned her in the dance. Phillip was still absent.

"I'd love to take you to an icehouse. Are you available tomorrow?"

Emma looked at him and gave a kind smile. "Thank you, Lieutenant."

"I'd appreciate it if we could move past the words *lieutenant* and *miss*. How do you feel about calling me David?"

Emma was taken by surprise and missed a step. She wanted to tell him no, because the only man she wanted to give permission to was Phillip, but he wasn't there. She worried she would have to settle for a marriage of convenience or stick with the goal of being a spinster, because she would never love another as she loved Phillip.

"I don't think it would be appropriate, Lieutenant. We have recently met."

Lieutenant Brady guided her from the floor as the dance ended and stood next to her longer than necessary. He brought her a glass of punch and stood off to the side as she danced with Mr. Cox. Unfortunately, when Mr. Cox took her back to her place, Brady was waiting for her.

Lieutenant David Brady was a nice man, but he was a bit of a bore. "Emma, have you ever been on a Navy ship?"

"No, I have not."

"I suppose it wouldn't be a normal past time for a lady."

"What did you want to tell me about the ship?" Emma continued to scan the room, hoping she would find Phillip at some point.

"When I was first stationed on the ship . . . " Emma stopped listening. She nodded when he paused. She looked amused when he laughed. She held back tears when she realized the night was nearing its end and she'd spent the majority of the evening listening to Lieutenant David Brady talk about his first year in the Navy.

"Is something wrong?"

"Hmm?"

"Are you unwell?"

"I'm sorry, Lieutenant. I—" Emma was saved the need for an excuse when Phillip approached.

"Miss Emma, I believe you are saving the waltz for me."

"Lord Arundel, Emma and I were just about to go back out on the dance floor," Lieutenant Brady said, putting his arm out for her.

Phillip hadn't asked her, but there wasn't a single man in the room she'd prefer to dance with. "I'm sorry, Lieutenant, but Lord Arundel asked first." It wasn't a lie, although her statement implied they had a prearrangement.

"I'll be waiting here when the dance is over," Brady said. Emma was certain his statement was more for Arundel's benefit than hers.

Phillip smiled as he led her to the dance floor. "It's fortunate I asked you for a dance before the lieutenant."

"He asked because you approached. He was more focused on talking than dancing."

"Tell me, Miss Emma, how is the Navy supposed to survive while the lieutenant searches for a wife?"

Emma laughed at his jest. "They'll cry from boredom, since he is their entertainment."

Before he put his hand on her, he leaned forward and asked, "Is it appropriate and do I have your permission to touch your shoulder blade?"

She swatted him on the arm playfully. "Just make certain you keep your hands in their proper places." She was blushing and found happiness as she looked into his eyes. His eyes never wavered from hers during the dance, which caused her face to turn even redder.

Phillip led her through the room as though she were the only one there. A flutter of excitement brightened her evening. By the time the dance was finished, she needed to leave the heat of the ballroom.

"Will you walk with me on the patio?" he asked as he pulled her out of the middle of the room.

"Yes." Her voice squeaked, betraying her nervousness to him.

"Miss Parker," he started. "I would like to start over and allow us to get to know one another."

"I don't think it would be good to start over."

He nodded. "I understand . . . If you prefer me to stay away, please don't hesitate to say so."

"I don't like you calling Miss Parker, Phillip. I want to continue from where we ended at Springhill Abby."

He took her hand in his and squeezed it.

Although exhausted from the dance at Almack's, Emma took herself down to the dining room to eat a little breakfast. She smiled to herself as she thought about the waltz and how Phillip held her.

She buttered her toast while imagining his face and eyes.

"What are you doing here?" Emma asked as Anne and Edward entered the dining room.

"We wanted to visit," Anne said with a smile. "We've missed the family."

"Miss Emma," the butler said, walking into the room with a silver plate.

Emma looked over to see a card. It was normal to receive flowers the morning after a party where she danced with any number of men. She picked the card up, opened it, and read:

> Thank you for the lovely dance.
> —Mr. Christian Bennett

The flowers were the same as he always sent—pink roses.

What is he talking about? Emma wondered. He was distracted the entire time.

"Who could those be from?" Anne asked as though she already knew.

"Mr. Bennett," she replied, trying to sound happy.

She handed the card to her sister and started eating her toast. Christian Bennett sent her flowers every time he danced with her. She knew it was a sore spot with her sister due to his courting of Anne during a previous season, but she was now married to Lord Edward and received flowers on a daily basis. As if the butler heard her thoughts, he walked into the room with a dozen red roses and took them to Anne.

"Edward, you don't understand the purpose of sending flowers," Henry said as he sat at the table with his meal.

"What are you saying?" Anne asked, admiring her flowers.

"Once you have the girl and you are married, you don't have to try so hard," Richard added.

"You are jealous," Anne said, admiring her flowers. "If either one of you puts wild ideas in Edward's head, you'll have to accept my wrath."

The butler again walked into the room with another vase of flowers, this time white daisies. He put them on the table in front of Emma, and she took the card from the plate.

"Are they from Phillip?" Anne asked. "Daisies would be his style."

"No." She could not help the disappointment from entering her voice. She handed the card to her sister.

Dear Miss E. Parker,

Thank you for the time you spent with me last evening. I will call this morning to take you to the icehouse.

Sincerely,
Lieutenant David Brady.

Anne put the card on the table, "There is still time."

"Are you going for ices with him?" Richard asked, picking up the card and looking at it with interest.

"I accepted last night when he asked. If Phillip sees me with the lieutenant, perhaps he will send me flowers and not behave as my brothers toward women." She grabbed the card from Richard's hand.

"What are you referring to?" Richard asked.

"You both go to these parties and dance with all the women you can and never send flowers to them. Are either of you ever planning to get married?"

The butler walked into the dining room again. Emma smiled as he brought another card to her. "Where are the flowers?" she asked as she took the card.

"They're in the morning room, miss."

"You couldn't bring them in here?" she asked as she opened the card. She looked at the words and noticed the rush of heat in her cheeks.

Will you be my Juliet?

"I believe you should see the full delivery at one time, miss." He smiled as he turned and left the room.

Emma ran into the morning room to find an overwhelming number of white lilies and red roses on every table, the mantel, and the window box.

"We should tell Arundel it's only necessary to send one bouquet after each party," Henry remarked with a shake of his head. "Edward, you'll pass the message on?"

Emma walked to one of the vases of roses to get a closer look. "If any of you advise him as such, I will no longer consider you my brothers." She blushed again and giggled like a little girl as she walked over to smell her lilies.

"Poor Lieutenant Brady," Richard quipped. "I don't think he can compete with her earl."

Their mother walked in the room. "Stop teasing your sister."

"Is this why you are here? To confirm the delivery came?"

Edward laughed. "Phillip wanted me to make certain it arrived before you went to get ices with the lieutenant."

"It is easy to lose yourself when a man shows his feelings for you in such way." Her mother pulled one of the lilies out of the vase to smell the scent.

"What are you saying, Mother?"

"Be careful and guard your heart until he makes it official." Emma kept thinking about the flowers and the card as she went back to the dining room. He had asked her to be his Juliet. He'd made the same request during the previous season, and she'd told him no. It almost seemed a miracle for him to ask again.

Emma dreaded the moment Lieutenant Brady arrived, knowing she would have to spend more time with the boring man. He didn't seem to understand she wasn't interested in him. When Lieutenant Brady picked her up to take her to the icehouse, Emma chided herself for accepting his invitation.

"I wish you would've rejoined me last night at the dance," Brady said as he helped her out of the carriage. She'd listened to him bemoan her absence for a quarter of an hour. "Lord Arundel and men of his type think it is their right to monopolize beautiful women."

"Lord Arundel and I are close friends, Lieutenant. His presence was most welcome. I enjoy being with him." She hoped Brady would take the hint, but he didn't. She listened and defended Phillip every time Brady made a derogatory comment.

Thankful the activity was coming to an end, Emma forced a pleasant but tight smile as Brady escorted her to his carriage. He held a hand out to help her when she saw Phillip walking with Marianne and Charlotte. Emma missed the step and scraped her shin, ripping her dress and stockings. She wanted to get into the carriage as quickly as possible to avoid his gaze. She didn't want him to see her with another man. Unfortunately, Brady made a scene out of the incident.

"Emma, my dear!"

Emma froze as he said the words *my dear*. She didn't know why he thought he had the liberty to address her as such. They didn't have an understanding. She denied him the right to use her Christian name.

"You're injured." He continued picking her up. He carried her to a bench outside the icehouse.

"Please don't concern yourself, Lieutenant." Emma turned sideways, hoping Phillip and his sisters hadn't noticed her.

"I must assist you. And I gave you permission to call me David." He looked hurt by her use of his title. He pulled her leg and lifted the bottom of her dress. Emma rushed to push her skirt back down.

"Sir, you do not have permission to touch my leg, nor to lift my skirt." She looked around and motioned for her maid to attend her. "Please leave me to the care of my maid."

"Emma, darling, I'm trying to ascertain if the injury is severe."

Emma pushed him away. "Do not refer to me as 'darling,' sir."

She didn't dare look up to see if Phillip was watching. Her maid helped her stand to go back into the icehouse. They could get water and clean the wound.

"Emma," Lieutenant Brady said, taking hold of her arm, "do you realize I'm your last chance at marriage? After the debacle with Lord Arundel last year, you're fortunate I'm willing to pay call to you."

Emma lifted her hand and slapped him. "Sir, I will find my way home. I prefer you no longer speak to me." She pushed him and limped away as Lieutenant Brady fell on the ground.

"Don't you ever speak to Miss Parker in such a way again." Emma didn't dare turn around as she heard Phillip's voice. In the window of the icehouse, she saw Phillip punch Lieutenant Brady for her.

"I am working to restore her virtue after you ruined her last year, Arundel. Have you now come to take her to your bedchamber?" the lieutenant provoked.

Emma closed her eyes as he finished the statement. Before she'd left Springhill Abby, she'd told her mother of her concerns regarding her reputation. Although she and Phillip had only kissed the previous year, society was under the impression that much more had occurred. She didn't realize how terrible society could be until she understood his implications.

"She is far more virtuous than you, Lieutenant. Clear off."

Emma looked up at the sky to fight the tears. She was ready to start walking when Phillip approached. "Will you allow me to escort you home?"

"Thank you, my lord. I appreciate your assistance."

He held his arm out and led her past the gawking crowd to his gig. Marianne and Charlotte both embraced her before Phillip helped her into the carriage. She looked graceless sitting with them in the carriage after she'd been on an outing with another man.

"Thank you for saving me, L—"

Before she could call him by his title, he raised his eyebrows at her. "Don't you dare use my title."

"I'm sorry, my lord."

Phillip again raised his eyebrows.

"What do you want me to say?" Emma asked as he continued to look at her as though every word she said was wrong.

"I want you to speak to me like you did last year. Last night we agreed we would start where we left off."

"Fine . . . thank you for saving me from the brute!" She took a deep breath and realized he was laughing at her. "Do you find this amusing, my lord? My leg is wounded. My pride is injured. And Miss Prim's scandal hasn't taken front row to last year's happenings. It doesn't matter it was all fabrication . . . What's so funny?"

"You are, Emma."

"I don't know what you mean."

"Your leg looks injured. Are you all right?"

Emma looked down to see the blood on her ripped gown. "It could be worse, my lord."

Phillip's eyes looked so intense her heart skidded to a halt. She wanted to ask him why he was looking at her with such intensity, but she had a feeling the answer would be he was in love with her. She wanted him to say the words, but not in front of his sisters.

"Do I have your permission to look at the injury?" he asked.

"No, my lord. I will have it cared for when I arrive home."

Phillip continued to gaze into her eyes as he said, "I respect your choice. I wouldn't want all of London talking about my rakish ways."

Emma worried he would kiss her in front of his sisters due to the intensity in his eyes. It was as though he had a rope tied around her heart, and all he needed to do would be to pull the end and bring her to him.

She turned as the carriage came to a halt. "Thank you for your assistance."

Phillip helped her from the carriage and walked her to the door. "May I call on you tonight?"

Emma's heart fluttered with anticipation. "Yes, you may."

As Emma readied for bed, she experienced a wave of disappointment. Phillip had asked to call on her, but he hadn't come to the house. She wondered if she misunderstood his request. She was determined to keep the tears from falling. She wasn't going to spend the season crying over Phillip and all the broken hopes and dreams.

"Miss?" Her maid, Abigail, stood behind her, taking her hair out of the pins. Pointing to the window she said, "There's someone outside."

Emma walked to the window and looked down. Turning back to her maid, she squealed, "Phillip!" She put her hand to her hair. "My hair is unpinned."

"Miss, open the window," Abigail said with nervous excitement as she helped Emma unlatch the lock.

Emma's hands were shaking too much, so she allowed the maid to open the window. A thrill of excitement fluttered through her as she realized Phillip was below her window. This was a romantic proposal, the best she could ever hope to receive. Most men discussed the arrangement with the father, and after negotiations regarding the dowry, the date was set and the banns read.

Phillip held a single red rose. "'But soft! What light through yonder window breaks?'" He reached his hand toward her as he spoke.

She didn't know if she should laugh or cry as she thought back to the day she suggested his name was Romeo. His response to her was only if he had a Juliet.

"'It is the east, and Juliet is the sun.'" He walked to the trellis against the house, put the rose in his mouth, and climbed. As he reached the top, he handed her the rose and kissed her hand. "Will you marry me?"

"I expected you to continue to quote Shakespeare," she said as she smelled the rose. She delayed in answering. "I never thought I'd want to hear words from Romeo and Juliet again after this last year." The pain of the poison was far too real.

"Are you going to answer him?" She turned to see her parents leaning out their window. Her mother continued, "You are going to wake the neighbors."

A window to the left of them opened, and Henry stuck is head out. "Have you always been so charismatic, or are you still suffering from a head injury?"

Phillip laughed and turned back to her. "Did I choose the wrong romantic gesture? I have a few other ideas."

"How can you think of Romeo and Juliet after what happened?"

"I'm not going to let it destroy my love of literature . . . Do you need time to think about it?"

She looked into his eyes as he spoke. She understood his desire to put the past behind him. "Yes, I will marry you."

He leaned toward her and they kissed. As he pulled away he handed her a paper. "This is the receipt for a special license—"

"A special license?" Anne called from her window, interrupting his monologue.

They laughed. She knew her cheeks were bright red as he called out, "Richard, do you have an opinion or thought to share?"

"Nope, no opinion from me, Romeo. I'm just enjoying the display," he called from his window.

"Edward, what about you?" Phillip called out.

"Will you get this display over with? I'm trying to sleep," Edward called over as he stood next to Anne.

Emma put her hands on her cheeks to cover the blush. Phillip reached forward and pulled her hands away. He whispered so only she could hear him. "You are beautiful when you blush."

She shook her head. "My face goes bright red, and it's embarrassing."

His eyes twinkled as he leaned forward and kissed her again. He couldn't kiss her the same as he had during those stolen moments at Springhill Abby, because her family was watching and he was hanging off a trellis and a balcony. But she enjoyed every moment of the exchange between them.

"Will you be able to climb back down?" she asked as he moved away from her. She touched her lips to make certain she was awake.

"Yes, I'll be fine. Good night, my love." He moved her fingers and kissed her one last time before climbing back down the trellis.

Epilogue

"MARRIAGE IS A GIFT GIVEN by God to the human family for our well-being and growth."

Phillip tried to focus on the words the sexton spoke, but he was distracted by Emma and the way she looked in her wedding dress.

The dress was lined in embroidered flowers and a pattern of swirls. Her veil sat on her head under a band of pearls and extended down her back. When he looked back at her face, he realized she was trying to get his attention with her eyes. He smiled as he noticed her nod in the direction of the sexton. He should be listening.

"The couple will join hands in a symbol of the union—"

Phillip stopped listening again as he thought over the previous year. It had been rough. He and Emma had been through a lifetime of anguish and heartache in a few short months. He wondered what the rest of their lives would bring.

"What were you thinking about?" Emma asked as he helped her into the carriage so they could go to Wentworth Hall for the wedding party. They would depart for a wedding tour the following week.

"My thoughts were focused on my great fortune of having the most beautiful bride." He pulled Emma to him and kissed her. He hadn't had the chance to kiss her since the day before. "Did you know a kiss after the wedding is a symbol of transferring the best part of ourselves to each other? Almost as though a marriage of souls."

"Where did you read such nonsense?" she asked, pulling away from him.

"How did you know I found it in a book?" Phillip pulled her back to him. He held her as the carriage made the short drive back to Wentworth Hall. He kissed her and twirled the loose locks of hair in his fingers. "Are you ready to meet our adoring families, my lady?"

He watched as Emma looked down at her dress. She touched her hair and tried to give him a disappointed look. Instead it turned into a playful smile. "Did you have to mess with my hair?"

He thought about helping her as she pinned the loose strands back into place but decided to admire her instead. She smoothed her dress out and nodded to him.

"I'm ready now, my lord."

She leaned forward and kissed him. Their families and guests could wait to congratulate them. He couldn't imagine a better beginning to their life together.

About the Author

ANGELA JOHNSON HAS A LOVE for the written word and the adventures one can take while reading. She writes the stories she wants to read: clean romance novels based in the Regency era. She has a BS in English from Utah Valley University, an MPC from Weber State University, and an MA in publishing from Western Colorado University. She loves to travel to collect ideas for writing.